A
Person
of
Significance

A Person of Significance

MARJORIE LAZARO

Matador
9 Priory Business Park,
Wistow Road, Kibworth Beauchamp,
Leicestershire. LE8 0RX
Tel: 0116 279 2299
Email: books@troubador.co.uk
Web: www.troubador.co.uk/matador
Twitter: @matadorbooks

ISBN 978 1785892 554

British Library Cataloguing in Publication Data.
A catalogue record for this book is available from the British Library.

Printed and bound in the UK by TJ International, Padstow, Cornwall
Typeset in 11pt Aldine401 BT by Troubador Publishing Ltd, Leicester, UK

Matador is an imprint of Troubador Publishing Ltd

For Cedric

Part I

CHAPTER 1

London, August 1952

Garrard halted at a crossroads, breathing hard. Traffic stoplights loomed over him, delivery trucks and vans pressed close with their stink of petrol and hot rubber and dust. His lungs struggled for oxygen, the thunder of heavy vehicles and the tread of many feet assaulting his ears. Huge red buses like elephants that could crush you in a moment lumbered along in procession, each with a place name and a number on its forehead.

'Here's the place,' his sister had said, the practical one, waving her magazine in the air. 'Right in the middle of London – look, you can't miss it. Regent Street, it says.'

It was unreal. At last he was actually in the city, that musical, starry, thrilling, exotic, daunting, longed-for destination. It was only three hours since his arrival.

The journey from Rangoon to London via Liverpool had been simple – a matter of saving his passage and packing his bag. P&O did the rest. Now he was alone, on foot, and needing to find the special place that would kit him out for the winter. A lightweight shirt and trousers were fine for the tropics, but the British Council representative had warned him to provide properly for the cold and fog that were to come. Against his nature, he had to be practical.

According to the map at the hostel, this was Oxford Circus – a strange name for a crossroads in London; it seemed to be the centre of the West End. But there was no way to tell which was Regent Street. Should he ask? People were milling around him, some directing curious glances at him. He looked straight back, unabashed. *No! I can do this myself! D'Silvas never admit defeat.*

He looked round again; then, attracted by its elegant curve, he chose the broadest street, which stretched away downhill in a perfect arc.

The buildings looked huge, long spreads of brightly lit display windows glinting in the afternoon sun. Peering to see what was on offer, he caught his own reflection amongst the bustling crowd, astonished at how conspicuous he looked amongst these tall, pale Europeans, seeing himself through their eyes – a small, alien figure, a round, dark face with hamster cheeks, bold eyes, curly black hair.

But suddenly there was the place, exactly like the picture in Weldon's: shiny, a large and imposing emporium. In the entrance he paused for his eyes to adjust after the sunny brightness. He went in. The cool quiet of the building was strange to him – shady, not hot and humid, no more clamour of voices and footsteps.

The store was practically empty, with a clean smell of cloth. Wooden counters stretched away into the distance, defending shelves of fabric, and dummies wearing smart outfits gazed at him, still and unblinking. The adverts had promised he would be able to choose material and have it made up to his own measurements, just like in Rangoon, where of course the family had its own tailor.

An assistant loomed up beside him. Garrard squared his weightlifter's shoulders in the crisp linen shirt before glancing up at the young man.

'I need a new suit,' he said.

'Yes,' said the assistant, not returning his gaze. His voice was neutral and his face gave nothing away.

Garrard took a second look. Yes, his manner really was offhand: not obliging in the least. He was young, too. He should learn some manners.

'So please show me your heavyweight samples, isn't it?'

The man's expression changed, a sneer perceptible. Garrard wondered if he had made a mistake – perhaps one of many in this new place. The pale youngster stood blocking Garrard's approach without meeting his eye. At the nearest counter, a customer leaned, examining a book of swatches.

Is everybody deaf?

'That's the sort of thing I need,' said Garrard, still polite, gesturing towards a dummy dressed in warm cavalry twill trousers and a grey tweed jacket.

Then he heard the young man say, 'I think a whole suit might be rather expensive for you, sir.'

Expensive?

'But this is the Fifty Shilling Tailors?' asked Garrard. By his calculation, fifty shillings was two pounds ten shillings.

'I'm afraid you are quite outta date, sir,' said the man, raising his voice. 'The cheapest we 'ave 'ere…' and he emphasized the demeaning word '…would be three pounds ten shillings.'

The other customer lifted his head to listen. Garrard hesitated, heat rising in him, the shock of such unexpected hostility putting him on the defensive.

'Yes? And?' Three pounds ten would keep him for a week – more than any music student could afford, and about three times as much as he would have paid in Rangoon.

He looked the man in the face. The man looked back. Garrard could not retreat now.

'Well, show me your, this thing, best cloth,' he insisted. His fists balled in his pockets, he moved towards the counter, his way still barred. His determination forced the fellow to stand aside; he followed, watching while Garrard flicked through a sample book.

'Have you nothing better?' Garrard said.

'Nothing – sir.'

'Hm.' Garrard looked through the book again, finally

pausing at a cream twill. He turned the page over, but there was no price on the back. He decided not to let this concern him.

'This one, then,' he said. 'I'll take a pair of trousers only, though. For a jacket, I'd need better stuff.'

There was a pause while the man digested this. Then, 'If sir would like to pay a deposit?' he said.

'Of course, of course. Just measure me up, please,' said Garrard, keeping control. He stood, legs planted, and watched the assistant kneel reluctantly at his feet to take his inside leg measurement and enter it in a book, before noting down the other necessary details. Then Garrard took out his wallet and produced the one, lonely pound note with a flourish. 'This should do for the deposit, I think,' he said. 'I will call back tomorrow.'

Another mistake. Catching the young man's expression, Garrard corrected himself – 'Or rather, next week.' He left, leaving no room for dispute.

Outside in the hot sun he wiped his face. *Such a tamasha over buying a suit!* he thought. *I'd better not trust to Weldon's mags in future.*

★

The full blast of Regent Street bruised him as he emerged: the white glare, the roar of traffic, with the red buses and the drably dressed people walking briskly along the pavements, skilfully avoiding each other without apparently trying. He had been brought up to think that London was a cosmopolitan city where everybody had a place – like Rangoon, with its Indian merchants and professionals, Chinese businessmen and shopkeepers, British administrators, Anglos with their skills in engineering, accountancy and so on, and everywhere, going about the work of the city, Karens, Karennis, Kachins, Shans and the warlike Burmans themselves, all part of the city's rich mix. Here in the West End all the faces were white – except his.

As he began to negotiate the crowded streets, following the only route he had so far learned – northwards from the West End towards the quieter squares of Bloomsbury – his was no longer the only brown face. Here, in the university quarter, the traffic thinned out, and he noticed more and more Africans and Indians on the pavements. The Africans liked to bunch together, he saw, sprawling apart in bursts of exuberant laughter. The Asians were more reserved, swimming like sleek pickerel compared to the African grouper fish.

Garrard began to relax, and the tension in his shoulders eased as he walked under shady plane trees. Clearly he had a lot to learn. At least he already had a room at the YMCA. The taxi driver who dropped him off had departed without helping him with his cabin trunk, so he hauled it up the stairs himself. But his college was nearby, and he felt sure of finding friends soon – girls, maybe. His feet began to feel more solid under him. He caught a glimpse of yellow skirt whisking away round a corner, his eye caught by the bright colour. Never mind the crass young shop assistant with his unhealthy skin and uncouth manners. You could find rude people anywhere in the world; he was probably not typical. 'Hold on to your dream, son,' his mother had said.

*

He went up to his room, kicked off his loafers and lay down on the bed. The place was small, plain and practical, clean. The black tin trunk with his name stencilled on it in white sat in the corner. He thought of his few European clothes, all too thin, and hoped his new trousers would be ready before the cold began to bite. The trunk held his cotton *lungyi* and a short jacket of heavy cream silk, a thick Karenni cotton bedspread with blue checks, two rough blankets, and of course his music. He still had to find a warm coat.

Like a loop of film, the long voyage through Suez and Gibraltar, across the bumpy Irish Sea to Liverpool, and so by train to London ran and re-ran through his head, his muscles still steadying themselves against an imaginary swell. HMS Salween, the P&O line. At the docks in Rangoon, his mother's face stony, but she managing a blessing at his embrace. He carried with him the warmth of her plump bosom and the silky touch of her coronet of hair against his face.

And her steely ambition for him.

His eyes closed in the warmth of his room, and he drifted off, dreaming... *he stands in the prow of a great ship, watching it cut through the waves, the wake streaming past him and far behind across the ocean like the long hair of women. The wind blows through his own hair, as he faces the blue ocean and the blue air, then inside the ship in a ballroom white with gold decorations and chandeliers and many points of light sparkling. He sits at a grand piano white with a candelabra, playing from his head as he loves to do and the people stand and applaud in evening dress, their smiling faces turned towards him. He smiles back and bows from the platform, only his hands and body are bound to the piano with delicate filaments, and grey strands like cobwebs enmesh him. He beats free of them and dashes out of the ballroom and into the engine room in the bowels of the ship where steam is hissing and pistons move on oiled cylinders. He finds a huge pair of shears and climbs up the companionway to the deck; he runs to the stern and chops at the cords that stretch back across the oceans to the shores of his homeland, chops and hacks severing hanks of hair and then smaller pieces until he has snipped every last wisp and thread and then he hurls the shears overboard into the heavy seas and they fall with a splash and sink at once. He races to the prow of the ship, and strains hard against the rail as if to urge it on, a figurehead leaning forward into the wind...* and he sank into a deep sleep.

CHAPTER 2

August 1952

Garrard woke chilled and disorientated. The light was beginning to go. He stretched, rubbed his arms and tried out his fingers, wanting to touch piano keys again, as he had done on the ship. The bed was strangely still. Leaning up on his elbow to look about him, he saw he was no longer in a cabin at sea, but in a proper room, his tin trunk in the corner, his leather loafers aslant on the floor.

England!

Everything came into focus, and he recognised that the ache in his stomach was hunger. When had he last eaten? On the train, probably, and the food there had been tasteless and dry.

He reached for his trousers, neatly folded on a bedside chair. In the pocket was the purse that he always carried, wrapped in a clean handkerchief to save the lining. There were a few coins. He counted them carefully. Six shillings and ninepence. That should do.

★

The racket hit him as he pushed open the door, that and the dense fug. The walls were yellowish, streaked with condensation, and the ceiling was sweaty. The place he had found was not promising, yet it was packed. He spotted one party getting up to leave, so in the echoing din he slid into a vacant seat.

The menu made his stomach growl. An appetising whiff of garlic and onions went straight to his taste buds, and he chose Spaghetti Bolognese, not sure what it was, but at one shilling and ninepence it sounded like good value, and he felt he could afford a cup of tea too. He was afraid it would be the same watery and bitter stuff provided on the train, but if this was how it was in England he had better get used to it.

A young waitress with stiffly curled blonde hair took his order and shouted it through a serving hatch. She gave him a friendly smile through the steam, moisture beading her upper lip. He took it that she knew he was hungry and would soon feed him. He leaned back to wait, humming under his breath, muscles clenched between unease and pleasurable anticipation.

The door burst open with a blast of hot air, and four young people charged in looking for seats. There were three boys and a girl, moving with the assurance of familiarity. Most of the tables were still full, so they advanced upon Garrard's with its empty places. One of the boys pulled over a spare chair, with 'You don't mind, do you?' and the others squeezed in round him. Garrard pushed back his chair to make space, wondering whether they expected him to move.

His plate of food arrived, and he thought of nothing but its soft, slippery deliciousness. Then he realised the girl was speaking to him – an unwelcome interruption.

'Always full here,' she said, looking into his face. 'It's because they have the best spag bol!'

One of the boys was intent on polishing the lenses of his spectacles, which had steamed up.

'I think that's what I'm having,' Garrard responded, and looked down at his plate.

'Good,' she said. 'That's the best.' He caught the smile before she ducked her head, soft fair hair falling over her face. It seemed she had adopted him.

They left him alone while he ate, twisting strands of pasta round his fork as he saw others do, making it last. It was savoury but he missed the tastes of ginger and chilli that he had taken for granted all his life.

When his tea arrived, the girl nudged her neighbour with a look of disgust.

'Er –' the taller boy put out his hand in protest '– you're not drinking tea with your spaghetti? It's awful stuff, you know.'

'Really?' Was it so obvious that he was new here, that they should be telling him this?

'Yes, really. You could have red wine – just a glass – or maybe you don't drink? I don't mean to interfere.'

Thinking of the lonely coins left in his purse, Garrard grasped at this straw. 'No, I don't,' he lied, trying to look virtuous as he remembered the whiskeys and chasers that used to skid across the piano lid in the Strand Hotel in Rangoon. People were always generous in those days – trying to get him tipsy perhaps – but he never let alcohol interfere with his music and anyway he had a good head.

'Oh well,' and the group turned back to each other, letting him be.

The generous mound of pasta had filled him with content. He lit a Navy Cut and drank his tea in slow gulps. It was thin and bitter, as he expected, but it suited his mood. He had been hungry, not just for food, but to absorb anything that was British, or at least adopted as British. Tea from India, spaghetti from Italy, he supposed – and it was only a few years since this country had been exhausted by the long war. As Burma still was. But England was reawakening; he could feel it. These young people were full of life and hope. He relaxed and sat back to inspect them as they ate.

Three of them were fair, and the fourth a dark-skinned young man with Southern Indian features. They seemed a little younger than Garrard, carefree and confident, and hungry, as he had been. There they were, tucking in and gabbling away with their mouths full, bits of scarlet pasta occasionally escaping on to a chin, only to be sucked in again, or wiped away with the back of a hand. They were all drinking red wine.

At last it was time for Garrard to move. A handwritten bill arrived on the table. He thought he should leave a tip, and got out his well-guarded purse to take out a new twelve-sided coin, the threepenny bit.

But the others had not finished with him. Their plates almost empty, they turned to him again.

'You have not been here long, isn't it?' This was the Indian boy, his turn of phrase instantly familiar.

'No.'

'Where are you staying?' The boy with the glasses leaned forward. He seemed to want facts.

'At the YMCA.'

'Oh, very fine. For how long?' The Indian boy again.

He shot them a glance, wary of their persistence. 'I'm all right, thank you,' he said, moving as if to go.

'Here, hold on a minute,' said the girl, laying a light hand on his wrist. He felt the warmth of her skin, damp from the heat, and paused.

'We're just interested, you know. And we've all been in the same boat.' The tall boy.

These easy, happy English people with their Indian friend? Confusion made him awkward.

'Indefinitely, I think. It depends…'

'On what?'

'On college – and how the money goes.'

'I thought you were a student!'

'Ah – money. Well, look. We have an idea.'

'Oh?'

'Yes. We're all students, as well – all of us – and…'

'Yes, so…'

13

'Well, we live in a place where...'

'... where you can live cheaply if you help out.'

'You take turns in the office, and you make up beds and wash up, and...'

Garrard flinched. He had not come halfway across the world to wash dishes; there was no room in his plans for such a thing.

'Well, no, I wouldn't want to do that.'

'...and you can come and stay for three days to see how you like it...'

'Come on. You'd enjoy it – and there's a vacancy.'

'But, is there a piano?' he asked.

They stopped in mid-breath. There was a pause. Then the tall boy spoke: 'Yes, there is, as a matter of fact. A Blüthner grand in the common room.'

This has just become tempting, Garrard thought. *Supposing the college cannot offer sufficient practice time?* It might be worth investigating after all, and term was still a few days away.

CHAPTER 3

Big Mummy's letter arrived the next morning – a good thing he was still at the YMCA. She must have written as soon as he left.

August 1952
AIR MAIL

My Garrard son

How are you? Are you keeping warm, and do you have enough money?

We are all fine, except for Amy who has an upset stomach and has been sick many times. She became so weak that we put her to bed for a whole day and gave her only water with a little salt and sugar. Today she is better, and drank some mohlet-saung, but I think I must call the doctor soon. She is very uncomfortable in the rains.

On Sunday last, Colin and all came over. Father O'Malley came too, and Sisters Angelica and Anna-Marie. I made panthe kaukswe and they enjoyed it very much. The children are growing sweetly and Donald took a photograph of all three of them. They have gone so big since Easter I hardly recognized them, and Violet's hair has grown nearly as long as mine. We made hot dry beef curry with ngapi for the Sisters, and thanatsone and green leaves too.

I miss your father and most of all you, son, and your music. How is your college, and do you have good teachers? Have you given any concerts yet? Remember to work hard always, and God will reward you.

Write soon, my son, love from us all, and a big God Bless.

Mummy

She would not let Garrard forget her cooking, and how like her to ask about his studies before he had even begun! Already she was weaving silver threads across the world; he knew the letters would arrive regularly, and he would have to answer every one.

CHAPTER 4

September 1952

Garrard went up worn stone steps to a pillared front door standing hospitably open. A notice saying INTERNATIONAL HOUSE in plain white letters seemed to mean that he was welcome.

His taxi was panting at the curb, his tin trunk still inside. If he shifted it himself, as he had at the YMCA, he was going to arrive hot and dishevelled. He called out 'One second' to the driver, and pushed open the inner door. The first person he saw was Lucy, the girl from the café, standing with one foot up a graceful staircase. She turned and broke into an open smile.

'Garrard, you've come. I thought you might have changed your mind. Come in, come on in, we're expecting you.'

He walked into a grand hallway, its lofty ceilings decorated with ornate flowers and leaves, incongruous in a place for students.

Torn between eagerness to see more and to take care of his property, he said 'Wait – my trunk is in the taxi', but seeing his hand go towards his pocket Lucy shook her head.

'Don't worry, the others will bring it in – you can settle up later.' She came down to him. She had an odd way of holding her head to one side, as if to question him, which he found strangely pleasant.

He was being taken over again. And how soothing that felt, after his long solo journey. Two figures lurched through the front door with his trunk and began to lug it upstairs. Life in London was like rafting white water: you never knew what would come at you next.

The girl led him into an inner room, a kind of office, cluttered with wall charts, a scatter of notebooks and scraps of paper and pencils. A noticeboard bristled with stickers, notices and rough notes. An older woman poring over these straightened, tucked back a strand of grey hair that had escaped from her bun, and put out a hand.

'Hello! I'm Elspeth Baird,' she said, 'and you must be Garrard – d'Silva, isn't it?'

'Yes, I am.' He regarded her with interest. Statuesque in her dark blue dress, it was obvious that she was in charge – he sensed a quality in her that he could respect, a kindly authority that was evident in her firm handshake. Despite their differences, perhaps she had something in common with his small mother.

Looking him over with lively dark eyes edged with laughter lines, 'So you would like to stay here while you study?' she said, straight to the point.

'Yes please, if you have a place for me?' He waited.

'Of course, we shall be interested to have you here. Burma, isn't it? I don't think we've had anybody from Burma before. And music? Lovely. Lucy, will you show Garrard to his room, please? Let's say for three months, to see if you like it here.' She turned back to her notes. It didn't seem rude – just busy.

And Elspeth can see if she likes me too, he thought.

On the way up to the third floor Lucy told him that he was to share a large room with Sam and Tony. Sam, the tall fair-haired young man from the café, was studying for his PhD in History. Spectacled Tony was working his way through medical school. Sanjay, a law student, had a small room of his own on the same floor.

Garrard found that his room was adequately furnished with beds, chairs, a wardrobe and a single-bar electric fire –

but how bearable is it going to be in winter? he wondered. He took comfort in his much-travelled wool blankets, and the memory that he had already survived cold nights in Simla during the War.

The three friends, with Lucy, made up the core of the House. They were the permanent residents, on whom Elspeth relied. It was not long before 'Garrard' was shortened to 'Gad', and so he became. He felt renewed. At home he had always been 'Garrard' or 'my son', and the change of name freed him from all that. For him, it marked a real break from the past, with its war and danger, its separations and its stifling intimacies.

★

It was not till later in the day that Elspeth took him to see her husband, who was busy working in a tiny den off a landing. From within, Rob had a worm's eye view of the hallway and could keep tabs on what went on, if he wished – which he seldom did, leaving all that to Elspeth. It seemed altogether too small a space for a tall man as he unfolded himself, his shock of grey hair almost touching the low ceiling. His face was craggy with a big Scottish nose and a remarkably innocent expression.

He stood and held out his hand to Garrard, with a hearty, 'Hello.'

Not sure how to address this big man, 'Hello, sir,' said Gad tentatively.

'Ha! Don't call me "sir"!'

Gad's eyebrows shot up.

'You can call me anything else you like, as long as you don't call me early in the morning!' Rob laughed uproariously at his own joke, so that Garrard could not help smiling too, though embarrassed at the man's sudden childishness.

Elspeth brought the conversation to a close, with 'I hope you'll be happy here. I'm sure you will fit in.'

Rob put in, 'Oh Elspeth! Of course he will!'

Aha! thought Gad. *So she's the worrier, he's the optimist!*

Learning the routines of his new home, he soon learned that these two ran a remarkable undertaking. Not content with providing short-term accommodation for young people newly arrived in London, the Bairds arranged a programme of regular lectures, discussions and concerts – their personal life took second place.

As he discovered how difficult overseas students, especially non-Europeans, found it to secure lodgings in London, Gad realised what a stroke of luck it was that he had dropped into that café on that day, at that time – especially on account of the piano.

★

One Saturday afternoon, Gad was coming to the end of his customary three hours' practice on the fine old Blüthner grand. Cursing to himself, he played again the run with the trill that he could never be sure of getting right. As usual, it was his right hand that let him down. The notes went up the keyboard this way, and the fingers had to lighten as they went so that the final shake would be clear and sharp: *like so – no, not like that!* He played it again – still uneven – and again, and – *yes!* He'd got it this time. It was there. He repeated it from memory – and again. Now his fingers knew the path, it would be in him for good. Pulling his hands away from the keyboard, he stretched and relaxed and got up, closed the piano lid and stacked his music neatly.

The sunny room where he had been playing was by no means silent – *so nothing new here*, he thought, remembering the school hall in Simla and the room full of family back home in Rangoon. But as far as music was concerned, he never had trouble focusing.

Tuning in now to the buzz of talk from the far end of the room where some 'regulars' occupied the circle of low chairs, he caught the faint smell of sweat – homely yet different from the bred-in-the-bone scent of his own family. There was a new girl, too, and there was something familiar about her – a *déja vue*?

'Well, what about tonight?' he heard as he wandered over, letting go after the intense concentration of the afternoon.

Tony: 'Tonight's fine.'

'But aren't you on duty?' asked Mary, one of the part-time secretaries.

'Am I, Robert?'

'You'll have to look at the rota.'

Dust motes danced in the sunlight. Tony continued to sit, apparently too comfortable to move. It was Saturday afternoon after all.

Gad remained standing, uncertain what was afoot.

'I think I did it last Saturday,' Tony said finally.

Suddenly awake, Sanjay sat up: 'No, you didn't, I did. 'Cos you went down to the Seamen's Mission with Rob.'

A nod from Robert.

'Oh yes, so I did. Well, the week before, then.'

'Oh, just go and look! Gad, you're coming anyway; no getting out of it.'

'Coming where?' said Garrard neutrally. Answering to his new name, co-opted into one of their schemes, he was learning to be part of the 'crowd'.

'To Guys and Dolls – come on, you'll love it.' Sam took over, while Tony strolled off to check the rota.

Gad chilled, thinking of his tiny British Council grant, his spare cash locked in the trunk – locked not against thieves but against his own impulses. Still, it was Saturday, and if they ate at the House first … He looked properly at the new girl. He saw short, spiky dark hair and cool grey eyes; she had wrapped her long legs round each other as she sat.

'Garrard,' said Robert formally, 'this is Thérèse Kutanguay. Garrard d'Silva.'

'Gad. Hello, Thérèse,' said Gad, looking for signs of interest.

''Allo.' She flashed a look at Gad for a moment, before shifting in her chair and looking away. *Wary. Low voice.*

'We can't go tonight – I'm skint,' said Sanjay.

Coming back into the room, Tony was not having this. 'Oh, you're always skint. We're going anyway. It's Estelle on duty; we've done a swap.'

Gad had had time to talk to Sanjay over the weeks, and had discovered that the young Indian sold pints of his blood to keep financially afloat – a regular but secret strategy for struggling expats.

'Come on, we'd better go,' he said, hoping to enlist him as one of the 'crowd'.

Sanjay returned a challenging stare. 'Meet in here at six, then,' he said.

*

At ten to six Gad climbed to the top of the House to get a little cash. He counted carefully. His family was a long way away. He could not risk running out of money.

As he came down again, he caught a flash of colour: Thérèse, racing out of her shared room on the first floor and flying down, feet in scarlet shoes and yellow skirt flaring. Now he remembered – those colours were striking in drab, post-war Britain. He followed her, and easing himself into position as the group gathered in the hallway, moved off with her towards the bus stop. He felt her restrained vigour as they crossed the square, a pleasant walk under tall plane trees, past a statue of Gandhi.

Strolling along, half a pace behind, he admired her neat rear and the easy swing of her skirt.

'Are you studying here like the rest of us?' he asked.

'Yes.' She glanced over her shoulder, without slowing. 'Folk music of Brittany. I came 'ere from the Sorbonne.'

Paris! But folk music? At home you only admired European classical music: a legacy of the British Raj – like the English inflections in his voice.

'And you?' she asked, looking out of the corner of her eye.

'Music too,' he said. 'Classical piano – performing.'

'Oh yes. You do play good.' Somehow they had fallen into step.

He was sorry when the rest of the group joined them at the 91 bus stop.

'Let's not wait,' said Sam, shifting his feet impatiently.

'I'm for the bus,' said Sanjay, and Gad knew he was thinking of his shoe leather.

'I'll walk,' said Tony.

Thérèse looked at Gad.

'Bus?' he questioned, looking back.

'OK.' And Mary too stayed with them.

The four of them went upstairs. Mary and Thérèse sat together, with Garrard and Sanjay behind them. Each bought their own ticket, Gad falling in with their habit.

Thérèse's voice, he noticed, was hesitant, her un-English accent, though different from his, giving him a sense of complicity. From his seat by the window, he could see into the upper windows of solid office buildings, box files stacked untidily on windowsills, and typewriters unattended this Saturday evening. Pigeons dived past, miraculously escaping collision. Cyclists wove in and out of the traffic, and taxis revved at traffic lights, as the bus trundled on to the wide-open space of Trafalgar Square, with Nelson's Column dominating everything.

Mostly, though, Gad watched the little strands of dark hair decorating Thérèse's white neck, the elegance of her head as she turned to speak to Mary, or bent to rummage for coins. He wished he was sitting next to her, to feel her warmth.

CHAPTER 5

Gad knew that his mother would be waiting for his next letter – he had only written once since arrival, to give her the address of the YMCA. But her letter had raised too many of the old demons to encourage him to reply immediately. He had read it only once, breathing with difficulty, overwhelmed by claustrophobia. The long voyage had, he thought, freed him; he had even conjured up gaudy dreams in which he broke, violently, from the past.

Finally he wrote:

November 1952
AIR MAIL

Dear Mummy and All at home

A big thank you for your letter, and I hope Amy is better now. Here it is getting very cold and foggy, but luckily I bought some warm trousers like you said, and also not a jacket, but a duffel coat like all the students wear here. I also need a scarf and will get one soon.

I have been very lucky and found a good place to stay, with all meals. The YMCA was expensive to stay long. At International House I hope to be taken on as staff, and will get reduced rates in return for some work. I shall know soon whether they will accept me. I hope so, because everyone is very friendly, and especially if you are living here you get to know everyone very well. I am in a big room with two other students, one medical and one historical. People come here from all over the world (there is one boy from India – Sanjay) and are very welcome. It is difficult to get accommodation in London now, because of the large number of people coming here. One fellow from Africa came with fish oil in his suitcase, to rub on his body to keep him warm, and it broke and made all his clothes smell rank! A lady came late at night, and when the secretary opened the door to her, she said, 'I come – from God!' Not knowing what to reply, the secretary said, 'Oh do come in and sit down; you must be tired.'

I have been at the college now for six weeks, and met all my teachers. It is difficult to tell you about it; everything is so different, and there is so much I don't know, so I must work hard to catch up. Did I say that the House has a grand piano and I can practise whenever the room is free?

Great Christmas wishes to you all. I will stay here at the House for Christmas. I am thinking of you, and send my love to you all.

Your son
Garrard

It was the best he could do. It hardly said anything that he really felt.

CHAPTER 6

6 February 1953

Early morning in the House. Elspeth got up early, glad to be downstairs while it was still empty – the first to go into the cave-like general office, its window looking out into a shadowed space, and its cluttered desk obscuring a handsome fireplace. The mess was oppressive. She decided to chivvy the secretaries about it later on.

Once the morning rush was over, the place was always quiet while Rob worked on his botanical studies, as was the arrangement. Mary and Estelle in their dirndl skirts would be entering bookings on the chart or greeting newcomers. Elspeth would be directing operations. In the evenings, with everybody back from work, Robert would be around, making his corny jokes, in the lovat jacket that seemed to have grown on him.

Elspeth gave herself the luxury of a moment to think of the silences, the open spaces and burning skies of Africa, where she and Robert lived for so long. She was still homesick for the smell of hot earth and yellow grass, the lusty brown boys Robert used to teach, the full-throated laughter of the house staff, which had brought them to this international centre in cold London. Few people in England knew Africans as they did, could understand how it was to face the grey light and the closed expressions they met here, could try to create a place that had a touch of home for them.

Elspeth remembered her African cook Daisy, raised in a mission school and knowing about English food; recalled their disagreements, when Elspeth would urge Daisy to use the peppery West African seasoning her own family longed to taste.

'Oh, madam, you would not like it.'

'But we might get to like it, Daisy: we are on the Gold Coast now.'

'No, no, I know better than that. I know you English like your plain food!' she would insist, and continue to serve her tasteless dishes.

And now there was Mrs Mockford, who really did not know any better. Breakfast was fine: Tony, Mary and Estelle and even Sanjay had all become experts with bacon and eggs and porridge, and Gad was learning fast. For lunch everybody was out. The trouble was supper, with its greasy lamb stew, or Wednesday's grey mince with the toast triangles, or Friday's vinegary fishcakes. They were lucky if they got carrots – Mrs M's cabbage was like rotting leaves.

Pulling herself together and glancing at the time, Elspeth began to survey the duty rotas. At that moment Estelle flustered in, followed by Mary.

'Sorry, sorry, we got talking…'

'Yes, well – never mind – good morning, by the way.' Elspeth took a moment to give them a fleeting smile. 'The first thing we must think about is tonight – there's the snake talk, remember? Canning – Robert knows him slightly from Edinburgh days; particularly wants to talk to him.'

'Snakes – not live ones?' asked Estelle in alarm.

'They are, but he'll bring them safe in baskets. He'll have you all handling them in no time!'

'Do we want to?'

'You will. We've got Fenner Brockway for next month – we must get the invitation list up to date – but we need a speaker for the month after that. Remind me to talk to Robert.'

'If he can tear himself away from his plants!' This was

Mary who, interested in botany herself, rather sympathised with Robert. She sometimes thought how much simpler plants were than people, especially new visitors to London. 'Who's going to introduce tonight?'

'It's Garrard's turn – let him do it.'

Mary and Estelle exchanged a look of resignation. Gad had acquired a reputation for absent-mindedness.

'Do you think he'll remember?' Estelle wondered, but the question remained unanswered.

*

Gad's opportunity to see Thérèse alone came at last, and unexpectedly. It was a college day, and after breakfast he went up to his room to fetch money for his canteen lunch. Coming downstairs again, he was overtaken on the first floor landing by Thérèse. He pulled back to let her dash past, instead of which she stopped suddenly as something bright flew out of her hand and landed in a corner. They exchanged a glance. Her eyes flickered, then she turned away and bent to pick up the object. He stooped politely to help her, but she reached it first and concealed it in her hand, though not before he had glimpsed a gold lipstick case. Lipstick? Uncommon in the House. The girls back home now – the dances and picnics, the rickshaw rides, a board piled with hot food and spicy kisses at dawn. He looked again at Thérèse, still flushed.

'I am – how you say it? – in late,' she says.

'In a rush?' He doesn't know what else to say.

'Yes.' She drops the lipstick into her bag.

The moment stretches. Gad feels the polished wood of the banister under his hand, and thinks about touching the back of her neck.

'Are you going to the Museum?' he asks, for no good reason.

'Yes. And you?'

'College, as usual.'

She has said she is in a hurry, yet here she is still, in the cold brightness of the early spring sun, at the turn of the stairs. Time slows. He catches the sweet power of talc and face powder as she moves to go down.

To keep her there a moment longer he says, 'Would you come out with me some time?' and holds his breath.

She stops and turns her grey eyes upon him, pauses. He sees her perfectly still for once.

'Maybe,' she says, and smiles. Then she sashays on down the stairs, slinging her bag over her shoulder. Gad lets out his breath and does a brief, wild dance on the landing before following her down. As he hotfoots it through the hallway he sees Elspeth in the office doorway.

'You haven't forgotten about this evening, have you?'

Gad halts, shifting his music case to the other hand. 'What?'

'The lecture? You're introducing it?'

'Oh – of course I haven't forgotten. Seven o'clock, isn't it? With snakes?' He gives an involuntary shudder.

'Yes, with the snakes.'

He leaves, instantly forgetting.

★

His feet felt light as he crossed the square, but his elation faded as he thought about how to manage the date. He wondered whether Thérèse was a novice in this game, and also how well she knew London. He wanted to choose something that, whilst not expensive, would stand out in her mind as special, something others might not think of, but that she would enjoy. Hampstead? No, too rarefied. The Wallace Collection, near his college – warm, free, a bit obscure; and it had a good tearoom where they could talk in peace.

Buoyed up by his small decision, Gad returned to his astonishment at the luck that brought him to this place, where Thérèse was. What were the chances of their long paths crossing?

★

The college day followed its usual pattern: a harmony class to start with, a lecture on Brahms piano quartets at eleven. Garrard loved old Brahms for his warm and genial spirit, and remained behind to ask questions.

'How unusual was it, sir, for the piano to lead in with a solo? Have many other composers have done this?'

'Sorry – er?'

'D'Silva, sir – Garrard.'

'Ah, d'Silva. Yes.' The lecturer kept on walking. 'Perhaps we could discuss this another time…?' he added vaguely, and slid through a convenient doorway.

Gad was left rooted to the spot. His hands went to his forehead in frustration. It was as if a lift had dropped suddenly, leaving him sick and dizzy. If he could not get his questions answered here in London, what was the point in coming? Maybe it was a small thing for the lecturer. For him, it was disaster.

At least Sister Mary, the nun who had started him on piano in Rangoon, had time to listen to him. But she had little knowledge to back up her fierce tuition, only a wooden ruler for wandering fingers. And the good Christian Brothers in Simla were even less interested in classical music. Gad felt as if he was left clawing at the smooth surface of a precious globe – this wonderful European culture – on which he could find no purchase, but which held the secrets of the universe.

He went to eat in the canteen, avoiding company. Clearly he had twenty years of learning to make up, twenty years when Europeans had been listening to great pianists playing the great composers – Bach, Beethoven, Brahms – let alone all the others. He had been on the wrong side of the world. He had never realised that such knowledge was important, had grown up believing that, if you played from the heart, it was enough – you could touch people. He pictured himself during the war, moving from country to country, earning his school fees by playing for weddings and funerals, improvising, picking up knowledge piecemeal, then drifting back to his war-torn country, using his gift in whatever way he could. And people who had heard him always remembered his music.

One time in London he recalled standing in the queue for the tills at John Lewis, waiting to pay for a wool scarf, when he heard: 'It's Garrard, isn't it? Garrard d'Silva?'

Gad searched his memory for this face. 'Er?' Just like the lecturer that morning.

'Yes – Dirk, don't you remember? Dirk and Marie – you played for our wedding?'

'Oh – yes, of course. Dirk Suarez? You wanted "Somewhere Over the Rainbow"?'

'You remembered! Yes, of course, and it was so moving. You put in some of your own music too, I think. Everybody loved it – it made our day, for sure.'

Thanking them, he thought now about the music of Burma, and why the people he mixed with had wanted so badly to hear Western tunes like 'Somewhere Over the Rainbow'. He supposed it was something to do with the American films that were beginning to penetrate the country. Yet there was so much other music that he heard drifting from people's homes around Rangoon, and that was played in the country areas – why didn't his Anglo friends want to hear that? Why should the sound of those locally made instruments, played by musicians who loved them, feel so alien? Instead, they lionised him for his ability to play European music on a European piano, even if it was in bars and churches or on Burma Radio. It unsettled him to think about it.

None of it counted for anything in London, anyway.

★

Garrard knew the ropes at the House by now, the winter programme of lectures and concerts. The committee would tap their contacts in order to hear about conditions in South Africa, or the Kinder Transport, or post-war social reconstruction in Germany. There were concerts too – later in the spring Gad was to accompany a respected visiting contralto of advanced years. The snake lecture was an unusual one. Robert had his own reasons for suggesting it.

Thomas Canning, herpetologist, turned out to be another tall man, one of those rangy Englishmen typically administering the colonies. His thin lips and pale, appraising eyes were familiar, too. Gad had no political feeling against such men: they just were, and their entitlement to respect was unchallenged. Since King Thibaw, Burma's last king, had been overthrown, Gad's family thought that Burma might be an even worse place without the British. Few people there worried about the long-term effects of government by a foreign power. The Raj was respected by many as a source of stability, and its occasional outrages were not publicly discussed.

It was with automatic deference, then, that the young man spoke to welcome Canning at the front door of the House, led him with his accompanying receptacles into the downstairs office, and gave him a mug of the despised tea, which he had now learned to make to an acceptable standard.

'Do you need any special arrangements?' he asked, gesturing towards the containers at their feet. *Do snakes need*

33

water? There were four baskets in all, two round and two oblong. They seemed quite heavy, and he felt no desire to look any closer. Why on earth did Robert inflict these things on them? Gad was amazed that he should bother to introduce dangerous reptiles into this house. Snake-charming, now – there was money in that.

'No, no. I have all I need, thank you,' said Canning with easy assurance, turning away towards Robert, who was hovering in the background. The two tall Englishmen fell into conversation. Gad knew about Rob's obsessive interest in traditional uses of plants throughout the world – for food and medicine of course, but also in aphrodisiacs and religious rites. Now he watched him in action, pumping Canning for information on the subject. His expertise, originating in the Gold Coast, was spreading its web across the world.

Typical Rob! thought Gad, listening disregarded from the side-lines, hoping to pick up some tips that he could use in his introduction to the talk. This was how it was: he lived on scraps from the tables of the knowledgeable.

CHAPTER 7

Early March 1953

The date started so well.

The air was fresh and sparkling as they crossed into the square. Gad held the gate open for Thérèse, amid the pungency of damp earth. Crocuses pushed their spears into the light. Tall plane trees had finally condescended to come into bud after a long winter.

'Where are we going?' asked Thérèse.

'The Wallace Collection – have you been there?'

'No. In fact, not to any of the galleries.' Her head was bent. She seldom smiled, he realised. *Does this mean she is not going out with anyone? Or only that her boyfriends are not the cultured sort? Well, at least this outing may strike her as original.*

Only a few cars passed as they found their way along back streets, but they could hear the pulse of the city beating not far off. At nine o'clock this Saturday morning the pavements too were almost deserted, so they walked leisurely side by side, enjoying each other's company in silence. Thérèse was wearing flat shoes. He knew she loved heels, so why? Certainly he was not tall by English standards, *but she is not actually taller than me, anyway.* Now she was trying to slow to match his pace.

'Do you like to walk fast?' he asked.

'Not "like" exactly,' she responded. 'I have a habit of hurrying, even when I do not need to.'

'Do you? Why?' He raised one eyebrow.

'I don't know. I honly seem to do it 'ere, in London – and

in Paris, too.' She hitched her bag up on her shoulder. 'I'm not like zis at 'ome.'

'On the farm, d'you mean?' He had learned at least this much about her.

She nodded. '*Mais regardes*, there, people take time. There is so much work to do, but it's hard and physical – you could not continue if you worked fast.'

They reached Tottenham Court Road, and Gad held her elbow lightly to keep her with him as they crossed. She flushed a little, and detached herself as they reached the far side. *Does she dislike my touch?* Her white skin felt strange to him.

'So who does the farm work?' Gad pursued.

'My father, of course. And 'e 'as two workmen. Labourers.'

'It doesn't sound like a lot of people,' said Gad. 'But then I have no idea at all.'

'No,' she said.

They edged past some rancid rubbish bins left out in front of a small café. A black and white mongrel sniffed round the base, its attention utterly focused.

'So, why did you leave home?'

She answered without looking at him. 'It was because of Alain, my broder – it was five years after 'e was killed. My fader would have liked that I stay and help, and my moder, too.'

'But you felt you couldn't?'

'No. I couldn't.'

They passed the great entrance to the Middlesex Hospital, with its ambulances parked in readiness for accidents and sudden death.

He pressed her: 'How did he die – do you mind telling me?'

'It was an agricultural accident. I will tell you some time,' she said dismissively.

They walked quietly for a while. His questions seemed to have upset her, and he felt he had reached an impasse. His instinct to entertain came to the rescue.

'The House is a weird place, isn't it? I mean, those snakes, last night?'

'They were beautiful! I could not believe how cool they were, and dry – and the python so 'eavy!'

'Maybe – I was too busy with my duties, remember?'

'You really did not want to 'old them.' She glanced at him then, laughing.

'No! I was brought up to avoid snakes in case they're poisonous. In India, people have a mongoose to keep the house clear. Or they're kept as sacred pets in temples. You don't just hand them round like parcels!'

'What – pets?' Her voice rose.

'Yes – they wrap themselves round the carvings. People bring them eggs and fruit to gain virtue or something – I don't know much about that sort of thing, but I've seen them.' He hoped she would not ask more.

'Do they stay in the temple, then, or do they escape?'

'Oh, they stay. They must have brains – they know which side their curry is spiced!'

She laughed again, and he felt better. So far she had shown no curiosity about him. Perhaps she didn't know where to begin; most people didn't. He was quite grateful that she had avoided the clichés: 'So what brought you to London?', 'What's it like in Burma?' and so on, but still... He hoped that it didn't mean the obvious – that she was really not interested. Well, here she was, with him, and the day lay before them.

★

After an hour spent with the art, they sank into comfortable chairs. They had had enough of English armour, and French oil paintings in ornate gilt frames.

Gad gave a sudden laugh. 'You know, to be honest, it's the

frames I like best! They remind me of the pagodas at home – especially the Shwedagon in Rangoon.'

'Oh! Why that one specially?'

'It's unbelievably beautiful. I used to love it – walked miles out of my way just to look at it. I remember, people would spend fortunes covering the domes with gold leaf, all to attain virtue. Reputation, more like – our Buddhists have some peculiar ideas! But at least it seems more far-sighted, don't you think, than putting such expensive frames round pictures – you come to see the paintings themselves, surely?'

She sat listening with raised eyebrows. 'Is Burma a rich country, then?'

His eyes clouded. 'It used to be. Heaven knows what it's like now. They always used to call it the rice bowl of Asia.' Brightening, he went on, 'Shall I tell you how I once crash-landed in a paddy field?'

'Yes, please.'

'Well, I used to navigate for Peacock Airlines, and...'

She interrupted. 'You were a navigator?'

'Oh, I didn't train or anything. I was very young. I just used to sit beside the pilot and read the maps. It was good fun.' He waved an airy hand. 'Anyway, this time, unfortunately, the pilot had had too many whiskeys and not checked his fuel level, so we ran out of gas, and had to make a forced landing. Good thing paddy fields are soft! My mother was furious.' He could see that she enjoyed this, though not sure whether to believe it or not. It was strictly true, but still he thought it was time to stop talking so much.

'Let's have something to eat,' he said.

★

In the enclosed courtyard, lilac bushes, not yet in bud, drooped their branches over them. Gad got out some sandwiches and a flask of good strong tea.

Abruptly, Thérèse began to speak: 'I suppose I must tell you about Alain – otherwise you will wonder.'

'No, really, not if you don't want to – it doesn't matter.'

'Well, I want to tell you, anyway. It was such a terrible thing – I still 'ave bad dreams.' She gave him a sideways look.

'Ok, then.' Lunch could wait.

'Yes,' she started then, in flat tones. 'It was 'arvest time, and Alain and I were helping with the harvest, as usual.'

Gad settled himself to listen. 'How old were you?'

'Oh – I was thirteen, he was fifteen. At *déjeuner* we were running across the field, with the sun in our eyes, and...' It sounded rehearsed, as if she had told it to herself many times already.

'Alain and I go to the wheat field in the trailer. It is bumpy, and my hands hurt from holding on to the metal sides. I am enjoying the morning air on my face. I am – brown – from the sun? Just like Alain.

'We get down from the trailer by the gate, and go to put our *déjeuner* under an oak tree – in the shadow. We have a bottle of our mother's cider and a blue tin box with eggs, fresh bread with cheese and apples from the orchard. We pull grass over to keep everything cool.

'The sun is 'ot already, and we leave our sweaters. I shake some grit out of my sandal. Then I follow Alain along the cut side of the field to the far corner, where the – er –machine?'

'The harvester?' suggested Gad tentatively.

'Yes, ze 'arvester.' She smiled faintly at Gad. 'Eet ees throwing out – piles?'

'Sheaves?'

'... sheaves of corn. We must set them up, six at a time, 'eads in the air to dry. We are hot and there is sweat in our eyes, and our arms and faces are hurting from the rough stems and my eyes from the colour of the poppies.

'Then we take a break for *le déjeuner*. I begin to walk to the tree. Alain sees and starts to race me. I run too, and we speed across the field with the sun in our eyes. Alain is running straight across the path of the tractor that pulls the big rake. Too late, I shout a warning. The driver shouts too, as he pulls on the brake. Alain dodges to one side. The corner of the tractor catches him. He grabs at the – mudguard? – but 'e cannot 'old it. He falls down behind the big wheel. The tractor stops. Jean is the first to run across, and then me. I hear screaming, try to make my legs move towards my brother. Jean is already shaking 'is 'ead. The rake has continued to lower its spikes to the ground. One spike has gone through Alain's right eye, and there is blood all over his shirt where two more 'ave entered 'is chest. We see his other eye tremble, his legs jerk, and then 'e stops breathing. Jean pulls a piece of sacking over Alain's face. We stand. I am crying. My throat is tight and my ears ring. Alain – Alain looks fine except that… Jean leads me away.'

As Thérèse falls silent Gad wants to hold her. He is shocked at the violence of the scene, does not know what to say. He puts a tentative hand on her shoulder. She seems relieved to have told him; he thinks she probably does not need his words at that moment. Her gaze is still turned inward as he stays with her.

★

In bed that night Thérèse dreams her dream again.

I am sitting with tears running down my face while sirens scream. I am on the shore at Trébeurden and Alain is there too, just the two of us; tourists are all over the beach, children building sandcastles and young men playing Jokari but Alain and I run across the crowd and straight into the sea in our clothes, laughing and shouting at the cold water and we fall into the salt waves. I fight the waves rough and playful as I kick with my arms and legs. I turn to splash Alain to play with him but he is far away and with him is another head, another person, another girl.

I swim strongly to find him to see where he is looking but the waves prevent me and I can't see who she is and I can't get near and I can't shout because my mouth is full of salt water; the water is too deep and pulls at my legs and I am not strong enough and they are far out where the currents are fierce and dangerous and will take them away. I save myself. I swim for the shore and when my feet touch the sand I say, 'Help! Help! Please help,' to the young men and I wave my arms and I point to the sea where Alain and the girl were but there is nothing, no heads, and the sea is smooth and they are gone.

CHAPTER 8

AIR MAIL
March 1953

My dear Garrard son,

Thank you for your long letter. I hope you got our Christmas card, and everybody here wants me to wish you for your birthday. I am glad you have a good place to stay, with a piano and all meals. I hope it works out that you can have the reduced rates. Is it run by the British Council? Son, do not mock one who says she comes from God – you must never make fun of great things.

Here it is very hot and we are waiting for the rains. You know what that is like.

Now, son, you remember Uncle Ned, Uncle Victor's brother-in-law? He used to come to see us on Daddy's birthday, but he lives the other side of Rangoon. He is going to England soon, to visit his sister Joyce who stays in London, in a place called Harrow. I am sending some things for you, so I hope you will go to see him soon. He is going this month. I have told him where you are staying. His sister's telephone number is HARROW 466.

Old Father Simon passed away last week. He baptised all your brothers and sisters; but he retired before you were born. He had been ill a long time, you know, but he remembered you and spoke of you. His Requiem Mass will be on Saturday, and I wish you were here, son, to play for it. There will be a big crowd, and many priests at the ceremony.

No time to write more. Write soon, my son, love from us all, and a big God Bless.

Mummy

It beat him how, in a few lines, she could still cause this mess of irritation, frustration, interest, sadness and affection to overlay thoughts of Thérèse, or music. What he really wanted to work out was how Thérèse would be feeling after her revelations. Regret? Embarrassment? It mattered, and he was not sure what to do next.

CHAPTER 9

March 1953

Thérèse spent several days in a grey fog, scarcely noticing others around her. The dream always did this to her. She didn't speak to Gad, and anyway, he was always busy looking after visitors.

Everyone at the House was talking about Stalin's illness – a minor stroke, was it? The office was buzzing. Churchill and Truman had sent messages, through intermediaries; he was a powerful, sick man, whatever he had done in his lifetime. There was fellow feeling there, as well as politics. For Thérèse, it was all beside the point.

If only her parents had talked to her after Alain was killed, she might have got over it better, but they had pulled the shutters down. They would never speak about her brother. They simply turned a deaf ear, so entangled in their own guilt and grief that they were unable to deal with her state of mind.

In a way it seemed to her quite natural: none of them had ever spoken about their feelings before, so why should they now? But Alain's death had not been natural. A boy should not die in a field, his lifeblood leaking into the earth like oil from a tractor. Anger at the waste of her brother's life still smouldered within her. And she asked herself, over again, whether she could have prevented it.

After the accident, Thérèse had gone off to Paris on her own. Perhaps understandably, her parents had worried not at all about any possible risks for her. If they had, perhaps she would never have made such a mistake with Guillaume.

With all this on her mind, Thérèse decided to leave the House and find her own lodgings. It was not that she disliked the company, or was not accepted on the same basis as Gad and the others, but the House could offer no proper place to work, and she longed to have a desk of her own where she could leave each day's papers set up ready for the next. It was not difficult for her: she scanned newsagents' windows until she found a room on the third floor of a house in Huntley Street at a rent she could afford, and moved in immediately. Living so close, she would not lose touch with the House and its inhabitants.

*

In the midst of these personal decisions, Thérèse was amazed to hear that Gad too had found a place to rent. It was a triumph – a whole flat to himself! There was even said to be a bathroom.

Thérèse had seen for herself the horrid signs: *NO IRISH NO DOGS NO COLOUREDS* when she had been looking for her own digs. She could not imagine what it would be like for Gad to look on the open market.

In fact, Gad had not even been looking. At the LCC Housing Department office where he had taken a Saturday job to help his finances along, a young Australian part-timer had tipped him the wink; it was a piece of insider information that perhaps he should not have used, but he did. He went straight for it and got lucky.

Sneaking a quick cigarette in the House office, Thérèse heard: 'It's in the middle of the rag trade, behind the BBC. That's halfway between here and college. What could be better?' Gad exulted, his hair standing on end with excitement.

'Furnished?' somebody asked. 'You know there's not much protection for furnished tenants?'

'Yes, yes, of course…' Gad ignored this, 'and no piano. Can I still come here?' he asked Elspeth, looking at her confidently.

45

'Just try and stay away!'

'When are you moving?' asked Sanjay. 'We'll come and help. We've got to see if it's suitable.'

'For what?'

'For parties, of course!'

It was settled. Thérèse saw that, once again, the 'crowd' had taken Gad over, and that he had let them.

★

4 March 1953, Saturday

On the day of the move, a motley procession embarked from the House: Tony and Sam lugged a battered tin trunk between them; Thérèse and three or four others were encumbered with an assortment of misshapen parcels; Gad staggered under a pile of music tied up with string; and Mary, Estelle and Sanjay had their arms full of oddments.

Progress was slow, but eventually they came to a narrow street edged with tall tenement buildings. Gad stopped them halfway along, went up some front steps and pushed open a filthy door. He beckoned enthusiastically. Thérèse halted to catch her breath, dreading to find that he had taken a hovel. Silently, the group bumped their awkward burdens up the steps and entered an unlit hallway.

Gad's front door faced them; he turned the key, flung the door open and ushered them across a tiny corridor into a reasonably-sized bedroom. All they could see was a vast wardrobe, dominating the room like some HGV on a country lane. Sunlight squeezed through a window that opened on to a solid brick wall topped with railings through which could be seen the feet of passing strangers.

'Just drop everything,' he said, 'till I show you round the estate.' His pride in the place, the first home of his own, was

46

obvious as he flattened his compact body against door frames to allow his visitors to look. On bare feet he was wearing a pair of strange rough slip-ons that she had never seen at the House – they seemed emblematic of a new Gad.

'Come into the sitting-room,' he cried, guiding them round a sharp angle into a small room full of more dark, lumpy furniture. Thérèse jostled with the rest to peer out of the window into a back yard. Gad shut the front door after them, revealing a passage with a peculiar bend in it.

'Great!' said Sam. 'And there's a bathroom?'

'Ah! Come along the corridor – past the lav.'

'A separate lav?' Mary marvelled.

'Yes. And this – this is the kitchen-cum-bathroom!'

In a small room leading out to the yard a stone sink, a gas cooker, and a cupboard huddled against a wooden counter with a huge boiler over it.

'We don't see any bath.'

'Walah!' Gad lifted the wooden counter top, which was hinged, to reveal a bath with a plug and both the usual taps. 'So you can have a bath and breakfast at the same time.'

'Super!' breathed Estelle.

The boiler loomed like a World War I bomb – heavy, solid, cylindrical. It was the size of a man's body. *You could use it for bayonet practice,* thought Thérèse, irrelevantly. *It must hold enough water for the entire building.* Underneath the water tank, narrow-bore pipes ran, presumably connecting to the gas supply, and there was a small hole through which you could light the pilot light if you had a long taper. She wondered nervously about explosions.

'You're not going to provide hot water for everybody in the building, are you?' she asked.

'No fear!' said Gad, finally smiling at her. 'I haven't actually lit it yet – thought I'd wait till you came!'

'Oh, thanks!' said Tony.

47

Thérèse surveyed the grey surface of the bath and felt sick, though not daring to say so. Her own place was small too, but clean and bright, with sunshine. In Paris she had had a romantic garret under the eaves, where she saw the sky and heard nesting birds; it had a sense of freedom. Here, in this underground hole, you could suffocate. But there was energy in the group, Thérèse saw. They wanted to get their hands on the place.

'Well, you'll need a lot of white paint,' said Tony. 'And that ghastly cream gloss on the boiler will have to go. It might be quite nice underneath.'

'Can you get rid of some of this furniture?' asked Sam.

'Any news of Stalin?' asked Sanjay. They shook their heads without much interest.

They must have painted and decorated rooms together before, they were so organised. Mary went out to get scrapers. They began work, in shifts, the boiler still unlit and the water cold. After half an hour or so, Thérèse's arm was aching and she stepped out into the yard for a cigarette. Rubbing her shoulder, she gazed up at the small patch of sky overhead. The dark brick walls towered on all sides, pressing inwards threateningly. The yard was only the size of a decent rug, and since the building had seven storeys in all, the patch of sky above, diminished by perspective, was tiny: a minute square of bright blue that on a dull day would hardly register. It was a trap, she thought; the promise of open space distant and unreal. But perhaps Gad would not mind: he did not strike her as an outdoor sort of person.

*

As they worked on the boiler they found that the tank was copper, but it had several coats of hard gloss paint covering it. The three colours – cream, dark blue and black – looked beautiful where they showed against the copper, at the edges of the scrape. Thérèse was tempted to suggest leaving it unfinished, to reveal its history, but she decided that the workers would take offence – they were enjoying themselves too much.

Like many of her thoughts, the idea remained unspoken. These people were so cohesive – a group that had lived and worked in the House together for so long, knew each other so well – that she never felt part of it. Finishing her cigarette, she moved down the odd-shaped corridor to the living-room, where those awaiting (or postponing) their turn were sprawled on the graceless furniture. Something in her was contemplating how it would be to live in this place.

Gad was a different person here: expansive, glowing with contentment. His face broke itself into little circles as he beamed: broad nose, plump cheeks, bold eyes and big laughing lips. She began to understand how contained he had been at the House – how careful.

Before long Gad called to Sanjay and they went out, returning with bags of cheese, brown flowerpot loaves, coffee and Merrydown cider from the German deli. A party unfolded, a newspaper spread over a low table. Gad had already bought basic crockery and utensils, cups and glasses, knives and plates, a stainless steel coffee pot and matches. Apparently, hospitality ran in his veins. He was in his element. Here he was host, instigator and provider.

'Come, come,' he called to the workers in the kitchen.

Everybody sat where they could, munching hunks of honest wholemeal bread and cheese, washed down with the strong cider.

'I'd rather this than Mrs Mockford's dinners, any day,' said Sam.

'Anything would be better than Mrs Mockford's dinners,' Mary agreed. 'How do we stand it?'

'How do Robert and Elspeth stand it?' This was Tony.

Thérèse had nothing to say: in her experience, all English food was vile, but this was not so bad.

'I suppose they inherited her,' said Gad, 'and can't put her out of a job.'

'Well, the point is we do put up with it,' said Tony. 'The point is, we don't really notice most of the time.'

'No, too busy,' said Estelle. 'But you're going to have to cook for yourself, Gad. Can you cook?'

'Haven't a clue. We'll see. There's always porridge. Come on. Let's finish the cider. How's the scraping going?'

'Slowly,' said Sanjay. 'It's going to take at least one other session. We'll be over tomorrow afternoon, shall we?'

'Fine. Thanks.'

*

5 March 1953, Sunday

On Sunday, Thérèse dressed for the job in an old pair of trousers and a shabby shirt, covering her hair in a bright scarf. Sanjay regarded her appreciatively.

'Hey, look at you. You look so different,' he said, lounging gracefully as usual.

'And you look just the same!'

'Elegant? Cool?'

'Lazy!' she said, smiling.

'Come on, let's get going,' said Tony.

There were only three of them in the working party today. Curiosity about Gad's new home satisfied, for others the novelty had worn off.

Gad threw open the front door with his big smile. He had cleared away the remains of yesterday's party. His bed was neatly made up with borrowed sheets and then blankets that looked rougher than any found in England; over them his beautiful blue-checked bedspread. The rest of his possessions were invisible, perhaps stowed in the great wardrobe that looked big enough to hide an entire ship's cargo. His music was stacked on the coffee table – the only surface except the floor. Thérèse was astonished to see how quickly Gad had made the place homely, and began to relax in his welcoming 'It's good to see you – I miss you all.' Not sure she liked the 'all'; she supposed it would have to do, for now. No mention of Stalin. Had he noticed her workmanlike appearance? If so, he didn't comment.

'Come on through,' he said, 'and have some coffee.'

'Yes, please.' They accepted with alacrity. Thérèse watched Gad as he deftly filled the bottom of his new Italian espresso-maker with water, spooned coffee into the middle compartment, and set the pot on the gas stove.

'I have to keep an eye on this,' he said, 'in case it burns.'

'It's a handsome beast,' said Tony with admiration, then went on, 'Anyway, let's get started.' He picked up one of the scrapers lying on top of the bath, and taking his station near the back door where the light was good, began to scrape. Tony was one of those people who, once started on a task, would always see it through, thought Thérèse. Neither she nor Sanjay was like that. Still, she followed his example.

'Shame!' said Sanjay. 'No room for me!'

'Oh yes, there is room,' Thérèse was quick to retort. 'We can move up. There's much of room.'

The coffee made a noisy gurgle as it forced its way through the grounds, and Gad took it off the heat before it could dry up. A rich aroma never known at the House reached their nostrils, and steam rose from their cups. Tony scraped on, waiting for his to cool.

'So, then, Stalin is really dead?' said Sanjay. He could not leave such urgent news alone – was always fascinated by what was going on in the world of politics – and actually, the topic was on all their minds. 'That's going to upset the Comrades.'

'The point is,' said Tony, scraping away, 'how did he actually die?'

'Don't they know?' Thérèse was startled. She listened to the radio but had not read what the newspapers had been saying.

'No. They say it was a brain haemorrhage, but apparently some people suspect poison.'

Gad said nothing. Leaning against the cupboard, he drank his coffee.

'Anyway,' said Sanjay, waving his scraper about, 'he's still dead, whatever happened, isn't it? Things will have to change.'

'Yes, maybe, but maybe not,' said Tony. 'Maybe things will just roll on exactly as before.'

'I think,' said Thérèse, 'the Party will try to continue, but the – Comrades? – will be afraid to lose him, their "Papa".'

The others looked at her, and she said no more. She was not sure what they would think. She had known a handful of Party members in Paris, after her break with Guillaume, but none here. Sanjay was quite cynical, she sensed; Tony cool and analytical as ever. But what about Gad?

'You know more than we do, then,' said Sanjay, and changed the subject. 'Are you going to get a piano, Gad?'

'Actually, I've been offered two already.' Gad was perfectly ready to talk now. 'It seems that many people have old pianos they want to get rid of. But they're probably wrecks.'

Was Gad ever curious about anything but music? She had seen his rapt attention when he practised, leaving ordinary life behind. He had listened to her story with interest – but she wondered whether he was, at heart, self-centred.

The doorbell rang, and a voice called, 'Anyone at home?'

Tony groaned.

It was Ronald – Ronald, with his usual look of shrewd

curiosity, who was a regular visitor to the House, always on the move, knowing everyone. Although a friend of long standing, his private life was mysterious, as lives could be in the big city. He came and went as he pleased, always alone, always interested in whatever the youngsters were up to.

'Come on in.' Gad unlatched the door. 'I wondered when you would show up.'

'Yes, like the bad ha'penny, always like the bad ha'penny. How are you all? Sanjay? Tony? And – who's this?'

'This is Thérèse.'

'Thérèse. Lovely,' said Ronald, looking anything but pleased.

CHAPTER 10

Dear Mummy and All at home

Thank you for your letter. I telephoned Uncle Ned last week, and will go to see him soon, but Harrow is a long way from where I stay, and trains are expensive.

Here the big excitement is the Coronation of Queen Elizabeth II. A whole crowd of us from the House went to see and wave the Union Jack flags. Of course, we had to go out very early in the morning, and wait for five hours, and we became separated because there were so many people, but I was with Sam and we saw the whole procession – the troops, and the soldiers on horseback in their plumed hats, and the gold carriage with the Queen, very serious, and Prince Philip in his navy uniform with all the gold braid. Girls, you should have seen her dress – all white and gold and sparkling, a diamond crown on her head and a bright blue sash with a huge diamond brooch on it. Some had come from far and brought blankets and bottles of tea. There were rows of people in front of us on The Mall, but we could still see well, and we both got flags to wave. Then we waited until she came back to the palace, and we saw her with the big crown on her head, and she was holding the orb and sceptre (see how I know?) and smiling at us all. Everybody shouted and screamed, 'God save the Queen!', 'Good on you, Liz!' and 'God bless you!' and all sorts of other things. We got so hungry we had to buy coffee and hot dogs in the street. Later the ceremony was shown on television, but the House has no television set yet so we did not see it. The next day we went to the news cinema near here, and saw the whole procession filmed from the air, and everything that happened in Westminster Abbey when she spoke the coronation oath and was crowned by the Archbishop of Canterbury.

I am sorry, no more room, but to say I am thinking of you, and send my love to you and the family.

Your son Garrard

PS I have just moved into a flat of my own.

There! That should satisfy their royalist hearts.

CHAPTER 11

One morning, soon after he had written, Gad heard the letter box rattle, and ran upstairs to find two blue airmail letters lying on the doormat. From the moment he read them, everything changed.

AIR MAIL
July 1953

My Garrard Son

Of course we here read all about the Coronation in the Nation, and it was so good to know that you really saw it all. We are all very loyal here, too. Julian wishes he could see it all, and then he could write about it for his paper.

There is not much news here, except that the Burmese are growing very restless and there are many rumours. Rangoon is going downhill – no street lights even – but we are all together and we are well. The Army and Navy will no longer send items on order, so we are short of some things, so would you please get some Stone's Ginger Wine and a large jar or two of Marmite and give them to Uncle Ned when you see him, and he will bring them over. Thank you, Garrard son, I know you are going to see Victor anyway so you could take them then.

No time for more, but write again soon, my son, love from us all, and a big God Bless.
Mummy

Rumours? What rumours? He tore open the second letter, which was in Wilma's careful handwriting.

July 1953

Dear Garrard,

I am writing to tell you that I think we shall have to leave Burma soon. Mummy will not tell you all the things that have been going on here, and I too must be careful what I say. The times are changing fast, and many of our friends are losing their jobs in the government, in the railways and also their businesses. Fortunately, Don has contacts with the Burmah Oil Company, and if he is able to find work that way, he and Veena will go to Borneo with the children, and of course Mummy and I will go too, to help them set up their new home and look after the family. Certainly, we shall have to leave Rangoon, and do not know where else in the country we could go.

Oh Garrard, it's so sad things are changing so much. Pray for us, please, and I will write again as soon as we are settled, to give you our new address. There is nothing you or anyone can do for us. We are leaving your brothers behind, but I think maybe Julian will go England – he can work for Reuters in London. Colin will stay on awhile – it is easier for single people than for families – but I will let you know.

In haste, with love from Mummy and all of us, and God bless. Take care of yourself.

Wilma

PS How wonderful to have a flat of your own – but will you not be lonely?

No! They couldn't be thinking of leaving Burma! His family? Weirdly, he thought of his father's bones, which should have been lying in the cemetery at Insein. Don and Veena to go to Borneo – and the boys here and there? That was not how families should be – and what about him? It was one thing to go sailing off into a future of his own while there was still a home in Rangoon. But this – he would be cut off at the root.

Rereading the letters in his hand more closely now, he heard the note of desperation under the loving words – what would ginger wine and Marmite matter, if they were all in transit eastwards? And 'Pray for us', his sister said? But as she knew, he was not the praying one in the family.

Are they actually in danger? What on earth can I do?

CHAPTER 12

July/August 1953

Thérèse returned from Cecil Sharp House one day, disappointed.

She had wanted to find out about Cornish women singers of the twentieth century, and hoped to find primary sources – photographs, sheet music possibly, programmes – having previously seen only sepia pictures of grizzled male singers. She had been looking forward to the visit, but found the Ralph Vaughan Williams library closed for redecoration. *They might have warned us,* she fumed. She made up her mind to allow at least a month in the autumn to explore the rich resources of this library.

At an unexpectedly loose end, she dropped into the House. Hearing Gad playing upstairs, she went up. As soon as he caught sight of her, Gad broke off and, eyes alight, exclaimed, 'Thérèse! Sweetie! Where have you been hiding?'

He did this now and then. Would use an expression that struck oddly on her ear, and she could never make out whether to blame her own grasp of English or his. At least, it was an advance on the silence of the past weeks.

'Gad, hello! Nowhere! How is the flat?'

'Good. Good. We lit the boiler – nothing blew up. It's all fine. Why don't you drop in?'

'I might.' She didn't want to 'drop in'. She wanted to be invited.

'Listen,' said Gad, jumping up and coming towards her with hands outstretched, 'I wanted to ask you – are you doing anything on Sunday?'

'Well…' She allowed herself to wonder why he had not taken the trouble to stay in touch. Since telling him about Alain – nothing.

'Because I have to go see this uncle of mine.' Uncharacteristically, he reached a hand out to her. 'It will take most of the day and I wanted to see you, and I wondered – you'd probably be bored stiff, but – would you come with me? We could see a film on the way back, if you like?'

This was unexpected. She laughed without meaning to. 'Oh. Where is this?'

'Er – somewhere in North Harrow. It won't be Buckingham Palace, you know.'

She hesitated, before: 'Yes, OK then. I'd like to.' There was a panicky flutter in her stomach; what were his family like? How did they live? Would they like her? What would they have to talk about? If there were children, how would she deal with them?

They made their arrangements. Thérèse sensed that Gad was admitting her to a part of his life that nobody else in London knew.

'Does he live alone, this uncle?' she asked.

'Oh no – didn't I say? Uncle Ned's come over from home – staying with his younger sister Joyce and Victor, her husband, and their children – four by now, I should think.'

Tony rushed in. 'Where's Elspeth, d'you know?'

'No.' Gad grimaced – not a moment's privacy in this place. 'No idea.'

Tony departed.

'I don't think Ned's younger sister Gertie has come yet,' Gad went on. 'She's still with her husband Royce. I think Ned wants to see first if he can get work, then he'll go back to Rangoon to bring them over. He works for P&O so he will get discounted passages.'

This quantity of information from Gad, so guarded up till

now, was revealing. He must be trying to live in two worlds – no wonder he sometimes seemed abstracted. His family was evidently scattered, always on the move. Could he be seriously worried about them?

'So, they have a big house?'

'No, not at all. You'll see. They all fit in, anyway.'

She saw that this sort of arrangement was completely natural to him. She resolved to ask him more about his early life on the proposed outing. Gad so seldom referred to it. *Why not?* she wondered, before realising that she behaved in exactly the same way. In fact, so did most of those at the House. They were all birds of passage.

★

There was only one train an hour from Marylebone to Harrow Road, so they met at the ticket office in good time for the 11.37. It was scorching hot. Thérèse managed to prevent Gad paying for her; although he had invited her, she did not feel like an official girlfriend, only one individual from the House group. The etiquette was not clear, but she knew that he was short of money. *All the same, this visit is going to be special.*

They waited on the dingy platform, she in her usual skimpy cotton dress and sandals, Gad neat with a large, heavy-looking shopping bag at his feet.

'What have you got there? I didn't bring anything!'

'It's OK,' he said, seeming embarrassed. 'It's just some things my mother asked me to take.'

'Oh? What?'

'Just a few things they can't get at home – Stone's Ginger Wine – she loves it – and a few jars of Marmite.'

Her amazement must have shown in her look, for Gad turned away, shutting a door quietly in her face.

They took it in turns while they waited to name the pigeons strutting around as though looking for company – there was little else in the way of pickings.

'That one's Pogo,' said Gad firmly.

'Pogo?'

'Yep.' He turned an ironic eye upon her. She felt undeservedly ignorant. Their references seldom matched.

'And that one is Elspeth,' she countered

'?' He raised an eyebrow.

'It's just like her. So busy!' she said, feeling that she had outplayed him.

Their train came in.

★

Thérèse decided to wait until they were on the move before asking Gad about his family. There would be three-quarters of an hour, time enough. They rumbled out of the station towards Harrow, sitting side by side. She felt the heat of his shirt-sleeved body and watched his supple hands, sinewy under the glowing skin, resting on his knees between gestures. How was it, with all their differences, that she was so much at ease beside him?

Through Edgware Road, noisy Paddington, Warwick Avenue, Maida Vale and Kilburn Park the rattle and echo of the tunnelled train made real conversation difficult. People got in and out. Thérèse waited patiently, hoping for quieter times on this unfamiliar trip.

Finally, with a shock of light, the train burst out into sunshine. Queen's Park. At last Thérèse turned to Gad, with 'This is better! We can talk at last!'

Gad looked alarmed.

'Don't worry – it's just that there is so little chance at the House – people always coming and going. And I really want to ask you before I meet your family: until you came here, what sort of life was it for you – you and your uncle?'

Gad raised an eyebrow in her direction.

'That's a big question!'

'Why?' She held his gaze.

He looked away with a slight frown. 'Because my life was never one thing or another.' His eyes met hers, appraisingly. 'We were on the move so much when I was young. It was all right before the war – happy little kids, you know. Then – things got difficult.'

She glanced out of the window. Grime-crusted railway gear; backs of unkempt houses with dusty, unloved gardens; blackened brickwork and then wilted bushes of mallow, golden rod almost ready to flower, and everywhere nettles. She turned back, trying to help. 'Did not the Japanese army attack you? Like the German army attacked us in France?'

'Yes. Well, we were away by then. Everybody knew they were coming, so…' His frown persisted.

'Yes? It was the same for us, but…' She shut her mouth, cursing herself for interrupting his flow. Her family stayed put, would never abandon their farm. She shifted uncomfortably, feeling the roughness of the seat.

'My parents sent me out to India by air – on the last plane that got away, as it turned out. I know you people don't think we in Burma did much to defend ourselves.'

This sounded like a challenge.

'Do we?' Thérèse's war had been different. Despite terror of the invaders, her parents had been obsessed with staying on their own land – holding on at all costs.

Gad leaned forward, lacing his fingers in concentration.

She glanced at a sign – Willesden Junction already.

'People here don't realise how little we had – we had no army at all, you know?'

'OK.' Was this because Burma was Buddhist? But then,

Gad was Catholic. Confused, Thérèse got up and stretched, resting her bare arms on the open window, staring at tracks that curved away into the distance.

'So I ended up in a refugee camp near the airport in India with Billy, my cousin – Auntie Amy's son. When she died, my mother adopted him – a mad boy – once he chased the *mali* round the garden with a hatchet!' She turned and saw his mouth widen in a laugh, as he remembered. 'The two of us ran wild in that camp!'

She sat down opposite Gad, the better to listen.

'It must have been unbelievably – scary?' she said, the questions tumbling out now. 'Did you 'ave good food? Who was in charge? Only you two boys alone! How old were you? Who other was in the camp – only people from Burma?' She already had a notion that there were various different groups in Burma, not to be lumped together under the portmanteau word 'Burmese'.

'Oh no, we thought it was good fun.' She saw Gad warm to his story, his defences down. 'I must have been thirteen or fourteen, Billy a year younger. We were all from Rangoon at that camp, because that's where the Japs had come – and some were actually Indian, those who hadn't yet linked up again with their own families. But you don't notice much at that age. Nobody bothered about us!' His eyes moved away from her.

'So what 'appened in the end?' She didn't want him to get side-tracked again. His story seemed so sketchy. It was as if he wasn't really there; as if it all happened to somebody else.

'Well, it was extraordinary.' He looked at her, eyes wide. 'You see, the others (my sisters Wilma and Veena, and my brothers) were already in the army – the Indian army, that is – so it was just us.'

'The Indian army…?'

'Yes – there was no Burmese army, remember? My mother

64

and father had left Rangoon by this time, walking from the railhead up-country.'

'Walking! Railhead – what is that?'

'Where the trains from Rangoon finish – because of the mountains, you see. Well, they walked over those mountains from Myitkyina to the Indian border, and from there the British helped them. But of course we didn't know anything about this till later.' He paused.

Thérèse sat down again, trying to understand the whole patchy story. The insistent rhythm of the train beat in her bones. Gad seemed to have forgotten about her.

Wembley Central – the football stadium? The heat struck at her through the glass.

'We used to run wild, like I said,' Gad broke in. 'The things Billy used to do – he would have been in such trouble if any of the family had been there. He would filch whatever he wanted from anyone – children, the market traders, even soldiers – but he always had this big smile on his face and people thought he was an angel.' He laughed again. 'We didn't lack for anything! And for company we used to spend hours in the market, chatting to the merchants and running errands for them for a bit of food or, occasionally, the odd rupee.'

'But which town was this?' Thérèse asked, to get a grip on something – anything.

'You know, I never knew!' His round eyes lifted to hers. 'All we knew was that we were safe in India – unbelievable!' His voice became lively as he got into his stride.

'About the market – that was so strange. One day we were talking to this tailor who worked there. Turns out he came from Rangoon – he left before we did, when the bombing started. He recognised us, but he didn't say anything. He could see we were OK – sort of – on our own. But the next day when we went to see if he had any jobs for us, who should be there but Wilma, in her captain's uniform! She looked like thunder.'

'Wilma was a captain?'

'Sure; in the WASB – the Women's Auxiliary Service of Burma. It was attached to the Indian Army. She was furious! All she wanted to know was why we hadn't sent any message. She didn't even look pleased to see us – just screamed at us, "Mummy and all have been worried out of their heads!"

'Of course, we explained, "But we didn't know where they were!" which was true enough, but she didn't care, she just yelled, "That's no excuse!" I can still hear her! "Go get your things, and come back here in one hour! I'll send you in an army truck – and make sure you make it up to Mummy when you see her!" Then we really knew we were in trouble!'

Thérèse listened intently. She sensed that Gad really didn't enjoy talking about all this – that he was making a big concession for her. Of course he had a right to forget if he wanted to – why rake it all up again? But she needed to know all she could – and maybe telling would be good for him.

Gad's voice ceased as a ticket collector came through the carriage, and he extricated their tickets to be clipped. 'On second thoughts, though,' he said almost casually now, 'it seemed quite nice to think of seeing the family again, and getting some good food. Perhaps it seems heartless to you? But we didn't have any idea what the others had been through. I suppose we thought my mother and father had flown out like us.' He was quite calm.

'So then?'

'So then we all met up, Billy too of course, and I played for weddings – to pay my way through school in Simla – and then we went home to Rangoon.' He turned and smiled at Thérèse. 'What a lark, eh?'

So that was that.

Thérèse could only give Gad a straight look that said, 'Don't think I am going to let you off the hook!' before lapsing into silence as they drew into North Harrow station.

CHAPTER 13

August 1953

Thérèse felt the tension of the journey ease as they approached Joyce and Victor's house. Gad's painful flippancy disappeared. They passed along a dull, grimy road, lined with little shops: newsagents, betting shops, laundrettes. A few buses trundled past, packed full, but most people walked in the heat, as they did. At last they turned off the main road and stopped outside a tall terrace house set back a little. As soon as they pushed open the gate, the green front door flew wide and she saw, in the doorway, two smiling brown children: a boy in short trousers who ran down the path towards them and then changed his mind and ducked back into the house, shouting, 'Uncle Garrard's here!' An older girl in a pink cotton dress waited shyly at the door as they approached.

'Hello!' said Garrard, beaming all over his face. 'And who are you?'

'I'm Luella,' she said, standing on one leg.

'I'm very pleased to meet you,' said Garrard, dropping his heavy bag and holding out his arms. 'So come and give your uncle a hug.' She sidled up and he put his arms tight around her, pressing his face to the top of her head. Releasing her, he walked up the path, the bag in one hand and Luella holding the other.

Thérèse saw a small, smooth-skinned woman of indeterminate age appear in the doorway, a tall man behind her, and the small boy bringing up the rear.

'Joyce! Victor! It's good to see you!' exclaimed Garrard,

giving Joyce a warm familial embrace and shaking Victor's hand vigorously. Thérèse followed him into the house, where a spicy aroma filled her nostrils. She sensed many people around, out of sight – upstairs, maybe. The hallway was narrow and dark.

'It's too long,' said Joyce in her soft voice. 'Why haven't you been to see us before?'

'You look well,' said Victor heartily to Gad, shaking hands, and then transferred his attention. 'And this must be Thérèse?' He stepped forward and took her by the hand also, holding her gaze with mild brown eyes. She was conscious of her crumpled dress and scuffed sandals. Joyce was far better groomed than she – black hair set precisely in place; round, light brown face carefully powdered. Slightly startled as Joyce stepped forward to embrace her, she felt her own hot cheek meet one that was perfectly smooth and soft, and scented with a sweet jasmine fragrance, a frame smaller and more delicately made than her own long-limbed body.

Joyce now took Thérèse by the hand and led her into a sizeable living-room, one end lined with comfortable old seats, the other set up with a trestle table and some folding chairs near a window that overlooked a garden riotous with flowers.

Two smaller children followed them in, merry dark eyes alert whilst their owners waited for the grown-ups to tell them how to behave.

'Stand there, children,' said their father from the hallway. They immediately lined up in height order, as if for a photograph.

'Good. Now, this is Luella,' he announced, laying a hand on her head. 'This is George. This is Susie. And this is…' but Patrick, not waiting for the seal of approval, toddled over to Thérèse with his arms wide and a gap-toothed smile, expecting the hug which she found herself giving, lifting the thin little boy up into her arms. He smelt of chocolate biscuit and gazed into her face with soulful eyes. Everyone laughed, and they sat down to wait for Ned, an older man who erupted suddenly into the house calling out in a cheerful voice, 'Have they come yet?'

'Yes, yes, they are here. You are late as usual,' Joyce scolded her brother.

He charged in, arms open, and the introductions must be made all over again. Gad handed over the hoard of goodies intended for his mother. By this time everyone was ready for drinks – glasses of water – and Joyce jumped up to serve the meal she had prepared, refusing Thérèse's offer of help.

Ned had the gleaming family skin, aquiline features, and looked athletic for his age – a man of some authority in the family. It was he who disposed the grown-ups round the table, frowning at the children to remind them that they would eat after the visitors, for there were only five chairs. He was in charge, and Thérèse felt at ease, knowing she would be looked after. There was no awkwardness about her welcome. Clearly the family was accustomed to mixing with Europeans, and saw nothing strange about Gad's bringing a French girl with him.

Joyce brought in rice, two dishes of curry, one of vegetables and one of beef; also a mango pickle, cool cucumber *raita* with salt and chilli, and home-made lemonade. She spooned the food on to their plates, leaving enough for the children.

'I hope you like to eat hot,' she said to Thérèse, who had no idea, having never met any flavours like these before.

'Just a little for me, please,' she said nervously. 'Where do you get all these spices?'

'Well, the family brings them over, of course,' said Joyce in surprise. 'Ned brought some *ngapi* this time too.'

'You may not like this,' Gad cut in under his breath. 'It's quite strong.'

Warned, she spooned a small amount on to her plate.

He was right: it was strong. Hot ginger and chopped chilli ran through a condiment made, she later found, from dried prawns fermented in the sun. There was not a single thing about this relish that was familiar to Thérèse, and she suppressed a gasp as the fiery mixture caught the back of her throat. Coughing, she reached for her glass of cold lemonade – only to be forestalled by Gad, who directed her expertly to the rice and cucumber instead. What a relief – so mild, and so cool.

'If you think that's hot, you should try *coringhee* pickle!' he said.

The afternoon wore on. Lunch was cleared, the children fed and sent out to play in the garden, and the conversation turned to family matters. Sleepy and satisfied, Thérèse sat quiet and comfortable, listening to their urgent talk with only the slight strain of following unfamiliar intonations.

'Rangoon is in an absolute mess, isn't it?' said Joyce.

'It's not so bad…' This was Ned.

'But didn't you say the streets are full of litter? And dark in the nights, because no electricity?'

'It's not so bad, sis.' He gave her a warning glance, with a tilt of his head towards Gad.

'Oh, I would hate that, the dark. Rangoon used to be such a lovely place, with the shops, and the churches and everything. It's so sad, the way things are going.'

'Well, the way things are going, you are better off here, and I will try to come soon too.' He turned to Gad. 'So what about Don and the others – he still has his job, ne?'

'Mummy doesn't say much, in her letters, but I can tell she is worried. Are people losing their jobs, really?'

'Oh yes, the government doesn't like us Anglos.'

'But they can't kick us out?'

Thérèse woke up suddenly: Gad said 'us' – so he was thinking about going back home?

'You hope! There was such a lot of excitement, you know.

The students – they've got nothing better to do, I suppose – and then the monks! It's all Burma for the Burmese, and we will be caught right in the middle. This government is a hopeless lot, anyway – can't even keep us in water. Big Mummy will be all right, you know.' He laid a reassuring hand on Gad's knee. 'Lucky she has her own well.'

'She is thinking of leaving anyway, I believe,' said Gad, cautiously.

'What? All of them? Where to?'

'Borneo, they think. Don has a chance of a job with Burmah Oil, and Veena can always get work there too. They can have a company house.'

'That Don, he always lands on his feet,' said Ned enviously.

Gad stayed quiet, not reacting. Thérèse wondered what lay behind this moment of tension. *Families!* she thought. Would she be expected to remember all this?

'And the rest?'

'Well, Julian has contacts at Reuters in London, so he may come here, and Colin wants to stay. I am sure he will be kept on, since the government needs railway staff.'

There was news of cousins from Western Australia to Tulse Hill: Ned's brothers still working for the railway company in Rangoon; another big family of brothers and sisters with jobs in insurance up and down England.

'What will happen to Annie?' Joyce asked suddenly. 'And the baby?' Their eyes darted towards Thérèse and away again. The men looked down at their shoes, not replying. Joyce answered her own question. 'Well, of course they'll go with Big Mummy.'

Thérèse could see there was an interesting story there, but no more was said. But how could they live with all this moving around, none of them knowing what lay ahead? The one solid thing in their lives seemed to be the family. She herself hardly saw her cousins. Her family depended not on each other but on the land that was theirs, that would support them if only they played fair with it. Gad's family was something else again.

They drank tea and ate fairy cakes, and Garrard received with appreciation gifts from home, from Wilma and his mother. Whatever were they? Brightly coloured folded cardboard, with figures of Chinese individuals mounted on the panels? Easy for Ned to pack and carry, bright, but…? Joyce gave Thérèse a little handkerchief, scented and embroidered with an English flower. She managed polite thanks, sorry that she had come empty-handed. It was only afterwards that she realised nobody had asked Gad about his music.

Part II

Part II

CHAPTER 14

August 1953

Time to leave.

Gad turned to close the gate, and Thérèse waved at the family clustered on the doorstep to say goodbye, wondering when she would see them again.

'Your family is so hospitable,' she said, smiling, as they walked back to the station. 'I felt very comfortable with them.'

'They love having company,' said Gad. 'I think they are rather lonely in London. They liked you, I could see!' His face smiled into hers.

Thérèse felt herself blushing. 'I'm glad! I wish I brought them something.'

'It didn't matter.' He took her hand and held it firmly, and they walked on in step. His hand felt warm, strong, a little fleshy. Through his shirt she could feel his arm and shoulder – their resilience. She was not ready yet to say more about their day. Gad walked quietly, humming to himself.

Some of the little shops were preparing to close, but most were in full operation, family businesses perhaps ready to trade until late at night. From a newsagent's window a headline caught her eye. It screamed, *MARGARET RENOUNCES TOWNSEND*.

'Oh look!' said Thérèse. 'So she has decided to end it, after all!'

Gad cast her a quizzical glance, as if wondering what her interest was.

The headline had brought the whole affair back to her

notice. It had been rumbling in the French press as well as the English for months; the public were sympathetic towards the princess, according to the papers. But something had forced her to give up on her lover.

Gad let go of her hand. 'Seems so,' he said. 'Look, I'll get the Standard and some ciggies too. Coming?'

'I'll wait out here.' She leaned against the wall, warm in the sunshine.

He came back with the paper and handed it to her, saying: 'We can read about it on the way back.'

'Yes… Do you know, I am exactly the same age as your Princess Margaret?' Thérèse said, feeling a curious sense of connection in this banal coincidence.

'Are you? And I am exactly the same age as "my" Queen Elizabeth! My birthday is the same as hers!'

'Well! So you are – how do you say it? – well connected!'

'But of course,' he teased.

'And not proud!'

'Aw, shucks!' He produced a parody of a modest smirk that made her giggle.

Thérèse turned her thoughts back to the serious question of Gad's situation – the loneliness of being here, in a strange country, with family responsibilities but few resources.

'Well, never mind all that,' she said. 'Joyce and Victor have all their cousins to turn to, do they not?'

'True. But they don't see them every day, and Victor has to work, and the children go to school – it's really not easy.' His face was closed.

Thérèse pictured the older children, brown faces standing out in a sea of white ones. There was a great deal not being said. She wondered if the other children picked on them – or even the teachers. For little Patrick, that was all still to come.

'How do – Luella, and George, and Susie – how do they get on? I heard Victor say they are doing well at school.'

'Yes, they work hard – but how many of the school friends invite them? Ask them when they last went to a birthday party with their classmates!' There was a touch of anger in his voice.

'Yes. I see. Joyce must feel it.'

'Of course she does, but she's not going to make a noise about it – mustn't rock the boat, you know. That's the way of the Raj.'

*

The train pulled out of the station and Thérèse glanced through the report on the 'Townsend affair', as it was beginning to be called, then threw the paper aside.

'It's strange about Margaret,' she said. 'For such a beautiful person with so much of privilege to have such troubles, no?'

The affair between Princess Margaret and Group Captain Peter Townsend, a war hero but unacceptable as a royal bridegroom because of his previous divorce, had been all over Paris Match as in the London press. She looked at Gad, curious to know how he would respond.

'You always pay for it in the end, I suppose,' he said lightly. His brown eyes gave nothing away.

'Pay for what?'

'Privilege.'

'You are fatalistic. Don't you think it is a pity she cannot marry Townsend? She is in love with him, I think.'

'Well, yes, I do. I am quite surprised. I didn't think the English church was so strict. I know we Catholics are. But I suppose it's special for the royals; they have to set an example.'

'Well, I'm a republican,' said Thérèse robustly, standing away from French sentiment. 'Do you think she will be happy now? Is she going to marry some aristocratic twit?' She was feeling her way here, knowing that her question was more than casual.

77

'I don't think that matters so much as where her true feelings are. She could be making a huge mistake. I feel sorry for her.'

'I suppose she could have rebelled?'

'Well, I suppose she could have. But I knew she wouldn't. She'd never give up her royal status. Too much to lose.' He said this quite casually, seeming to understand perfectly.

Thérèse wondered again where this mind set came from, who his friends had been in Burma, what his connections were. And how much importance he really gave to love.

Then she looked at him, sitting beside her so open-faced and companionable, and banished the thoughts. If he had any secret 'baggage' as she had heard it called, surely he would not have brought her to visit his family. There were so many contradictions in their ways of thinking, it was confusing.

She bent to her newspaper again, reading in the sunshine that succeeded in reaching her through the dirt-stained window.

★

It was late afternoon before they rattled into Marylebone, and still fine and warm so, unwilling for the day to end, they wandered into Regent's Park. Fluffy clouds still floated in the blue sky; the air was soft on their skin; music from a band came gently across the grass – a tender waltz tune. They had all the time in the world to dawdle, fingers lightly linked, towards the canal, where jade-headed ducks with their V-shaped wakes caught their eyes, and narrow boats nosed quietly past the Zoo with its animal grunts and yelps. This afternoon, there was nobody in the world she would rather be with.

'You may have to pay to see the animals,' said Gad, 'but you can get the sound effects for nothing!'

Thérèse smiled to herself at his instinctive frugality.

But as they left the canal behind and headed for bus routes, something changed – as if the day urgently needed crowning. Gad drew his hand away from hers and laid a heavy arm across her shoulder, pulling her close so that they walked hip to hip and Thérèse could feel the length of his body against hers – then – a big old tree; she found herself leaning against it, and the rough bark against her back and Gad against her and she saw his glowing face close – then his lips enveloped hers and she was lost in the kiss; lost in the moment when it seemed her mouth had always belonged to him.

CHAPTER 15

BY AIR MAIL
September 1953

Dear Mummy and All at home

Thank you for your letter, and I hope you have received the ginger wine and Marmite I took to Ned in the summer. My new friend Thérèse (she's French) came too. Victor and Joyce are well and gave us a fine dinner of beef curry and pilau rice, with brinjal pickle and ngapi, and plenty of gin thoke afterwards. I had almost forgotten the taste of home cooking. Nobody here knows how to make a curry, so now I have a place of my own, I will learn to do it myself.

I shall be very busy the next few weeks, because I am playing in a big concert at Westminster Central Hall, and I shall meet the Duchess of Gloucester! I shall play the Chopin Nocturne that I first learned at home, but now I play it so much better, and two other Chopin pieces. I would rather have played Brahms, but my Brahms Ballade will not be ready in time. The programme is made up of six of the best students each playing a group of pieces. Two of the others, a girl and a boy, are amazingly good. I shall have to hire a tail suit, and that will be very expensive, but it is expected.

Did I tell you how my friends from the House came to help me decorate the flat – Tony, Sanjay, Thérèse and some others?

So you see, your son is on his way!

Love to you and all the family, and I hope that Burma will settle down soon.

Your son Garrard

Gad laid his pen down with a sigh, folded the airmail form and stuck it down, feeling curiously defeated by his attempts to keep up a connection with his closest family while his whole self was crying out to think about Thérèse, about the implications of the day they had spent together.

He moved restlessly about the flat, knowing it needed cleaning but unable to concentrate on it. So, with posting time approaching, he picked up the letter, inadequate though it was, and his Bach Fugues to practise on the way back, and went out to the post box at the end of his road. Somehow, he found himself continuing past the back of the BBC and the neighbouring small restaurants and newsagents, towards Thérèse's room.

There was a public call box on the way, but he had come out with no money, only his front door key. He had never yet made an unplanned visit to her home, though of course he knew where she lived, and she had never yet invited him. Ten minutes' walk and he was there, standing on the pavement and looking up at what he presumed was her window, as if expecting to see her lean out at any minute.

There was no sign of her. Perhaps she was sitting at her desk, working. Or – perhaps she had a visitor. There was only one way to tell.

The house door was solid with a shiny letter box and a row of neatly labelled bell pushes beside it. He saw her name, 'Kutanguay', against the top button, pressed it and waited. Nothing – then a window thrown open and a 'Catch!' as a key ring came flying down on to the pavement at his feet.

Two keys, both freshly cut Yales. At the second try he got the right one, and entered a tidy hallway with a row of wooden pigeon holes on the wall. It struck Gad as remarkably civilised. Soberly, he climbed the three flights of stairs to her place.

She stood at her open door, waiting. He halted near the top to say, 'Is it OK if I come up?'

'Of course, yes.'

He went towards her, reaching out, but she only retreated into the doorway and stood aside to let him pass, dropping her eyes. He noticed that she was in a drab old sweater with holes in the elbows.

He went in, finding himself in a large, light room furnished for one occupant. By the window was a table bearing neat piles of papers; others were strewn around the floor by the chair with its green Rexene seat, which had been pushed back in a hurry, presumably at the sound of the doorbell. The heavy sash window was still open. There was her bed in one corner and an all-purpose cupboard for her clothes, then a heavy old radiator and finally, in the far corner, a kind of cooking arrangement that included a gas ring, a small sink and some open shelves. There was no curtain.

'So how are you?' he asked, meaning it.

'I'm fine. What are you doing here?'

'I just wanted to see you.'

At that, she closed the door carefully behind her, and moved into the room. There was only the one chair.

'Well, here I am,' she said.

'Yes, so I see. You are working?' with a glance at the table.

'Yes, I am getting my notes in order. I need to go back to Cecil Sharp House soon.'

'With any special focus?'

'Of course with a particular focus – but you surely didn't come here to talk about my work, did you?'

'No, I suppose not. Look, can we sit down?' he asked, with a vague gesture that included the bed and the one chair, but leaving it up to her to choose.

Thérèse turned the chair around to face the room, and waved Gad towards it, herself making for the bed, where she propped herself against the wall and drew her legs up comfortably, saying nothing.

Gad leaned his elbows on his knees, trying to make a link across the space between them.

'You know, that day with my family – I hope it wasn't awkward for you?'

'Awkward, no! I told you – they were so nice to me,' she said politely.

'Yes, I know, but… There was so much family stuff after lunch – talk about Rangoon, and how things are with the people we know. You must have been bored.'

'Bored? Bored?' Her voice became animated. 'Don't you see how fascinating all that was – so different from here, and from my home too? I mean, it's like opening a door on things I didn't even know existed.'

It was a good response, but it didn't answer the real question.

'And afterwards?' he said, tension in his voice and urgency in his eyes.

'Afterwards…' she repeated, looking directly at him. 'In the park?'

'Yes.'

She took a breath. 'In the park was simply lovely,' she said, casting caution to the winds – she couldn't help it. A smile started in her eyes, her cheeks flushed red and her eyes sparkled.

'Really?' cried Gad in delight. 'Oh, what a relief – it all happened so quickly, I wasn't sure it was OK. Anyway, I wasn't actually thinking…'

'It was very OK,' she said again, still smiling, and then she uncurled herself, went over to Gad, pressing herself against the back of his chair and dropping a feathery kiss on his ear.

Quickly then: 'But now, you'd better go before I get myself a bad name!'

'Oh – yes, of course,' he said, jumping up, suddenly aware of the risk she had taken in letting him in. 'But come out again soon, will you? Soon? We could go and see that film. Saturday?'

'Saturday then. Will you pick me up here?'

'Of course. I'll see what's on and drop a note in. Thérèse – thank you!'

'Go, go,' and she held the door open for him.

CHAPTER 16

September 1953

It was the first of many dates. Whenever they could spare the time they roamed London, walking the streets to visit free museums and galleries, carrying food in their pockets to eat on the riverbank or in parks and garden squares.

There was a Saturday, which they had planned to spend together, when their enthusiasm wore a little thin. First they walked far across Hampstead Heath, but it was still the dog days of summer, sultry, and by late afternoon they felt exhausted, finding nothing new to say to each other. On the lookout for entertainment such as another good film, they ambled down Heath Street.

Gad caught sight of a poster for *The Little World of Don Camillo,* a story that he had come across as a small paperback, read and treasured so that it was still standing on his bookshelves.

'What about this?' he asked, turning to Thérèse. Rain clouds threatened to burst. 'Shall we see it?'

She smiled back. She had come out in a thin cotton dress and sandals, carrying an umbrella. He saw she was reluctant for the summer to end. His eyes stroked her long bare arms and legs, drowned in the intense colours she wore, yellow chrysanthemums on jade green, with the scarlet accent of her umbrella. He loved her; sometimes it was almost too much.

'Fine,' she responded now, with a burst of energy. 'Yes, OK. Let's walk down the hill, then.'

Gad wished again that he had not brought the duffel coat, which had become his second skin in London's changeable climate. Whether he wore it or carried it, today it was a burden, hot and heavy and smelling of the last shower of rain. He slung it over his shoulder and reached for Thérèse's hand. He could taste the wetness in the air, clammy and tantalising. At home, in the days before the monsoon, there was always tension and people would break into rows for no reason. But Thérèse's fingers intertwined with his, and he felt reassured.

They stood waiting in the cinema queue. Gad watched a boy with dreamy eyes moving his hands up and down his girl's waist, gently, slowly, utterly oblivious of watching eyes.

It was cool in the cinema where the sun never reached, but smelt of stale cigarette smoke. They sat down close together, and during the newsreel Thérèse lit her own fresh cigarette as she always did, right elbow cupped in left hand. Gad laid his arm across her back, moving his thumb under the loose little sleeve that veiled her shoulder, longing to explore the soft hollow of her armpit. But Thérèse finished her cigarette and leaned forward to stub it out in the ashtray, settling back again companionably to watch the main film.

Gad knew she had not read the book; it told of a combative Catholic priest in a small town in the Po Valley. Don Camillo and Peppone, the fiery leader of the local communists, had once fought side by side against Fascists, but now they competed for the hearts and souls of the people. Gad loved the film's knockabout humour, but found his mind turning back to the Church wrapped firmly around his own family at home, protective but ultimately tight, suffocating. You could not criticize. Well, he had escaped now, and could enjoy Don Camillo's furious conversations with the Lord: the priest never quite managed to achieve his higher calling any more than Peppone could altogether toe the Party line.

The film wound to its close; Peppone had his children baptised with several names, which in the end did not include 'Lenino', though he had been tempted. All ended happily – if you happened to be Catholic – and in any case common humanity triumphed. Everybody came out of the cinema smiling.

Gad was thinking how much he enjoyed seeing the Church at such a distance – a battleground with caricatured opponents; a good joke to be relished. At home, religion was full of warning voices: beware of sex which means wickedness and disease; beware of freedom which will lead you astray; honour your father and your mother; obey them and your priest in all things. Gad wished he could be as single-minded as that boy, just to enjoy the moment.

★

'Well, where now?' asked Thérèse.

It was about six o'clock, that awkward time of day when afternoon switches into evening. It was a Saturday. The film had been entertaining, but it hadn't helped to resolve the tension that seemed to have developed between them. He didn't know what to do with her, and she seemed to want him to decide for them both.

Gad wrenched his thoughts back to the present. Somehow he had lost his joy in the day. There were too many things going on in his life. The worry about his family was constant, most particularly because he didn't even know where they were at any moment, whether they had been able to leave Burma and, if so, whether they were comfortably settled in Borneo. And then, there was Thérèse.

In such a frame of mind, only music could rescue him; what he badly needed was to practise.

'What do you want to do?' he asked, shifting his cumbersome coat to the other arm.

She stopped and her eyes widened. He pulled himself together.

'I'm sorry, but you know, there's this concert that I've been picked for at Central Hall in two weeks' time. Some VIPs are coming. It's really important to me, and I absolutely must put in some work.' He looked at her uncertainly.

He could see she was impressed. But still: 'On a Saturday? Don't you ever take a break?'

'Course I do,' he said, nettled. He already had, to spend the day with her. 'But not just because it's Saturday!'

They walked southwards in silence. A shower began, large drops hitting the dusty pavement with a splash, the cheesy smell of new rain rising.

'Well then, call me,' she said abruptly, and dived into the Underground.

He couldn't leave it like that, and sprinted after her, catching up at the ticket office.

'Thérèse,' he said, taking her arm. 'Come on. Please don't go like that. We're fighting over nothing.'

Jerking her arm away, Thérèse turned to face him.

'Nothing? Zis 'as been a nice day,' she said, her accent sounding more pronounced than usual. 'But I see you 'ave things on your mind, and so 'ave I. For me, it is not easy either, you know.'

'No? Why?' He did not need to ask – it was obvious that people in the street always looked curiously at the pair of them, sometimes with open hostility. He really didn't know how she felt about all that; had never enquired.

'Because – zere are sings you don't know about me.' She stuck her chin out, belligerently.

He was nonplussed. 'But you told me – about your brother.' It was all he could think of.

'No, no. Other things.'

'Well, what?'

'Maybe some time – but not 'ere, not now. I 'ave to go… I really enjoyed today.'

She turned and went through the turnstile, giving him a small wave as she disappeared.

*

Gad did not see her for the next few days. His tutor put pressure on him to memorise his pieces at once, not to delay until the last minute. Given his facility for improvisation, Gad knew the danger – that if he stumbled over a phrase, he could always cover his tracks without the audience noticing, but it was a bad habit, and he would not always get away with it. Note perfect was an absolute requirement now; after that, true artistry could begin.

By Wednesday he had the music in his bones – had played little else – and surfaced again, to think about Thérèse. Her sudden departure had seemed to be a minor disagreement over how to spend a Saturday evening.

But he thought it was more – she was not a girl who took offence. Yet there had been a lack of feeling that day, boredom almost.

Then he knew – it was becoming impossible. If he was honest, he would never be satisfied until he could hold her, touch and explore, love her. There was no stopping now. But what could he offer her? It was not just the colour of his skin, which seemed to be such a huge problem in this wonderful city. That didn't help, but more than that, he was just a poor student with ambition but no prospects and nothing yet to show for all his work. There was too much to kill their joy in each other, and that was the worst of it.

He made up his mind. It was altogether impossible for him to keep on seeing Thérèse as well as living his music.

Walking around London, he thought of nothing else. At

the House, he could not concentrate on anything. Elspeth had taken to looking at him questioningly, and he would look away, knowing her shrewd instinct where her young tenants were concerned, and unwilling to have his feelings made public.

He decided to break with Thérèse. He must speak to her – it would be cowardly to leave things unsaid – but he did not want her to come to his flat. A public place would be better.

He sent her a note asking her to tea at the big Lyons' Corner House at Marble Arch; as unromantic a place as he could think of.

★

She came through the entrance and his heart turned over. She had on a loose coat that swung as she walked, and high heels.

'Hello, Gad,' she said, unsmiling, holding out her hand to him. They sat. 'Just tea, please,' she said.

'The same for me,' he said.

They waited until their order appeared, and then: 'How are you?' he asked. 'Shall I take your coat?'

'No, thank you. I won't stay long.'

He heard her, and immediately felt a pang of – disappointment? Love? No, more like aggrieved irritation – this was his line.

'Oh,' he said.

Thérèse straightened her back, and then, looking into her teacup as she stirred, round and round: 'We should stop seeing each other,' she said. 'It doesn't feel the same as it did – your music is everything to you. You must just get on with it.'

His eyes were on her face; he saw colour rise in her cheeks as she said this, and knew she was lying. He badly wanted to deny his ambition, to pour out his feelings for her, to challenge her doubts once and for all, but his determination held.

Bowing his head, he sat back in his chair. 'Well, I'll go along with your decision. I'm sorry it has not worked out, but glad we've had this chance to talk. We'll see each other at the House.'

The words came out of his mouth without passing through his brain. He could not remember any of them afterwards.

Leaving her tea unfinished, she picked up her bag and stood to go. He rose to his feet. There was a single, uncomfortable moment and then she held out her hand for an English handshake, turned and left.

CHAPTER 17

October 1953

The world was a colder place without Thérèse. Gad felt sick when he thought of what he had lost. He could have kicked himself for being so passive. He had sat there while Thérèse put an end to their future; he had silently consented.

It was true that he had wanted the break, or so he thought. He wanted and didn't want it, was anxious about his music and uncertain about how his life and Thérèse's could possibly mesh together in the long term. Yet their few months together had been wonderful.

But then again, she had said something – he hadn't paid much attention – something about 'things you don't know about me'. Perhaps it wasn't all about him? He couldn't sleep for wondering. They were not children, to rush blindly into such uncertainty. Gad thought of lovely Luella, sturdy George, little Susi and baby Patrick in their house in Harrow. What about his own children, if he were to have any? Every child deserves security. *Could Thérèse and I manage that?*

*

February 1954

That winter, at a low ebb, he caught flu, and sweated under heavy blankets in his poorly heated flat, thinking with longing of the boiled rice and ginger his mother would make when she saw the yellow-grey shadow of sickness show through the brown of her son's skin, and the ochre tinge that would stain the whites of his eyes, the legacy of his childhood bouts of malaria. Wilma had told him of the efforts Big Mummy made to save her frail youngest; how she had circled herbs around his head in traditional Burmese style but also, as a good Catholic, pledged her diamond earrings to the Church if he recovered. He did, and the earrings were gone forever.

For the first time Gad realised that here, his illness might not so easily be recognised; might even be misdiagnosed. English doctors were not used to his difference. There were no dark shadows showing under his eyes; his hair still sprang curly over his forehead, instead of hanging lankly as often happened with Sam or Tony when they were out of sorts; there was no obvious pallor. The signs were there for those who knew what to look for, but doctors here might not have that experience.

He was desperately lonely, too – had brought it on himself by signalling to his friends that he would be immersed in work till further notice, and would not welcome visitors. Of course, he had no telephone. Nobody missed him, or knew that he was ill.

For two weeks he crawled around the flat alone.

Then at last he began to feel life returning. He cranked up the boiler to run a much-needed bath, and put on clean clothes.

Finally he got himself back to college, and dived into work once more, practising with a new intensity, and finally earning praise from his most discerning tutor Murray Smith. Yet as he sat in one of the stuffy little practice rooms in College with only the piano, a stool and a dusty pile of music stands for company, he felt his isolation complete.

He seemed to have lost a vital connection with the music. When he lifted his eyes from the keys he saw only dusty scrubland, trackless with shifting sand, unbroken by softer signs of life: a blade of grass, a thorny shoot, a palm tree to give shade.

He would play mechanically, repeating the notes that he had once heard as magical, his mind following the tracery of counter melodies with nothing within him vibrating in response.

It was not that he was missing Thérèse, exactly, though he was, with all his senses. He would get flashes of her head turned towards him and a slow smile beginning in her grey eyes; bare legs curled under her as she relaxed on his sofa; the salt taste of her skin; a sun-burnt shoulder with that soft hollow beneath.

But this, now, seemed to be a different sense of loss – as of an underground stream that used to bubble spontaneously within him and that he could no longer find. At the end of a piece he would sit still, his hands on the keys, and feel the silence in the room as the echoes died.

He would walk home alone, to his empty flat where nothing stirred after he left in the morning. A mug was still draining in the kitchen; yesterday's newspaper was on the floor where he had dropped it; the bed was untidy; a bedroom curtain hung askew. He had been too successful in warning his friends not to come.

★

One morning, waking early to the usual grey prospect, Gad had had enough. Summoning up his spirit of enterprise he dressed, combed his hair neatly and walked over to the church he had been attending: St Xavier's in Holborn. It was a well-known Catholic church that had once been chapel to a European royal family but was now the venue for a polyglot congregation made up of medical staff from two local hospitals and greengrocers working in nearby Covent Garden.

The organist was a highly qualified musician of uncertain temper, and Gad knew he had upset two of the priests as well as a number of the parishioners. He thought there might be a niche for him, for weddings and funerals at least.

He went into the church, charmed as always by its rose-red hangings and white alabaster, a lamp burning steadily before the altar. One of the priests would often be there, but today the place was empty. He bowed his head and thought a quick prayer of intercession before going round to the presbytery at the back of the building.

Father Martin himself answered his knock.

'Garrard, my son,' he said. 'What brings you here?'

Gad spotted crumbs of toast round Fr Martin's mouth; he must be having a late breakfast after saying Mass.

'I would like to talk to you,' he said. 'I hope it's convenient – not too early?'

'No, no, not at all. Is it me you want? Come in, come in.'

He took Gad into the house, and led the way to a small parlour, bare and not at all comfortable. They sat on upright chairs at a table. There was a stale smell that had in it whiffs of incense and fresh varnish and toast.

'Now then,' said Fr Martin, looking at Gad expectantly.

Gad rested one wrist on the shiny table, not sure how to start.

'I wondered,' he began hesitantly, 'whether there would be any opportunity for me as an organist here.'

'Oh,' said Fr Martin. He looked surprised. Perhaps he had been expecting a spiritual dilemma of some sort. 'But we have an organist.'

'I know,' said Gad and then, choosing his words carefully, 'He's brilliant, isn't he? I just thought – there might be times when he would be away, or unable to be at a midweek funeral. Perhaps I could deputise occasionally? I used to be an organist at home – for years, in fact.'

He had mentioned this to one of the priests when he first arrived, but was not sure it was Fr Martin, or if he remembered anyway.

'You were, eh?' said Fr Martin. 'I see. And have you any experience with choirs?'

'Oh yes, I trained the choir at my school in Simla – masters as well as boys.'

'Hmm.' Fr Martin looked at him, one hand stroking his chin. 'Well, there isn't much of a choir at the moment – only two where there used to be eight or ten.'

Gad knew that others had dropped away, daunted by the present man's overbearing ways. 'Perhaps we could contact the old members?' he suggested.

'Well, sure, we could see if we can retrieve them; perhaps recruit a few new ones too; build the choir up again,' said Fr Martin. 'What do you say?'

Despite this sorry situation, Gad did not hesitate for a moment. It would be the kind of music he knew well, and it would mean he could practise on this organ – each instrument was different, and he looked forward to experimenting with the stops so that he could make the instrument roar like the Lion of Judah or coo like a Holborn pigeon.

'Of course I will do that, Father,' he said. 'Tell me, who are the other choir members that you'd like to bring back?'

'Ah. Well, you have John Flynn already – a fine tenor, a very fine tenor indeed. He is a joy to listen to.'

Gad detected a touch of reserve in this praise, and wondered what the unspoken 'but' might be.

'And Mrs Flynn, of course. She's a tremendous strong woman with a wonderful tuneful voice – and her vibrato... Do you know that she cooks Christmas dinner for thirty? Yes. She's always at Midnight Mass, though – she puts the turkey and sprouts on before she comes out.'

Gad thought of Mrs Mockford's dry meat and soggy sprouts. 'Oh. And the others – those who have left?'

'Let me see. There's Niamh; she's a marvellous musician – knows the way everything should be done.'

'Oh.'

'And then Declan, the one who lives at the Irish Club off Oxford Street; he's more of a baritone. He was a priest.' Fr Martin avoided Gad's eye. 'Then there are always Phillipine nurses working at Great Ormond Street and the National – they come when they are not on shift, but there always used to be at least three or four of them. They were trained in the mission schools, and they read music well. And of course Juanita, from the British Museum; an expert in flamenco, though her English is not very fluent.'

Gad had thought of trying out the austere disciplines of plainchant, which he had been studying this term. After Fr Martin's report, he felt that was out of the question – at least for the time being. He would find a style that would better suit the singers' natural talents.

'I'll tell you what,' said Fr Martin, getting to his feet. 'I'll visit them myself, and see if I can persuade them to give the choir another try.'

CHAPTER 18

November 1953

Dear Mummy and All at home,

I am hoping that you are still in Rangoon, otherwise this letter may never reach you. I hear no news, and keep wondering how you are and how is life for you all?

I have not heard from you since Thérèse and I went to visit Uncle Ned and all, and gave him the things you wanted – is he back, and did those things reach you? Thank you so much for the things from Burma – I will treasure them.

I have no more to tell you now, except that I have asked Fr Martin at St Xavier's for some work in the church, and hope that he will find me some. Of course I am busy studying.

Please send me news soon.

Your loving son,

Garrard

November 1953

Dear Garrard,

We have not heard from you since September, and we have not written because we have had to move, and I am now writing from Borneo. Don has a contract here for a few months, and we can decide whether to stay or not. It is very different here from Rangoon. We are in a big company house but it does not feel like home. Don has a nice car.

The children are settling in well.

I hope your concert went well. Write soon, but if we move
again your letter may not reach us.

  Your sister

  Wilma

Gad read this on his way to college, and it stopped him in his
tracks, late as he was. Had he been blind and deaf? Had he
really not written home for two months, knowing how unsafe
his family were feeling? Too late, though – now they were
out of reach, making the best of things as usual – and now he
hadn't even got an address to write to.

CHAPTER 19

March 1954

Fr Martin had been as good as his word, and Gad got along well with his multinational singers. Moving round as they sang, in order to hear individual voices, he began to understand their particular abilities and limitations, and saw that they had begun to trust him. Before long, he managed to persuade his disparate bunch to modify their swoops and wobbles and to sing out in a clear, natural tone without losing expressiveness. Regular members of the congregation had commented on the improvement, and he knew that the music was emerging more clearly.

Missing Thérèse and constantly worried about his family, he was grateful for the new interest.

As for his own progress, he realised that there was none – that he had reached a plateau. This happened sometimes, and it was always unpleasant. Searching for inspiration, he heard of an adult master class in a college near Waterloo. He imagined it to be something like the daily class taken by dancers: a workout, the performers responding to a sharp, experienced eye who could point out faults of which they were not aware. There would be advanced players, and the tutor was renowned and not under pressure to prepare students for examinations.

He signed up.

★

April 1954

On the first Monday in April, Gad arrived early for class, a sheaf of music under his arm. There was already somebody there – a slim woman in a dark blue dress, studying a register that lay on the table. Alert for first impressions, Gad approached. High windows kept out the view; the chairs were the shabby plastic kind that stacked; there was a battered Broadwood grand. It didn't look promising.

Anxious to impress, he had dressed carefully – a polo neck sweater tucked into his well-pressed trousers, a twisted leather belt. He had brushed his glossy hair back at the sides, leaving some to fall over his eyes. She looked at him and sighed a little.

'Good evening,' said Gad tentatively. 'Am I the first?' How lame!

'Looks like it,' she said with reserve. 'Good evening. I am Eva…'

He nodded, noticing the darkness beneath her eyes.

Elsewhere in the building doors opened and banged shut, and voices called to each other. The last of the sun shone through the grimy windows. The college, though solidly built, was set back only a few yards from a busy main road, and the sound of traffic outside was loud. Gad heard buses stop and start. A motorbike revved up and a heavy lorry droned by. He thought about how his Schumann would sound against this background.

Footsteps clattered past the door, and excitable voices were raised. The door flew open, a dishevelled head appearing.

'Sorry,' said its owner, dangling an untidy haversack by one strap. 'I thought this was First Year Drama.'

'No,' said Eva. 'It's Piano Master Class.'

The head withdrew with another apology. Eva smiled professionally at Gad.

'So, are you sure this is where you want to be?' she asked.

Gad regarded her, and decided that it was. Her eyes were large, dark, liquid, almond-shaped. He felt he could trust her to be honest.

'Yes,' he said. 'Please.'

He gave her his name, and she ticked it off on the register, using her left hand as he did, the silver pen flashing with quick, incisive strokes. She looked at him gravely, a small tightness at the corners of her mouth.

'Doesn't it bother you, all this noise?' he asked abruptly.

'Noise?' She seemed mystified, lifting her eyebrows in perfect arcs.

'Well, the traffic...'

She laughed gently. 'This is London,' she said. 'Haven't you noticed? We can't be so easily distracted.'

'We?'

'Yes.'

Gad liked that – to be included. It was all he wanted.

Eva moved over to the piano, taking a pile of music and laying it on top. She was about his own height, with a neat figure. She tried the pedals with one foot, then stooped to inspect one of them. Her silky hair hid her profile. Nobody else had arrived yet.

'Can I play you something?' he asked.

'You had better wait till everybody is here.' She came to stand in front of him. 'I have a particular approach, you see. It's better to start on the right footing. Have you played much in public?'

'I had my own radio programme at home, if you count that,' he said, striving for a modest tone. 'I've played for weddings and funerals for years.' He decided not to mention the bars and clubs that had helped to provide income. 'And then, of course, I give concerts at college.'

Eva smiled. He could see she was unimpressed, and this riled him, spurring him into action. Leaving his music on a chair, he marched over to the piano, sat on the worn stool, adjusted it for height and began a theme from Schumann. Before long, he let his imagination take off and his fingers go their own way into a fluent and lively improvisation.

Eva had not moved from where she stood. A spark of anger showed in her eyes and a flush of red on her thin cheeks. He stopped.

'No,' she said. 'You can't do it like that here.'

He took a breath. 'I thought you might be the one to help me.'

'Perhaps, but I don't work like this. It may be a nuisance to you, but music is serious for me. I can't play games with it.' She turned away from him.

Gad still sat at the piano, his spirits dropping into his loafers, and coughed gently. 'I didn't know improvising was "playing games".'

'Well, it's a bit like a church organist on a Sunday morning, isn't it?'

This stung. Providing music for church services was his job, which had put him through school in Simla, and now St Xavier's was paying the fees for her classes.

'So what is serious?' he asked.

The question remained unanswered. The door opened wide and students began to drift in as the clock showed seven o'clock.

CHAPTER 20

Gad walked out of the class alone, as he had entered it. Under the dark sky, he muttered to himself, 'Idiots! Morons!' and kicked a lamppost. 'Can't even damn play!' His pace quickened. 'Stopping every damn minute to discuss "the phrasing"! What's discussing got to do with anything?' He stood stock still and said, furiously, 'And I've paid for a whole damn term of this!'

Astonished to find himself near home already, he turned into his local all-night café, drank several cups of watery coffee in quick succession and smoked more cigarettes than he usually allowed himself in a day.

'What's up?' asked Annie from behind the bar, flapping the dirty tea towel ineffectually over the counter top.

'Nothing!' he growled.

'Pardon me for asking.' And she turned her back like an offended cat.

At last, he got up and paid the bill with a mumbled apology. He liked Annie, and had not meant to take his frustration out on her. Not knowing what to do with himself, he went home but could settle to nothing.

This was no good. Why was he so out of gear with everybody else in this blessed country? Pacing up and down the crooked corridor, he decided to tackle the issue head on.

★

Eva laid down her fork, with a little sigh of appreciation, though there was no one else to hear. The salmon mousse and salad were good; you had to hand it to Walter's Deli. Now she sipped her black coffee, relaxing in her pale linen-covered chair as the Saint-Saens cello concerto unfolded on her record player. She never liked to listen to piano music in the evenings; this was her time away from its demands.

The doorbell shrilled; she tensed. It was already after nine o'clock, and friends seldom dropped in unannounced. Reluctantly, she uncurled herself, set down her coffee on the low glass table and went to see who it was, switching on the hall light. She peered through the peephole set in the heavy wooden door. It was drizzling, and the outside lamp shed its fuzzy beam on Gad's downcast face. Startled, she thought he looked terribly sad, standing there in the wet. She undid the locks and swung the door open with a little hesitation, not exactly afraid but apprehensive as to what Gad could want at this time in the evening.

'Hello?' she said, on a rising inflection.

'Eva?' He raised his head slowly. The light rain drifted down.

'Garrard. What a surprise.'

'Yes, I'm sorry. I should have called. The phone boxes are always out of order.'

He took a half step back. She could see a thick sweater under his duffel coat, and his hair damp and curly from the rain. He was holding some music under his arm.

'No, no. It's all right.' She held the door open further. 'Would you like to come in?'

Gad stood, obviously undecided. Then he braced his shoulders, and a smile began in his round brown eyes, seeming to make some connection with her. 'Thank you.' He stepped over the threshold into the house, wiping his feet carefully on the mat. She saw him notice her long pale dressing-gown, tied at the waist, and wrapped it tighter around herself.

Taking a moment to relock the front door, she turned to face him.

'Well,' she said. 'So here we are, then. What is it?'

'I really didn't mean to disturb you. I didn't realise it would be so late by the time I got here. It was just… When I got home from the class, I thought…'

'Yes?' she prompted, puzzled.

'It's going to be hard to explain.'

'I see.' Eva sensed an appeal, such as she found hard to resist. 'Here, give me your coat.'

'It's wet.'

'I know. I'll hang it up.'

She watched him shrug off the shabby coat and hand it to her, shifting his music from arm to arm. She took a wooden hanger from the hall cupboard and hung the heavy garment near the radiator as carefully as if it had been cashmere. He rubbed a shoulder with his free hand as she led the way into her music room. He paused on the threshold, evidently impressed by what he saw, cocked his head towards the record player, still quietly playing the Saint-Saens, and glanced at her coffee, cooling on the glass table.

'I am sorry,' he said again.

'Yes. Never mind. Just sit down and make yourself comfortable. I'll get you some coffee.'

She picked up her cup and went off, needing a moment to collect herself. 'What is serious?' was the question that Gad had asked; maybe he was here to find out.

Returning, Eva saw him silhouetted against the soft light, gazing at her many photographs. He stood still before the one of her parents when they were young, and she saw afresh as if through his eyes an attractive dark-haired couple dancing dreamily in each other's arms under a string of fairy lights, the man bending to hold his partner close, gazing into her upturned face. Eva looked again, too, at the other couples seated at small tables behind them, at the waiter weaving his way to bring their tall drinks, at the black-haired musicians seen at the very edge of the picture, their eyes sad and knowing. Another picture, the head-and-shoulders shot with '*Alles liebe* – Elena' scrawled across it; next, the same young woman in a laughing group leaning on a rock with pine trees.

Gad's expression remained tense until she handed him his cup, and then at last his face relaxed, he smiled and sat down.

'What you said at Greville,' she began, settling into her chair, 'I've been wondering – what did you mean?'

'About what?'

'You said it hasn't been easy – in your own life? Was it political? In – Burma, is it? Were there difficulties for you there?'

He looked startled. 'Difficulties?'

'Well, yes. I mean, I know nothing about the situation there, but…'

'No, no. Nothing like that. I don't get involved in politics.'

'I thought maybe…'

'No.' It sounded final.

'You don't give me much to go on.' She picked up her cup.

'I'm not good at explaining. This may sound stupid, but can I just play to you?'

'Play to me? You can do that in class.' The teacher in her was immediately wary.

'I know, but… I mean, really play. In the class I feel that I shouldn't take up too much time. That you have to say things that will be helpful to everyone. That the others are in a hurry to play, themselves.'

'Yes, that's the deal with a class. You have to share the attention. But I do listen, you know.'

'Look, I just want to play. Couldn't you forget you're a teacher, just for now?'

The curtains were not drawn, and the rain whispered on the window panes, fine drops catching the light from within. Faces gazed down from the walls.

Letting go her breath, she said slowly, 'I suppose so, since you've come all this way. Well, all right, but not for long – it's late.'

Gad got up at once, exchanging his cup for his damp pile of music. He went to the piano that occupied most of one end of the room, and laid the music books on the turned-back lid unopened. He sat down, and she set herself to listen.

Frowning slightly he spread his fingers over the keys; paused, biting his lip, then leaned forward and let his hands fall on to a soft chord, meanwhile pressing both feet on the pedals. The strings responded and she heard the quiet sound start and then die. He struck another chord, tilting his head to listen while the hammers met the strings, which vibrated into silence; and then he picked out some single notes and listened to the discord of their sounds. Then he took his foot off the pedals and picked out a tune she had never heard before, and when he had listened enough, he began to play with the melody, repeating and diverting it, raising his hands to free his fingers for runs or trills, and dropping them for heavy chords that made the pencils on the music rack rattle. Arpeggios, runs and ornaments were all there, too. The music seemed to flow straight through his shoulders and arms to the fingers touching the keyboard, and she wondered at the heart and imagination that generated it.

What he played that night was his own, and nobody else's. In it she could hear childhood songs, music that must have been popular at weddings and dances, tunes to entertain guests in hotel ballrooms, and sounds he might have heard in college – and also rage; a rage whose source she could not fathom.

Eva listened intently. This was a kind of music that she, brought up by her father in the strict European classical tradition, could not play. Her ear was attuned to every nuance of European style, knew the exact phrasing appropriate to each period and each composer. She had heard many great performers and considered their different musical approaches; but she could only play music written by others. Interpretation was her language – her voice. She was both envious, and repelled. How tasteless, was one thought. But how wonderful, was another. There must be a whole culture there – friends, family… She heard nostalgia and also unease, as of insecurity and homelessness.

Then she thought, *What can I say? How can we discuss this?*

Gad stopped at last, taking his hands off the keyboard with a final showman's flourish, and smiled expectantly. Up until now, he had always found it easy to make people listen.

She said to him, 'This is quite strange to me. You were not just playing games, were you?'

'No,' he said, remembering.

'I don't know what to say,' she said at last. 'I don't mean to be negative, but I don't know if I can be much help to you.' She knew he would hear it as a judgement. She lifted her hands helplessly and let them fall into her lap.

There was a strained pause. Then, abruptly, 'I see,' he said, huge disappointment in his voice. 'I should have stayed home – wherever that is now.' He stood, picking up his music. *He must have brought it as a kind of passport*, she thought. She stood up also.

'I'm sorry,' she said, and then again: 'Look, I just don't know what to say to you. I'm afraid I am failing you.' She bent her head, and the dark wing of hair fell over her face. She was in real difficulty.

'It's all right,' he said, smiling with some effort. 'Don't take me too seriously. It was just an idea. I shouldn't have bothered you. I'll go now.'

He straightened the unused music in his arms and came briskly towards her. At the last minute he checked, reached out and touched her shoulder gently. 'Don't worry about it,' he said. 'I'll see myself out.'

He went, and she heard him unlock the front door and then close it quietly behind him.

Eva stood still for a moment before moving to the hall to lock up. Without warning, tears came to her eyes; she could not think why. Like an automaton, she went to her medicine cupboard for a sleeping pill. Then she went to bed, sad and uneasy, knowing she would not see Garrard again, and eventually fell into an exhausted sleep.

CHAPTER 21

April 1954

Gad turned away from the door without looking back. He wanted to be away from Eva, from the knowledge that she occupied a territory that was closed to him. But then, so was his territory closed to her. He could not be angry with her. It was nothing personal.

The fine drizzle had stopped, but the pavements gleamed like a seal's back in the lamplight. He put one foot in front of the other, head bent, as he started down the hill back to where he was beginning to feel he naturally belonged. Hampstead, he thought: they're so damn high-minded.

He shook his head in fierce denial, and the pain of disappointment began to ease with his headlong progress. He had no intention of using a bus or burying himself in the Underground. But after exhausting his first burst of energy, he leaned for a moment against a wall, catching his breath. The surface was smooth to his hand, part of a shiny shop frontage, and cold. He wanted to deface it somehow – scratch it if only he had a sharp tool. He looked for a stone – there were none.

It was going to be a long walk.

At the steepest point of the hill he passed a doorway where a shabby young woman crouched. Her pale face was upraised to his, though she didn't speak. She was huddled up in an old eiderdown that smelled strongly, even through the rain and fresh air. From force of habit, he drew aside in case she asked for money, but she did no such thing.

'Are you all right?' she asked. Her voice was soft, intimate.

He stopped in his tracks, looking down at her. 'Why? What do you mean?'

She went on staring up at him.

'You look done in,' she said. Her features were small, pinched.

'I'm fine,' he said firmly. 'What about you?'

'Oh, I'm OK – just broke.'

So, here it comes, he thought. As usual, he had very little money in the pocket of his duffel coat, but began to feel in it for some coins anyway.

'Oh no, I wasn't asking…' said the small voice. 'As long as you're OK…'

He held out a handful to her, the entire contents of his pocket, urging her to accept, then dropped them on to the wrecked quilt wrapped round her knees. Mostly they stayed there, but he saw her pick one out and hold it up in her outstretched hand.

'Here,' she said. 'You can't carry on without any money at all – go on, take it. And thank you.'

He took it, pocketed it slowly, then held out his hand to her. They shook in silence. He wanted to give her a smile, but none came.

★

As soon as he regained the flat Gad sat down with an unquiet heart. It was high time he wrote home; he had left it too long already. How easy it was for people to lose their homes, even in a place as solid as London!

112

Dear Wilma and All at home

I wonder how much longer I shall be able to write those words. So you are all leaving Burma – for good this time? When we escaped in 1942, none of us knew whether we would ever return, but we all did. Now I am here, and soon you may be even further away, somewhere with Burmah Oil, and I hope safe if not sound! If only you could come to England – then I could show you around (see what an old hand I have become!).

Things are not so easy for families here, but I am sure we could find you somewhere to stay, perhaps a little outside the centre of London. Work might be a problem. Think about it.

Dear all of you, I have hurried to write this in case it doesn't catch you. But surely you won't be leaving in such a rush? We get no news of Burma here, now that the British have stopped governing the country. Is it really so bad?

Please write me your new address just as soon as you know it.

I send my love to you all, and a big God Bless.
Your loving son,
Garrard
PS You must stay in touch.

These words in blue ink on thin airmail paper looked insubstantial. *Is this all I can offer?* he thought, the weight of distance upon him as he took his letter to the post.

★

Into Gad's barren landscape, Valerie plunged like a lightning bolt.

At college one day, early in the afternoon when he as always had to fight off sleep, Gad was trying to summon the energy to spend another two hours preparing for his next tutorial.

Draped entirely in unidentifiable black garments, a whirlwind figure burst through the door, a chunky necklace positively clanking, long black hair flying away from the shiny black comb that was trying to hold it.

'I've been looking for you!' she said, plunking herself unceremoniously on the spare chair beside the piano. 'Where have you been all this time?'

'Valerie! Good to see you. I've had flu. I've been back for a while.'

'Oh, so that's it. We thought you'd got lost!'

'Maybe I did.'

'What?'

'Nothing. Who's "we", anyway?'

'Ah. Just listen.' Valerie leaned forward eagerly. 'Here's the thing.' She laid a finger on his knee. 'It's my family – you know that my family lives in London?'

'Of course – north, isn't it?'

'Spot on. Hampstead.' His heart flinched away. 'Well, this is it…' She caught sight of his fingers straying to the keys. 'Are you listening?'

'Yes – yes of course.' He forced himself to pay attention.

'This is it,' she said again. 'My parents are arranging a party for their cousin who is coming to live in London – and for charity at the same time – this is what they do…'

'Charity? What charity?'

'Any. Does it matter? They'll dream up something. They always do. Anyway, this is it: they want me to sing!' She threw her hands open towards him in a dramatic gesture.

'They do?' Gad was listening now.

'Yes! So of course I'm going to need an accompanist!' She looked at him expectantly.

'Yes?' Gad never took anything for granted.

'Oh come on, you know perfectly well what I mean! Will you be it? Murray wants you to!'

'What? You've already spoken to Murray?' Gad stood up abruptly and slapped the piano with his hand. Valerie had spoken to his tutor?

'Of course! You don't think Ma and Pa would risk their precious daughter's career on just anyone? And won't we look fantastic together – like a great ruby and a little black diamond? I'll wear dark red, you see – it will be tremendous!' She had a smug smile on her face.

Winded, 'Oh,' was all Gad could think of to say. The idea of being a diamond to her ruby was... He was jolted by a flash of memory: his grandmother had always called him her 'little black diamond'. He had not thought of it till now. How peculiar, he thought, and how odd it sounds from this strange woman.

Valerie had been gushing on, and was now standing with her hand on the doorknob. 'So come on, then!' she was saying.

'Come? Where?'

'To Murray's room, of course! They're all waiting!' The doorknob rattled in her hand.

'They're here? Your parents? I've never even met them!' Gad was panicked: he had no idea what they were planning for him, had no time to think about the proposition.

'Oh, come on! They won't eat you.'

'Oh, OK,' he said, capitulating with a shrug. 'Let's see what they say. What are you thinking of doing?'

She led the way out, and they left the room talking about the Schubert lieder her singing teacher had suggested.

'Those accompaniments are not easy, you know!' he warned.

'I know. That's why I've asked you.'

He thought of the times he had heard her sing at college concerts, and had admired her mezzo voice, bold and warm. He laughed to himself now, realising, *I can do something with you!* and followed in her wake to Murray's office.

CHAPTER 22

May 1954

At the end of that week, Thérèse was standing outside Boar House, Stow Ferrers. This was not a typical English country house, Thérèse thought.

It was a Friday. She had travelled up from London alone after an early evening concert, successfully changing at Woodham Fitzpaine on to the clanging branch line, and arrived at Stow Ferrers Station just before ten. Following directions, she walked the short distance to Boar House, the poorly-lit road near the station brightening as she entered the village proper. It was still warm, fine and dry, the sky clear and star-studded. The house was in a dominant position at the centre of the village, opening straight on to the road. Hearing voices bubbling cheerfully from a half-open window, she approached the front door and paused, reluctant to disturb the magic circle. The occupants were quite happy without her. Conversation came so naturally to some – not to her though, especially in English. Ideas, phrases, jokes that might be crowding her head got stuck in there – never fizzed out at just the right moment.

And then, Elspeth had warned, there would be Gad from whom she had parted on bad terms so many months ago. There were many things left unsaid; the break had been sudden, and remained unexplored. She hadn't really wanted to split, but felt forced into it. She wanted to come first in his life, but feared that nobody could fill the gap left by his loss of family and home. Music was his passion, his obsession, his family.

So this weekend, it was probably best to keep her distance. It would be safer, more comfortable. There would be others there too – Mary, Tony, Sam, Estelle and Sanjay. She would keep things general.

The road remained quiet as she stood hesitating, her small bag at her feet. There was not a soul about. At the back of her mind she could see herself shelling peas on a sunny doorstep, the only sound the popping of little green globes into her enamel bowl and the roar of a tractor: she had been happy then.

With a tremor of anticipation, she raised the heavy iron knocker and let it fall.

★

It wasn't difficult at all. Elspeth greeted her as if she were the last piece of a jigsaw – the one she had been waiting for. Despite herself, though, Thérèse's eyes went straight to Gad, and then away in confusion. The others sat down again round the big kitchen table to keep her company. For the moment at least she belonged to this large family.

As she ate two helpings of shepherd's pie, Thérèse learned that Elspeth especially had long wanted to have a place she and Rob could call their own, a retreat from the hubbub of the International House they had run so successfully for so long – ten years or more. This house had once been a pub – which was ironic considering Robert and Elspeth's stance on alcohol. They had always been quite firm about it: none was allowed in the House; but Thérèse missed wine with her meals.

Elspeth and Rob clearly loved their weekends in the country. Yet no sooner had they bought the place than they could not help inviting people down for sociable weekends.

'Are you not sorry, though?' Thérèse wondered, putting down her fork and wiping her mouth, and then, greatly daring, 'What happened to the peace and quiet?'

'No, the point is,' put in Tony, 'that we are selected people! We know how to behave – we wash up and make our own beds! We are no trouble!'

There was a general laugh. Rob, with his rugged, open face, deep-set eyes under the overhang of bushy eyebrows, pushed back his chair, crossing his long legs as he sat at the head of the table. 'You know,' he said with his gaping smile, 'we're so used to living with people around us, I don't think we would survive without it. Our children have deserted us; they're off into the big wide world. What would we do for company without the House?'

'Yes, but you have your botany. You can spend the mornings upstairs on your own.' This from Mary, who knew his habits well.

'True!'

'But how about you, Elspeth?'

'Oh, you know me. I love to know what people are up to,' said Elspeth. Her eyes rested on Gad as he absently toyed with a knife. 'People are endlessly interesting. I don't find it a strain – mostly.'

Thérèse was not sure she wanted to be one of Elspeth's 'interesting' specimens, and without thinking she blurted out, 'Doesn't anything upset you?'

'It upsets me if people are not straight with me.'

So she wanted to know all their private business? Even their secrets? Thérèse looked back at Elspeth, wondering how much she knew, or suspected, about her past, saying nothing.

★

The night had clouded over, and Robert took them out to a wood that backed on to their small garden, to see the fireflies. Trying not to disturb the undergrowth, they crouched close together in the pitch black until bright pinpoints of light appeared one by one, glowing steadily for moments at a time, gleaming like tiny lighthouses signalling to ships across a void, alternating to allow time for their meaning to be understood. It was warm and dark, and they heard each other's quiet breaths. Sparks glimmered amongst the trees, flitting uncertainly. Gad was there, at the other end of the line, part of the breathing.

★

Saturday afternoon was fine, and Estelle suggested a walk. As they all clustered at the garden gate, Gad stepped back, and said to Thérèse, 'Why don't we take the bikes? I like bikes, don't you?'

Thérèse was taken off guard. 'Yes, I do, but...'

'Well?'

Gad was looking intently at her, his body tense. She felt the force of his desire to be with her, thought of turning him down, and failed. The others were already moving out into the road. Some mysterious link clicked into place. She spoke on impulse.

'Yes, let's.' It was more than simple agreement.

She bent to tighten her sandals, aware of Mary's curious look.

★

They took the two aging bicycles left fallen on their sides in the garden shed, adjusted the saddles and set off away from the village, pedalling idly in the May sunshine, warm air caressing their skin, and soon turned up a side lane. As they left the main road grass verges ran alongside, a lively green, and there were hedges thick with dog roses and old man's beard. Gad rode on the outside, to protect Thérèse, she supposed, though there was no traffic at all. He sat on his bike relaxed and easy,

120

one hand on the old-fashioned handlebars, one hanging loose, his face raised to the breeze. She could see in him the boy that perhaps he had once been, dawdling along deserted roads with his head full of dreams.

'I'm glad you came,' he said at last, reaching over perilously to touch her arm, looking into her face rather than at the road. Taken by surprise, she flinched and swerved. 'What happened the other day? I didn't mean us to quarrel.'

'Well, why did we, then?' She pedalled vigorously. 'And now you ask me to go cycling – why can't you say what you mean?'

'I don't know.' He shrugged helplessly, taking both hands off the handlebars. 'I don't know how.'

She braked, put her foot on the ground. 'But you made it clear that you didn't want to be with me!'

'Well, I had to, that day...' he said, pulling his bike round in front of her. They were on a dangerous bend, confronting each other.

'But another hour would not make any difference to your practising?'

'I didn't really think – I'm not used to thinking about anyone else's feelings...'

'It's time you did think, then!' She jerked back into the saddle and swerved round him to ride on, chin up.

The lane was rough and little pebbles skidded under her tyres.

'So now, do you want to go back?' he called, putting on a comical, pleading voice as he set off after her. 'Don't – please?'

'Oh, don't be so silly!' She felt impatient, knew she was being manipulated, tried to keep a straight face and again failed to resist him.

He caught up with her.

'You're so obvious!' she cried in exasperation, at him and at herself. 'I don't know what it is about you – you're like a shadow, you keep disappearing!'

'How can I be so obvious if I keep disappearing?' he said, smiling into her face as he homed in close beside her.

'Well, I don't know, but you are. And you do! So there!'

She rode along, stubbornly silent, feeling childish.

Gad seemed to be thinking about what she had said, but 'Is your work going well?' was what he finally came out with.

She felt he had taken several steps backwards – another of his 'disappearances'.

'Yes, thank you,' she said, with exaggerated formality and a sort of bow from the saddle of her bike. 'And yours?'

'Very well, thanks,' he returned politely, then added, 'There – you see? I never actually asked you before, did I?'

She knew she hadn't given him much to go on. A few petals from the hedgerows drifted over on the warm breeze, one sticking to her bare arm. 'No, actually. No one ever does. Brittany? Folk music?' she said a little wearily. 'I mean, who cares?'

He couldn't take his eyes off the petal, she saw. He grinned. '*Touché*. Trouble is, I don't know where to start. Being intelligent about it, I mean.'

'Well, fine. I'm going to Cecil Sharp House again next week to see if they've got anything new – I'll tell you about it when I get back.' She stopped abruptly, fearing she might have taken too much for granted. Then she spotted Gad's covert smile. 'Let's walk for a bit,' she said, to cover her confusion. She was tired of trying to balance on the ancient bike whilst working out what on earth Gad was really feeling.

'OK then.' He got off and leaned on the handlebars, like any old farm hand. 'I did some work at Cecil Sharp House once.'

'You did? I didn't think it would be…' she hesitated, 'up your street?'

'Well, playing for rehearsals – they paid me a bit.'

'And then…?'

He said awkwardly, 'Actually, I couldn't stand it! So knowledgeable about so little – so precious! So irrelevant. Sorry – I don't mean to insult you or your work.'

There they were, still fencing, she thought, as they stood in the middle of this deserted road in the middle of nowhere. She began to feel desperate, but hadn't the words to break through his defences to find something real.

'Well,' she said, frowning. 'At least that was honest! Anyway,' she added almost spitefully, 'is playing classical music so – relevant?'

'Yes, well. You'd think that if we're both into music, we'd have that in common, but…'

'Oh, it doesn't always work like that; you should know.' She shrugged, walking on again. 'You should hear the feuds that some of the folklorists go in for!'

'Really? Good Lord! I thought they were all so well-behaved!' He cocked an eyebrow at her, then grinned at her expression of distaste.

This is just a smoke screen; he's disappearing again, thought Thérèse. *How can I get through to him?* She jumped onto her bike. 'Race you!' she cried, childishly, and at least Gad rose to the challenge. Her legs pumped the crooked pedals – she wasn't going to hand him victory. Her old bike ran smoothly along the white lane, but glancing behind her she saw Gad swerving wildly across it as if no other traffic could possibly exist, wobbling headlong onto the bumpy grass verge, and pitching off into a bed of nettles. She skidded to a halt, dropped the bike and ran back, to be transfixed by the sight of a pair of upturned shoes, smartly polished but holed on the bottom, and a round face sporting a look of comic astonishment as Gad lay on his back in a ditch, winded. She tried not to laugh till she had made sure he wasn't hurt. He began to struggle up, but fell back again feebly, head down in his dry ditch, from which he looked up at her in mock appeal.

'Help me!' he croaked, wedged as he was. Suppressing her merriment, she hauled him to his feet. It was only when he was upright that Thérèse began to laugh aloud; he looked so ridiculous as he stood there trying to hold on to his dignity, ruefully rubbing the back of his neck, and it was only when she had become quite helpless with giggles that he finally gave way, breaking into a hoot of joyful laughter.

★

For the rest of the weekend they found themselves gravitating towards each other whenever possible. They didn't actually intend to, but it happened all the same.

After supper was cleared that first night, everyone sat round in comfortable old chairs in the small living-room. Watching Gad, Thérèse found he was delivering a mini-lecture about his new passion for the music of Manuel de Falla – at the same time so fiery and so delicate, so different from the long, smooth melodies of Schubert or Brahms – and smiled to herself. So he was joining in the hidden competition for best-informed person in the party!

She found she could contribute something, at last. 'He was interested in Spanish folk music too, was he not? *Cante jondo*, is it? From the south of Spain?'

A light came on behind Gad's eyes as he turned towards her. 'Of course, you're right,' he said. 'I haven't really looked into that yet, but I shall. It's mostly in his vocal work, anyway.'

Elspeth watched and listened.

'Can you play us something of his now, Gad?' asked Sam.

'Now? Are you sure?' At a general nod, 'OK,' he said as he went to the old upright piano. 'I'll play *Aragonesa* – it's the one I remember best. I wish he'd written more for piano.'

Thérèse could hear how easily he caught their attention with the piece's deceptive simplicity; how he made you feel as if he were discovering it at that moment. Robert nodded sagely as he listened. Elspeth put her head on one side, making agreeable sounds in her throat. The others, so full of themselves when they talked, seemed to lose themselves in another world while Gad played. And then the percussive middle section, and back to the quiet ending. Thérèse remembered that Falla, unusually for his time, had written for harpsichord as well as piano, and saw how this would work. She watched Gad as he played, his face totally absorbed, his hands weaving with beautiful economy over the keys, his body still.

*

Elspeth had gone into the garden to pull some vegetables for lunch, and Thérèse stepped out of the back door to enjoy a cigarette in the sunshine while everybody else was deep in the Sunday papers.

Seeing Elspeth bending to the vegetable patch and feeling she should offer, 'Can I help you?' she asked. This was familiar ground. There was spinach to cut, and a lettuce or two to pull; and there seemed to be some early carrots. Somebody here knew what they were doing, and for the first time she began to see how capable and resourceful this pair was.

'Thank you. I'll hold the basket, otherwise it always flops over.'

Elspeth held the receptacle open, offering an inviting hollow into which Thérèse started dropping dark leaves cut from the spinach, then the fresh, lighter green of round lettuces, lastly, fine whiskery carrots with their feathery tops frothing out of the top of the basket. The sappy smell of green and of the brown earth crumbs sticking to the roots came up to her with a tug of homesickness.

She straightened her back and took the basket from Elspeth, ready to help prepare the vegetables for lunch.

'Thank you,' said Elspeth. 'It will give us a chance to have a chat.'

Mais non! Et maintenant quoi? Thérèse busied herself scrubbing and chopping, while Elspeth moved energetically round the kitchen, preparing meat for roasting and pudding for reheating. What was this about?

'You had a good time with Gad yesterday?'

'Oh yes, thank you.'

'What happened? He had vetch sticking out of his hair! I've never seen him so untidy!'

'Oh! Oh, he fell off his bike; that is all!'

'Oh, I see. And you both came back looking so cheerful!'

'Did we? Well, it was a lovely day.'

'Mmm.'

They went on working.

'Only, you see, I am always concerned about the people who stay at the House.'

'Oh yes, of course.'

'Because, you realise, you are so young and far away from home and family – in fact, everything familiar. You may not always understand what you are doing.'

'Well, I suppose I am like that, although I do not live at the House now.'

'Yes, but Gad is a very long way from home.'

'Yes,' she said, keeping her voice neutral.

'You know,' said Elspeth, coming over to stand at the sink near Thérèse, 'he could really have a great future if he were to meet the right people who would help him.'

'Yes, I know.' She kept on scrubbing carrots.

'Have you met Valerie?'

'No, never.' Valerie – who was she?

'Has he told you about her?'

'No.'

'Well, you could ask him. She comes from a good family

with all sorts of contacts in classical music. I think he ought to think seriously about them – perhaps even about Valerie.'

Thérèse's hands were still. 'That is his business.' She held on to the sink with both hands.

'Oh yes, of course.' Elspeth moved away. 'After all, you and he stopped going out together months ago, didn't you?'

'We did.'

'Well,' concluded Elspeth, gathering up the prepared vegetables. 'Thank you very much. I'm so glad we had this little chat.' She smiled warmly before reaching for a saucepan.

Thérèse went to the back door, opening it wide in order to breathe free air.

CHAPTER 23

June 1954

Throughout that weekend at Stow Ferrers, and ever since he came back, elated from the renewal of his – whatever it was – with Thérèse, there was a dark undertow in Gad's thoughts: what was to become of his family, and had his own letter been too callous, too hasty, too altogether self-centred?

He moved restlessly from room to room in his tiny flat, smoking and worrying. Wilma's sketchy proposal for a future away from Burma seemed so ill-considered that he suspected the situation was becoming desperate. She seemed to be suggesting that his family would scatter across the globe. She and the closest relatives were planning a move to Borneo. He had no image of Borneo or the people there, and was full of questions. *So Julian might come to London. Does he know what to do, or will he depend on me? And Colin deciding to stay in Burma – will he be safe?*

Borneo was even further away than Burma! And Gad had never been there, could not even visualise it. It began to dawn on him how hard it had been for his mother to imagine his life in England.

Should I return east to the family, help them resettle, be an extra pair of hands? Does the family expect it? Do they need me? He did not know whether Borneo would become their permanent base, or if they would be moving on, if indeed they had not already done so. He hoped most of all to get a contact address for them. He spent the next day at college, preoccupied, unable to share his concern until he had more definite news.

★

September 1954

The brass catch of Gad's smart new music case caught the sun as he emerged from the crowded Underground station (the deepest in London, he had been told). He was at the crossroads in the heart of Hampstead Village. Two roads led upwards, two down. A quick check – yes, that was Heath Street, the way down to Fitzjohns Avenue. He was relieved to be going in the opposite direction from the cinema he had visited with Thérèse; he felt he couldn't stand going over all that again.

Today was a brilliant day, sharp with autumn, chill and dry. He had to step carefully through fallen leaves so as not to scuff his only decent pair of shoes. Colours jumped out at him from trees and garden hedges, the crimson of sumac, fading pink roses with brown edges to the petals, the yellow fans of horse chestnut leaves. Sunlight, weakening now but unsullied in these lofty heights, touched his face.

Distracted by all this, he found he was already outside Valerie's house, the number that he had been given displayed on brick pillars flanking high metal gates. A driveway swept past garages to an imposing porch with its own white columns. A side gate with a latch allowed him entry.

His heart was beating fast as he walked up to the front door, looking forward to setting eyes on the venue for their concert, but wondering what else would go with it. He had already felt the need to look presentable; now he wondered about the occasion itself – would he have to meet the guests? It might not just be a question of playing and then departing into the night; there might be social obligations too.

129

It was Valerie who opened the door, followed closely by her mother Adèle, the chic woman he had already met in Murray's office. Even at this early hour of the morning, she was elegant in soft shades of grey that fell gracefully, her pearl cluster earrings drawing attention to her smooth skin and shining dark hair. She held out a well-manicured hand, and Gad immediately felt at ease with her, more so in fact than with her flamboyant daughter.

The hall was spacious, with a curving staircase and a chandelier. Gad followed Adèle over a muted Persian carpet amid the seductive scent of lilies, a complacent Valerie beside him. The room they entered was a very large L-shape, overlooked the garden, and was dominated by a grand piano in the angle, a gleaming Steinway grand. It was perfect.

'Look,' said Valerie. 'The audience can sit in the two arms of the L. I shall have to make sure I look at them all in turn – we can't have anybody feeling left out.' Gad looked at her in amazement; he had never before given such close attention to audience reaction.

Adèle cut in with, 'Drinks can be served in the hall as they come in, and the main party afterwards will be in the dining-room on the other side of the hall; a buffet of course. You will have a chance to talk to everybody then. Valerie already knows most of them. For you, this could be a big chance, Garrard. If they like you, I'm sure other invitations will follow.'

★

The two of them settled down to rehearse. They had been studying the songs independently in college, and were already note perfect; now they would concentrate on working together, agreeing their interpretation, the connection they would make with the sophisticated audience. Songs from *Winterreise*, expressions of grief and regret. He would underpin the voice with a wintry accompaniment, suggesting frozen streams, bare trees, cold inhospitable towns and fierce storms, simple yet demanding. He was glad Valerie had chosen lively songs too: *Die Forelle* (of course), *Heidenröslein* and others, and *An die Musik* to finish. They had decided to stick with Schubert for such a short recital. He of all composers could provide the variety they needed, particularly on the pains and sorrows of love.

They had just embarked on *Heidenröslein* when the door opened and Valerie's father, Bernard, strode in, advancing across the carpet with hand outstretched, unembarrassed to be interrupting their work. At their first meeting, in Murray's office, Gad had seen him as strong, watchful, silent, a hunter lying in wait. This was a bear-like man, with bristly grey hair and a high complexion. Gad could see Valerie's likeness to him. Now Bernard enveloped his hand in two huge paws and pumped his arm vigorously, while the face speaking to him looked down from a great height. It seemed more like a demonstration of strength than of friendliness, for though the greeting was cordial, it was almost too hearty, Bernard's eyes remaining cold.

'Garrard, my boy!' he boomed, Gad's hand still captured.

Gad found himself drawn to his feet in mid-verse.

He saw Valerie lower her music and smile at her father as he said, 'What a pleasure to meet you again. I hope you have everything you need?'

'Certainly, sir. This is a wonderful instrument.'

'And the room? You like the room?' His eyes watched Gad, who felt that his manners were under scrutiny.

'Of course. You have a lovely home.'

'Well, we have high hopes for this concert. Valerie needs someone she can trust. You play well for my little girl, now!'

With a final, curt nod of his head, Bernard left, just as Adèle entered from the other door.

'Garrard, we'll be having lunch soon. You'll stay, won't you?' she said, smiling. 'We don't bother with the dining-room when we're on our own, just eat in the kitchen.' She left with a smile, not waiting for an answer, though Gad had opened his mouth to say, 'Well, thank you very much, but...'

Valerie shrugged and opened her hands as if to say, 'What can you do?'

Plenty, thought Gad, but it didn't look as if Valerie ever raised objections in this household. The place ran on oiled wheels, and you just fitted in with it. Your own concerns had to be kept to yourself.

★

September/October 1954

It was on his next visit that alarm bells rang loud and clear. It was the last rehearsal before the concert, which promised to be well-attended. He had travelled up early, in order to practise and get home again before lunch. He was going to make this clear from the outset.

A housekeeper came to the front door this time, taking his coat and showing him into the drawing-room, where Valerie was busy closing a sash window.

'Morning,' she said cheerfully, adjusting a purple wrap around her shoulders. 'Are you OK?'

'Fine, thanks. I must just let you know, though, that I need to get back for lunch today – I've got lectures this afternoon and choir practice this evening.'

'OK,' she said casually. 'Mummy will be disappointed, though. She's asked an agent to be here for lunch. He could be useful to you.'

'What? I didn't know! Why didn't you tell me?'

'Didn't I? Oh dear. I must have forgotten. Mummy always

arranges everything – even I don't always know what's going on.'

'But – this is very awkward. I can't miss the first lecture this afternoon, or I'm going to be in a mess with my essay. What can I do?'

'Oh, I don't know. It's up to you,' said Valerie carelessly, turning away. 'Shall we get started?'

Valerie was not going to get involved in this; she was used to having her life organised for her. He guessed that for her, it was simple: if one opportunity was lost, another would be arranged. But he felt sure he would not get a second chance. He would have to be available.

Gritting his teeth, Gad took his seat at the piano and they rehearsed, but the rapport of the past was broken. When Adèle came in to tell them that lunch was ready, he packed up with unusual alacrity. He had not enjoyed the session, and Valerie had sung flat. Adèle shot a curious look at him as she led them through into the huge kitchen where food was spread out for them.

Bernard was not there, but a small man with old-fashioned pince-nez was standing by the window. He turned to kiss Valerie first on both cheeks, and then greeted Gad with courteous formality.

'I hear good things of you, young man,' he added. 'Do you mind if I sit in on your rehearsal after lunch? I'm Charles Bouvier, by the way. You may have heard of me?'

'Well, I hadn't planned on staying,' he demurred, bypassing the question. 'But…'

'Oh, surely,' Adèle cut in with that smile. 'We thought you could stay the night.' That wasn't a question, and Gad was in danger of submitting to her charm. Somehow he found it a struggle to say the 'no' word to her.

Nevertheless he managed stoutly, 'I'm afraid I have to be back in Holborn to take choir practice.'

'What time?'

'Seven o'clock.'

'Well, we'll let you off dinner this time. Bernard can send you back in the car,' said Adèle.

This still left the matter of the lecture. *It's a game of chess*, he thought. *I'll have to sacrifice a pawn.*

*

As the applause continued, Valerie and Gad glanced at each other in mock surrender and consented to give their short squib of an encore, after which they bowed themselves out. In the corridor outside, Valerie gave a stifled scream of delight and enveloped Gad in a suffocating hug. Discreetly removing a strand of cashmere from his mouth, Gad did his best to respond appropriately despite his misgivings, snapping his eyes and squeezing his cheeks into fat cushions as he beamed back at her, holding her arms to stop her from falling over in her enthusiasm. Adèle bustled out to congratulate them, and Bernard followed with Charles, who said to Gad quietly, 'Well done, young man. I'll call you,' before opening his arms to Valerie: 'Marvellous, my dear! Simply marvellous! We must hear more of you!'

As soon as he could, Gad slipped away to the little room allotted to him high up in the house, to stow his music away. It was quiet up here. He surveyed himself in the full-length mirror, wiping his face. He looked good, he thought: quite a handsome figure in his hired dinner jacket, neat and capable-looking, radiating energy. He knew he had played well. The audience had loved them. Why, then, did he feel deflated? Something to do with the instant burst of sociable chatter that rose from the audience as the applause died?

Time to face the music, he thought, grimacing at the terrible pun. He walked down into the wall of voices, needing a drink: whiskey for preference. It was always whiskey at the Strand Hotel, glasses sliding to him across the lid of the white grand.

He could see that Valerie, her mother at her elbow, was at the centre of a lively crowd, and Bernard was standing with some of his cronies. Edging his way towards the buffet table with one eye on its mouth-watering dishes, Gad had just managed to reach for an unpalatable glass of champagne, the only drink that was on offer, when Bernard spotted him and raised a glass in the air.

'Ladies and gentlemen, now that we are all here, let's drink a toast: to my daughter Valerie, who has generously given of her time and talent to sing for us tonight! To Valerie!'

'To Valerie!' came the response.

'And,' Bernard continued, 'we must not forget our little friend from overseas, on piano, Garrard d'Silva! To Garrard!'

'To Garrard!'

'Ladies and gentlemen, please make free with the victuals, while Garrard continues to entertain you with a little light music. My boy, the piano is all yours!' And making his way through the well-dressed crowd he took Gad by the arm and steered him firmly towards the drawing-room. 'Ah, I see you have a drink. Good, good. Do come and find some food when you feel ready, but first – a little jazz, hm?'

'Jazz, sir? I think you have me confused, sir, with an American. I don't play jazz.' He could hear his mother urging him, 'Play, son, play what they want!'

'You don't? Oh! Surprising. Well, anything you like then. Just strum a little something they'll like!' And he turned on his heel.

Furious, Gad closed the lid of the piano, none too gently, and sat astride the piano stool to sip his 'tarts' drink', as he had always called it. So he was not to mingle with the guests! Not up to the mark, socially. He could, he knew, play them out in the old Strand ballroom fashion and they would love it; it was second nature for him to be agreeable, not to disrupt a smart social occasion. But first he was going to take this minute to himself; he was not going to be steamrollered. He lit a subversive cigarette and inhaled with pleasure and relief.

He heard the hall door rattle, and to his surprise saw Charles enter, bearing a large plate of food.

'Peace offering,' he murmured, carrying it carefully over to Gad. 'And how about a real drink? I can find you one.'

'God, this is good of you,' said Gad. 'I just can't believe Bernard! Does he think I'm his lapdog?' It was unwise, but who else was there to listen?

'He's like that,' said Charles, putting the plate on a low table where Gad could reach it. 'I've known him for many years – grew up with him, really. He's larger than life, and he can't see that anyone else has a life of his own. No respect.'

So he felt it too. 'How do you deal with it?'

'I don't have to. I toe the line when I'm here. Adèle is lovely but she will never cross him, and nor will Valerie. I like a quiet life. You don't want to get caught up with this lot, you know. It's all social – getting Valerie showcased? She's quite a girl, don't you think?' He looked carefully at Gad as he said this.

'She's a bit much for me,' responded Gad candidly, thinking fleetingly of his Thérèse, with her pride and her quiet ways. He stubbed out his cigarette and put a whole canapé into his mouth: 'Mm, tasty, thank you, thank you very much, Charles. I'd better play a bit, at least sing for my supper, you know.'

'Yes, I know. I'll get you a – whiskey, is it? I thought so. You carry on, but listen to me while you play. I'm sure you can do that.' He went out, returning quickly with a Scotch on the rocks, the way Gad always drank it.

'That's exactly what you are doing, singing for your supper! I know you haven't been paid a brass farthing, even fares.

And Bernard will milk you for all you're worth, in the nicest possible way, if you carry on dealing with him. As for Valerie, she is going to depend on you more and more, and then, if you ever let her down in the smallest way, there's going to be hysterics from her and God knows what from Bernard.' He gave Gad a warning look. 'He knows a lot of people, and he only has to put the word out.

'What you need – no, keep on playing...' Charles laid a bony arm across Gad's shoulders, '... is someone who can promote you without strings; who will have your best interests at heart; who will see that people pay you properly and respect you for your work.'

He stopped speaking. Gad played on to the end of *Night and Day,* with ripples.

'It won't be easy for you to get established here, you know. You need contacts, a professional agent. You need to learn the ropes. I can do this for you if you will put yourself in my hands.' He removed his arm.

The voice dripped on into Gad's ear, promising the world. Gad dropped his hands at last and turned to look Charles in the eye. Their gaze held for a moment, before Charles bent his head, his lizard's tongue flicking out to lick his lips. In that moment Gad knew that he should never trust this man, who was so ready to rubbish his friend to a stranger, the friend who provided him with so much hospitality.

Did any of the family know he was alone in here with Charles? He turned back to the piano and played on loudly, plunging at last into a dizzying cascade of arpeggios, syncopating a little as he went, and ending with a deep rumble of discontent near the bottom of the scale.

'There,' he said, rising with a flourish and decisively closing the lid once more. 'I'm done here.'

'Think about what I've said,' pressed Charles. 'Here's my card. Call me any time, day or night.'

Gad took the card by one corner and stuffed it carelessly into a pocket of his hired suit. 'Thank you,' he said politely. 'I'm grateful for your interest.' But his eyes were averted as he left Charles standing.

It remained for him to change back into his own clothes, pack away the dinner jacket and his music into the small bag of a traveling performer, and leave by the back door, expending the last of his money on a late taxi home.

CHAPTER 24

October 1954

In the noisy college cafeteria Valerie proposed a new scheme. Gad, head down, was methodically chewing his way through a tasteless chop when he heard her familiar: 'Oh, there you are!' as if he had deliberately disappeared.

'You never said goodbye to my parents; what happened?'

'Didn't I? Sorry. I got tired, that's all.'

'They missed you,' she said reproachfully.

Perhaps he had been a little rude. He didn't regret it, though. Somebody barged past their table, causing Gad's tea to shiver and spill into the saucer; he saved the cup just in time.

'What the...?'

'Sorry!' said the burly Russian, his violinist friend.

Turning to Valerie: 'They were pleased, then?' he said.

'Pleased? I'll say. In fact, they've got another plan!'

No! he thought. *No!* He took another mouthful of greasy lamb.

'Yes.' She hitched a chair up, leaning her arms and bosom on the table. 'There's a festival on Capri. It started last summer, in a scrappy way, and next year it's going to be bigger and better. They're getting a festival orchestra together, and guess who's conducting – Martin Ferris!'

Gad recognised this name of a young conductor beginning to build a fine reputation.

'It's going to be absolutely super, and – wait for it – we are invited to do a recital!'

Gad thought: *sunshine!* And was tempted. The meat in his mouth would not go down.

'And,' she went on, one of her large flourishes knocking over the salt, 'Daddy and Mummy are taking a villa so we can all stay there! Oh, Gad! It's going to be so smart, so international! Can you imagine?'

Yes, I can, only too well, he thought, retrieving the salt. The servility that would be required. Himself in tow behind this hurricane. A picture flashed into his mind, by some seventeenth-century Englishman – was it Dobson, William, perhaps? – a small black boy in crimson velvet and white silk raising his arm respectfully towards a moustachioed gentleman wearing a broad embroidered sash, a white horse bending benignly towards them. And there were others – he'd seen the pictures – little black boys in the bottom corner, alongside the dogs and attendant horses. *No!* he thought again. He finally managed to swallow.

'When is it?'

'May and June.'

'I think I have to be in London then. I'm sorry.'

'But you can't! What can there be for you in London, for heaven's sake?'

Thérèse! rang in his head. *There is Thérèse.* 'It'll be coming up to finals, you know. It's just a very bad time. Impossible, in fact.' He pushed his plate aside decisively.

Valerie flounced in her chair. It creaked alarmingly. 'But what can I tell Daddy? I said you'd be sure to come!'

'Well, you should never have said so. I just can't, and that's that.' He frowned. This was getting difficult.

She tried wheedling. 'Oh please, Gad. I've never enjoyed singing as much as with you.'

He held firm. 'No, Valerie, you'll have to find another accompanist.'

She put her head on one side, a caressing hand on his

arm. 'Please! Not even if Daddy can get you a concerto with Martin?'

'Oh, so he knows Mr Ferris, does he?' Gad wondered how much money Daddy had put up for the festival.

'Of course.' She smiled, showing even white teeth.

This made it less, not more, tempting. 'No, not even then.' *How much harm can Bernard do me?*

'My God, Gad, I wish I'd never met you!' She pushed her chair back violently, sending it screeching across the floor. 'After all the kindness Daddy has shown you! All that hospitality! Mummy was beginning to think you were one of the family! You've certainly led me on! How far do you think you can go on your own? What am I going to do without you? You don't think everything falls into people's laps, do you?'

'No,' he said soberly. 'I don't.'

'And anyway,' she added spitefully, standing hands on hips, 'who do you think you are? Get off with you? I wouldn't touch you with a barge pole!' And with this telling fusillade she swept away, flinging her stole around her shoulders.

His violinist friend at the next table, interrupted in his meal by the fracas, summed it up nicely: 'You are well away from that one – she will eat you for breakfast.'

★

Thérèse had had a good session at Cecil Sharp House, and even spent some time in the garden, reading in the sunshine. A gardener plodded to and fro with his wheelbarrow, first full and then empty, nodding to her each time he passed. He was knobbly and whiskery, she saw, like one of the singers in her old photographs. There was earth on his hands. And he reminded her of home.

Finally she left, with as many books and sheets of music as she could carry. She always wrote best in her own room.

The labour of extracting material in the library and carrying it home seemed to calm and focus her mind, so that when she sat down to her orderly table her fingers would fly around the Imperial portable without hesitation.

Walking briskly out of the building, she bumped into a rotund male figure who was leaving at an easy stroll, empty-handed.

'Dr Hetherington!' she exclaimed, drawing back and bending to pick up a fallen book. 'Sorry, I didn't see you.'

'Didn't you?' He let her get on with it.

She stood up then and took a cool look at him for the first time outside his office. Not much taller than herself, rather portly, a shabby tie with stains on it, hooded eyes and an expression that was hard to read.

'Working, I see?' he said then. His voice struck her as unduly resonant for the situation.

'Yes. You too?' She straightened her back. He would probably think her impertinent.

'No. Just visiting,' he said. 'Where are you heading?' His eyes moved.

'Oh – home with this lot.' She weighed the books in her arms. 'Easiest to walk, I think.'

He didn't attempt to help her, so she was surprised to hear, 'I'll walk with you.' She felt his glance on her, and realised with a small shock of recognition that here it was again, this assumption that she would of course comply with his wishes. *Eh bien*, she thought, *que pourrait-il bien se passer?*

They turned, side by side, towards the park, and once again she found herself moderating her step to please another. This man beside her was too heavy to walk fast, and Thérèse felt her arms begin to ache. She could carry loads more lightly at her own natural pace.

'Dr Hetherington...' she began.

'Roy, please. Do call me Roy.' There was something ingratiating in his tone.

'Well, if you like. Roy, then. I really need to get this stuff home. Please excuse me if...'

'Oh, don't rush off! Surely you don't need to rush off? Here, I'll take one for you,' and he leant against her arm to seize the heaviest of the volumes, threatening to upset the rest of the pile. She found herself in a sort of grappling hold, in which she struggled to retain possession of the book – it was her only chance of escape – while he tugged away at it. It was in this very moment that Thérèse saw – felt – the presence of a giant hornbeam; the bark was familiar; the tree arched over them, blotting out the grey sky, and she leaned her shoulder against it for balance, twisting her body to regain her hold on the book, making sure her elbow stayed between herself and this 'Roy'.

He panted a little, disorientated. 'You don't have to behave like that,' he said, 'you little slut.'

The sudden insult was a warning. His face red, he moved heavily towards her, trying to trap her with his tweedy arms. Awkwardly, she ducked under them and backed away into the open, leaving him floundering. She glanced up. Yes! it was the tree – the same tree where she stood with Gad all those months ago. Her body flooded with recollection, his neat body with its sturdy warmth pressed against hers. This blundering idiot must be got rid of – he was nothing to do with her, and she worried how much he had had to drink.

She turned her back on him and simply walked off. Let him sort himself out. She heard him call, 'You'll be sorry!' He would not follow; and she knew he would not look at her again.

She walked, fast now, across the grass, putting distance between herself and Hetherington. Why did she not see it coming? It must have been a spur-of-the-moment thing. She was there, so he pounced because he was in a position to help her with her work, or not. Was this what he banked on? He was hardly an attractive figure. But, at any other time, would she have gone along with what might only be a mild flirtation? She knew she had reacted badly – more violently than the situation warranted. She must be more involved with Gad than she thought – imprinted somehow. There was no room now for anyone else. One thing was certain: she could never repeat the massive mistake she had made with Guillaume, to imagine that she had any resource against a well-established man who, when it came down to it, would always put his work, his 'career', before any minor hindrance – like an unwanted baby. The bitter memory welled up in her: the terror and pain of that quiet Paris street, the tree-lined avenue, the brass plate with its discreet legend, *'Maison de Retrait'* and the number 23 forever etched on her retina. And her lost baby who would be four years old by now, a little boy or girl to whom she could not even give a name. To have trusted such a man now seemed ridiculous. Guillaume so confident with his well-modulated voice that could never be interrupted (though she tried), his easy ability to dominate a situation and impose his will. *It must have been part of the attraction*, she thought, stumbling slightly as she climbed a little rise. She must have thought she would be safe with Guillaume, that he would look after her.

At the top of the rise she was ready to rest on a bench, taking the opportunity to roll some sheet music carefully and fit it into her bag, with the books in a heap beside her.

Trees and green, space and sky – Gad called the park his back garden. She loved Gad, she knew it now, and it was inescapable. Safe or not, acceptable or not, this was the man she wanted. She wanted his genuine modesty ('Gad, modest?' she heard his friends exclaim). She wanted his warmth, his guileless humour and, more than anything, she wanted his way of looking at people in their essence, never mind their social standing. She wanted him here, now, his hand on her shoulder, drawing her close, his face close to hers, his kisses.

She leaned back against the bench, lost in dreams, until a sharp gust of wind brought her back to her rootless self and her head snapped forward, her eyes blinking against the dust that swirled around her. The grass beneath her feet was sparse, but wherever you were, it was still earth, the same as in Brittany, and she still felt that pull. She smiled to think of the old photographs in the library – those men were far away from what passed for city smartness and wit. She didn't understand how people could stand living with nothing but bricks and concrete around them. For a moment she was not sure whether she was in London or in Brittany.

★

November 1954

Finishing his shift at the big Royal Mail sorting office at Mount Pleasant, Gad decided to go across from Farringdon Road to the House on foot. He smoked as he walked, and his face kept breaking into an irrepressible smile. It was something his supervisor had said to him as they worked: 'So, if you're from this Burma place – next to India, you said – how come you can speak English proper?'

'Well, you see,' he had replied, trying to hide his amusement, 'we were brought up under the British Raj. All the good schools taught in English.'

'Well, were your parents British, then?'

'No, not exactly. My father was half Portuguese and half Goanese, and my mother was half Scottish and half Burmese. Her mother was a Miss Barrett.'

'Oh, so you're a right transcontinental fuck-up, then!' said the supervisor, and he roared with laughter.

★

Alone with Elspeth in the office, Gad was deep in conversation when he heard someone come through the front door of the House, and looked up to see that it was Thérèse, looking upset and avoiding Gad's eye.

'Oh, I just want to see Louise – is she around?'

'Ah,' said Elspeth. 'I think she's still up in her room – I didn't notice her going out.'

'OK, thanks.' Thérèse glanced at Gad, who was looking at her but saying nothing. 'I need a bit of light relief.'

She went out. Gad thought that she looked a bit down, and that she was lucky to have made friends with Louise, someone who could speak French with her. Louise was in the fashion industry and would be at the House for at least a year.

'Louise is a nice girl,' Elspeth said. 'A pity she's allergic to making beds – too tall to bend her back, I suppose.'

'I suppose.' Gad laughed. How sharp Elspeth could be if she didn't like you. 'Perhaps she hopes to be a model,' he said. He remembered asking Thérèse what a Parisienne could possibly learn about fashion in London, only to be told rather briskly, 'There is more to fashion than pretty pictures in a notebook, you know. You don't understand these things at all!'

Elspeth turned back to Gad, picking up the threads earnestly.

'Now listen,' she said, leaning towards him, 'I want to give you some advice. I remember when Rob and I got involved, and before we knew it we were headlong in love. We hadn't two pennies to rub together, so my parents thought it was a very bad idea – which it easily could have been.'

It was strange to think of Elspeth and Robert as young and single. They presented such a united front; rock solid, you would think.

'But luckily, we had enough going for us...'

'Such as?'

'Well, energy for a start – we both liked walking.' She

looked surprised at herself, and Gad thought it didn't sound much. 'But you know, I was brought up a Wee Free and he was not, and that caused all sorts of problems…'

'To you or to other people?' *Goodness knows what a Wee Free is.* This was getting interesting, as he thought of his mother's staunch Catholicism.

'Well, to other people, really. To the Elders and older friends. But listen, never mind that. All I'm saying is, be careful. It seems like a different world now; you all meet so many people. But still, remember the fuss when Seretse Khama was going to marry Ruth Williams?'[1]

'Yes, because of racial prejudice?' Gad wondered where this was leading. Briefly, he considered Elspeth's position in relation to the International House and those who sponsored it. It occurred to him that perhaps she did not wish to be seen as encouraging mixed marriages.

'Well, there's no apartheid policy in Bechuanaland, so I don't suppose mixed marriages were forbidden there. But South Africa is an important neighbour, and for him to be an effective chief would be difficult if South Africa would not recognise his marriage.'

'As the son of a chief in his country, Seretse was in a special position.' Gad had been following the news with interest, considering the issue carefully. 'Perhaps he should have consulted his people before entering into the marriage.'

'Perhaps. Both he and Ruth had quite high status. She was only a clerk in an insurance company, but she was a white Englishwoman and their standing was an advantage to them. Of course, they married in England.'

'And that meant everybody was watching them!'

'They would watch you and Thérèse if you got serious!'

---

1 Seretse Khama, son of a Paramount Chief in the Protectorate of Bechuanaland (now Botswana), came to London in 1946 to study to become a barrister. In 1948 he married a white English girl, Ruth Williams.

Silence. Gad was winded. Now it was out. He deliberately sidestepped.

'Well, Princess Margaret couldn't marry Townsend, because of his divorce – but ordinary people do, don't they?'

Elspeth sighed. 'Yes, since the war all sorts of things have happened that never... Oh well.' Then, more vigorously, 'But people have to understand what they are doing, what the consequences will be. If ordinary people do an extraordinary thing then they become extraordinary – people see you differently.'

They could hear Thérèse and Louise clattering downstairs, cheery with talk and laughter.

'You do realise,' Elspeth said urgently, 'your marriage would be unthinkable to many people? This place is not the whole world, you know.'

Gad shifted in his chair. It all seemed so rocky. In his mind's eye he saw life in Rangoon before he left: boys and girls light-heartedly partnering each other to dances, driving round the city in tongas late at night, eating their picnics, celebrating; the invasion of Burma over, the Japanese vanished, nobody wanting to think about the deep scars that remained; the bitterness between those forced to collaborate and those who escaped; the half-Japanese babies and their mothers. And now? Who knew what was going on now? Gad had left all that behind, come to Britain only to find a different set of complications in which he floundered, struggling to find his bearings. What was it for, all this prejudice?

For a split second he was back in the Fifty Shilling Tailors, expectations disappointed, assumptions dashed, a sense of shame and anger washing over him.

Then Thérèse stuck her head in. She hesitated and glanced from one to the other, raising her eyebrows a little.

CHAPTER 25

January 1955

Thérèse was coming back – that was all Gad could think about. Longing for her was making his chest hurt. Without her, Christmas had seemed endless. He had played for Midnight Mass and the choir had done well, not rushing, even in *The Holly and the Ivy*. He had stayed for sherry and mince pies at the presbytery with Fr Martin and his two assistants, Frs Peter the intellectual and Connor the fey. He had endured Mrs Mockford's 'Christmas dinner', and the subsequent 'hands across the sea' exchange of greetings and presents by the Christmas tree. It was very well meant, but made him long for the familiar presence of those he had known since birth, the gossip and backchat, the great spicy dishes served up after Midnight Mass and, above all, the quiet presence of his mother, who had such mysterious power over him. Tiny and erect, a long plait twisted around her head like a coronet, she was the one you deferred to, loved and were in awe of.

Where is she now? He had heard nothing for months. She was lost to him.

He had a quick memory of her arriving at his school like a vengeful spirit every time she heard a whisper of any defection on his part or that of any of his teachers; she was completely uninhibited by any feelings of propriety or hierarchy and would go straight to the point. 'Did you not know that Garrard was falling behind in his maths homework?' she would say. 'You only have to tell me, and I will make sure he makes it up.' Or 'I hear that Garrard stayed out too long playing and was late back to class. Did you punish him? Good! I will punish him too!'

All this had been on Gad's mind during the festive season, when everywhere was closed and he had felt too restless even to practise. But now, Thérèse was coming back, after spending 'Noël' at home in Brittany, and he would see how things stood between them.

★

The day after Boxing Day, before the New Year celebrations could get underway, Gad got a welcome airmail: he saw at once that it had been delayed in the Christmas post, and that it had an American postmark; he tore it open eagerly.

30 November 1954

Dear Garrard

We are all so excited, and so tired! Here we are in the US of A, staying in a convent outside San Francisco, but soon to move into a house of our own! It will be small, but right opposite the church of Holy Mary Stella Maris in Oakland, near the Bay. Don't write to us here, because we shall soon be on the move, and our address will be 1398 Medlar Street, Oakland, California, USA. Mummy will be able to go to Mass every morning as she wants, and we shall quickly make friends here.

Garrard, never forget how good the Church has been to us, to help us come here from Borneo. We did not belong there, but here we can make a new start and there will be good education for the children. They will be Yanks!

I hope everything goes well for you. How are your friends, and especially your good friend Thérèse?

A big God Bless from us all, and especially from Big Mummy. She is busy helping the Sisters make a Burmese curry.

Your sister
Wilma
PS Write soon, and remember the new address.

★

He had not promised to meet Thérèse at the station but, suddenly energised by the thought of seeing her again, he put on his duffel coat and did so anyway. She had crossed the Channel by ferry to Southampton, and was due at Waterloo at four in the afternoon. Would she make straight for her digs, or come to see him? Either way, he could not wait.

Standing near the barrier, he caught sight of her far down the platform, as she descended amidst a crowd and turned to manoeuvre a heavy suitcase after her. She wore a new scarlet beret with her wool coat, and her soft red bag dangled from one shoulder. She looked flustered.

He sprinted along the platform. She looked up and saw him. Her face lit up, as if a hundred-watt bulb had been switched on behind it, and she stood stock-still to watch him. Skidding to a halt, he felt himself smiling all over his face, and gave her the biggest bear hug, burying his face in her hair and inhaling the scent of train fug along with her own fragrance. She felt small, her arms wrapped tightly round his neck, though he was aware again of her long limbs – like a little spider, he thought.

At last they pulled apart, and Gad bent to pick up her bulky suitcase and haul it along the platform through the station to the bus stop.

'D'you want to go straight home, or...?' he asked.

'Could we...'

'Go to my flat?' he finished jubilantly. 'Yes, yes, of course. We could go out and eat later?'

'I'm not hungry,' she said. 'Nothing else to do on the boat.'

They made it to the bus, and sat downstairs because of the suitcase. Her shoulder was pressed against him and her hand was in his. Being with her again was bliss.

'So how was Christmas?' he finally thought to ask. 'How is your family?'

'They're well, thank you. Did you think of me?'

'A bit.'

She smiled and squeezed his hand.

'It's always sad for us at Christmas, though,' she said. 'We miss Alain.'

'Yes.'

'But did you miss me?'

'Not much,' he teased. 'Too busy having a good time!'

She glanced at him suspiciously. He must get out of this habit, he thought, or she would never know when he was being serious. He could not understand how she, so lovely and desirable to him, could be so unsure.

They trundled over the river, riding above its watery traffic, glancing up- and down-stream to Parliament and St Paul's.

'No, but really,' he said, 'it was fine. Just – impersonal.'

'Yes, well, you need a bit of – racket?' (he nodded) 'at Christmas. You know, music and neighbours in and out, and visits and – general chaos!'

'Was it like that for you?' asked Gad.

'No, not really. I saw a few old friends. We missed Alain,' she said again.

'And there's no young man at home who has been looking forward to seeing you?' His tone was light, but he watched her anxiously as she replied.

'No, nobody, not since Guillaume. And he wasn't from Brittany.'

'Oh, so who was he?'

It was Thérèse's turn to dodge. 'What is this?' She looked him full in the face. 'You want to know everything, suddenly?'

'Well, not everything. If I wanted to know everything, you would ask too.'

'And you wouldn't like that?'

'It's just that I feel like a freak – everybody asking about my background all the time.'

'Well, you must be so interesting!'

'Or they are so ignorant?'

'People can't know about everything in the world. Be reasonable. How many people have been to the Far East at all, let alone a small country like Burma? I don't know anything about it – only that I have looked in the atlas to see where it is.'

'You have?'

She blushed. 'We're here,' she said.

Gad wrestled the suitcase out of the bus, and they turned into his street, the narrow link between two main thoroughfares, a chasm between dark brick tenements occupied mostly by workers in the rag trade, he being the exception. Today, a weekday, they had to dodge rails of clothes seeming to wheel themselves, in various stages of manufacture, from one workshop to another, and as they reached his flat they could hear the treadle machine going upstairs, where his neighbour Carmen was hard at work.

Thérèse let Gad manhandle the suitcase down the stairs to his front door, and following him down, said as she had before, 'You need a light on these stairs.'

'Oh, to hell with that – come on into the warm.' He dropped the case in the middle of the bedroom floor and turned to gather Thérèse as she came through, opening his arms wide and enfolding her tightly as he kicked the door shut. It was not actually very warm in the room, never was. Together they fell onto the monumental bed and found themselves in an impenetrable thicket of clothes, to be fought through like brambles. Shoes flew in all directions and Gad ended up making love with one arm still in his shirt; not that it mattered. She was wonderful naked, that was all he could think: small, warm, quick and loving. Afterwards, as they lay panting in the cool air, he managed to pull aside the heavy covers and get them both underneath, where they lay with legs locked as became their habit until their heat warmed the bed and they slept.

But not for long. Gad woke soon, stirred by an urgent and unusual need to speak. He dreamt they were talking and woke up to find they were not. He felt that there was something to be settled, and that words were needed. What he felt was mostly relief – at last they were where they were always meant to be. He eased out of bed, gently displacing Thérèse's arm which lay across his waist, and pulled on his old, rough dressing-gown. So as not to disturb her too abruptly, he went into the little room that served as both kitchen and bathroom, ground a good measure of coffee beans and put them in his Italian coffeemaker. As the water bubbled up noisily and the rich aroma spread down the corridor, she woke up, calling, 'Gad?'

'Here I am. Is black coffee OK – I forgot to get milk?'

'Mmm, lovely. I'm coming.' She did, first throwing on her big black sweater, a pair of pants and her long boots. Gad pulled her to him, enjoying the thought of his hairy dressing-gown scratching her bare thighs.

'You are lovely,' he said.

'Am I, really?' She leaned back against him and nuzzled his neck contentedly, before raising her head again to ask, 'Do you love me, though?'

'*Naturellement*,' he said, and she smiled her beautiful smile. Still, this felt inadequate. He knew his moment had come, and turned her to face him.

'Listen,' he urged. 'I've got to talk to you.' Her eyes widened. 'Come into the living-room.'

They sat down close on the bulky chesterfield, and he took her hands in his while he gathered himself. The forgotten coffee fizzed on the stove.

His mother's voice sounded in his ear, as she had spoken when his brothers brought girls home: 'She is a lovely girl. Is she a good Catholic?' He knew Thérèse was not. His stomach clenched when he remembered that they had made love without worrying about any possible consequences. There was nobody in London that he could talk to about such things, no brother Julian. He was on his own, and it made him feel young and ignorant. So now, he must get this right.

Feeling Thérèse's hands warm and live in his, he drew in his breath.

'Thérèse, we have to talk seriously. I've never felt like this about anyone before. I love you, that's all, always will. You're like no one else. You're beautiful and…' He broke off, feeling the inadequacy of his words. 'How do you feel about me?' It was banal, but it was what he desperately wanted to know. He could not even look at her till he knew.

'Oh. Oh Gad.'

No! She was going to say 'but'.

'Gad, you are the most – solid – thing in my whole life.'

Her breath was warm on his face.

'Solid?' he exclaimed indignantly. He waited for the word 'but'.

'Oh, I say it badly. I do not mean to be rude, at all.' She pulled a face.

'What do you mean, what d'you mean?' he said urgently.

She lifted her eyes to his. 'I mean, I have known other men – boys and men – and it has not always been happy.'

'I see. Guillaume?' He leaned back. She's turning me down!

'Yes, Guillaume.' She looked again at him. 'And others. I

like to explore, you know? I should perhaps be more careful. But if I were I would probably not be here now, with you.'

'No! But the question is, are you really with me?'

She nodded slowly. Where he had seen hesitation, he began to see acceptance.

'Then that's all I need to know! Marry me! I know it's risky – I've been thinking about it all ways round. Have we run scared? We shouldn't! These feelings I have for you – I can trust them, I know. Can you say the same? If you can say the same…?'

Again the nod, and Thérèse began to smile. 'Oh sweetheart, surely that's all that matters, how you and I feel about each other?'

He grabbed her and she threw her arms round him hugging him, laughing.

'How we miss each other; how I feel when I see you again. Who cares what others think, we can make it together, I know. What do you say? Say yes, my darling Thérèse, please say yes!'

CHAPTER 26

The morning light seeped into the bedroom without much brightening the room. The huge mahogany wardrobe loomed over them, and the feet of strangers passed within a yard of their window. The Sally Army was off duty on weekdays, so they had been able to sleep until nearly nine. Gad lay warm against Thérèse, his body weightless as his mind wandered. So, he thought, the die was cast. They were to marry. In the cold light of morning, it all seemed unlikely. Two small figures lost in the enormity of London, the centre of the universe, fragile as moths attracted from far-off planets.

★

Two hours later they stood in a cold drizzle, looking up a narrow, winding street that held no promise at all. But, as they set off away from the bustle of Kensington High Street, Gad was relieved to see the first of what turned out to be a series of small antique jewellery shops, lining both sides of the road. He had heard about these.

'Let's browse,' he said, taking Thérèse's arm with a sense of ownership that was new and pleasant. He saw her hair, spiky with rain, random strands sticking to her wet cheeks. Her eyes glowed.

'I shall not know what to choose,' she said uncertainly.

'Don't worry – we'll choose together. What about here?' he said, and they peered into a window streaked with rivulets of rain, falling more heavily now.

The window was full of heavy pieces of semi-precious

jewellery – amber necklaces, amethysts set in silver, jade and ivory earrings, jet brooches and agate rings.

'No, no good,' he said, moving Thérèse on, although she was inclined to linger.

The next window was full of unpriced rings set with brilliant solitaire diamonds that reflected the spotlights directed at them. There were, too, five-strand pearl necklaces paired with large drop earrings, and gold wrist clasps that looked like handcuffs. He hoped that these would not appeal to her, and was rewarded: '*Ma fois*, no,' she said, pulling him away.

As in the fairy tales, the third try was the right one: they saw a window with a great variety of treasures chaotically displayed, poorly lit behind a none-too-clean window. There was a steady gleam of light inside, though, and an old man holding a lens to his eye.

'Coming?' said Gad, pushing open the door, which emitted an old-fashioned 'ping'.

The old man smiled with one side of his face as he removed the lens from his eye and looked enquiringly at them.

'Can I help you?' The words came sideways out of his mouth. Thérèse looked as if tempted to giggle, and Gad gave her a warning glance.

With no particular system, they began to search through the trays of offerings; Thérèse at random, as if trying to form an opinion, Gad with a hunter's eye. He knew exactly what he was looking for, and indeed soon found it – a Victorian half-hoop of graduated diamonds held by delicate claws within a grooved gold ring. It was perfect – smooth with not a clumsy feature, precious, yet possibly affordable. He showed it to Thérèse: she liked it, amongst others, which included an opal and a tiny rosette of diamonds set in platinum.

'This is the one, though,' insisted Gad.

'Is it, though?' Thérèse demurred.

'Yes, it's the one. The diamonds are good quality, and the ring is Victorian gold, not a modern alloy. And don't you love the way the stones are integrated into the ring – part of it, you see? A smooth curve.'

'I see.'

He took it to the counter before she could change her mind, and asked the price.

'That one? It's thirty-six pounds.'

Gad had brought forty pounds, most of his savings. He had not yet learned the standard question, 'Is that your best price?' but in any case thought it was fair. He took out his wallet and paid the sum asked.

*

The rain was coming down in a steady downpour, so it was in the shelter of a doorway that Gad took the ring out of its box and formally placed it on Thérèse's finger. Their mouths were hot in their cold faces as they kissed, and Thérèse thought that if he was prepared to buy her a diamond ring on a day when she looked so bedraggled, there must be something real between them.

She took hold of his hand, the right one with the signet ring of soft Burmese gold on the little finger, and pressed it, saying, 'I didn't know you knew so much about jewellery?'

'Not jewellery, really: just stones.'

'But how…?'

'Many of them are mined in Burma, you know.' He looked at her, smiling. 'My mother used to have the jeweller call – he'd come to the back door and bring leather bags of stones to spread out on the kitchen table. I used to watch.'

'And did she get them set, then?'

'Oh yes, she told him what she wanted and he would cut and set them.'

'Like a hairdresser, really?'

He laughed at her. So like a French girl!

'So,' she went on as they ventured out again into the rain, 'your mother used to wear lots of jewellery?'

'Not she; it was all for her daughters and cousins and nieces. She lost most of what she still had, on the trek.'

'Lost?'

'Yes – stolen, or swept away in the rivers as they crossed.' Suddenly, he looked irritated, as if bored with explaining himself yet again. 'Never mind that now. Are you happy?'

'Oh – yes,' Thérèse breathed, not sure all the same if what she felt after the gift of the ring was happiness – was she 'happier' now than she had been an hour ago? She liked the unfamiliar circlet, but receiving it on her hand was such a new sensation that she could not work out yet how it might change things. She looked at it on her finger, twisted it and admired the sparkle.

'Thank you, thank you, darling,' she said, experimenting with the endearment, which seemed appropriate to Gad's intention: *Cheris pour diamants*, said a little voice in her head.

★

The morning finished oddly. Thérèse had assumed they would perhaps go to one of their favourite cafés for a celebratory cup of coffee, or maybe back to the flat. She was surprised when Gad stopped a few paces further on, outside a jeweller's shop that was quite large by Church Street standards.

'Listen, Thérèse – would you let me have the ring back for a moment?'

Taken aback, she hesitated, then held her left hand out without speaking.

He drew the ring from her finger, and put it back into the box, which he produced from his pocket.

'Wait there, will you?' he said, and leaving her standing in the doorway, he dashed into the large shop.

She shivered, chilled by more than the rain.

In a moment he emerged, smiling.

'It's all fine, sweetheart. Here, let's put it on again.'

'What was the matter?'

'Oh, nothing – I just wanted to make sure I paid the right price. It's fine; he valued it at an extra five pounds!' He beamed, triumphant at this confirmation of his expertise.

★

January 1955

Thérèse had first encountered the parish priest at St Xavier's one evening when she had gone to meet Gad after choir practice, and found him a sensible, rational sort of man. She had it in mind that he had been a grammar school master, as Gad had once mentioned, and she expected that it would be quite possible to have a conversation with him, despite her inherited atheism. So when she opened the front door that winter morning she was surprised to confront a young cleric, one she had never seen before.

'Gad!' she called. 'It's not Father Martin!'

Gad emerged from the kitchen, where he had been preparing coffee. 'Oh!' he said, looking startled. 'Is it not?'

'Never! I'm Father Diarmid,' said the young man, standing perfectly still in the dim light of the stairwell, sniffing the air, which held a delicious aroma. It was quiet at this time of day. Fr Martin would have saved precious time by marching straight in.

'We were expecting Father Martin. But anyway, come along in, Father,' said Gad, holding the door wide in his role as host.

The young man ambled in, looking round him, and Thérèse saw that he had shining, ruddy cheeks and big red hands dangling against the black cassock. He reminded her of the workers on her father's farm.

Glancing into the bright, empty sitting-room, the young man headed straight for the kitchen, rubbing his hands together. It was relatively warm there, with the soapy dampness from their morning bath, the crumbs from their breakfast toast, and now the bubbling coffee.

'Ah!' said Fr Diarmid, 'they told me in Dublin that you would all be drinking coffee in London! I have to try it – heaven must smell like this!'

'When did you arrive in London, then?' enquired Thérèse.

'A month ago! Christmas! Isn't Father Martin darlin'? But such a big, gloomy house!'

It was going to be hard to talk religion to this man, Thérèse thought. She must remember that he was here to instruct her in the Catholic faith – to her a dark notion. She remembered a procession following a great brass crucifix bearing a brutally-tortured body; angelic little boys in their white surplices and frills; and lastly a crowd of village people with a tail of ragamuffin children hopping along behind. She saw the brightest colours ever seen in the hardworking farming community – no wonder people were attracted. The priest was gorgeously decked out. But where was the carpenter of Nazareth? She found a perch on the edge of the bath while she thought about this.

Gad had poured coffee into mugs, and now watched Fr Diarmid raise his and taste, eyes closed – and saw his face contort.

'Why, it's not at all like it smells! It's bitter!' Diarmid smacked his lips, inhaling again the aroma. 'It's odd. There's the taste – like bitter leaves – and then this heavenly...' he flapped his free hand, sending wafts of steam up to the ceiling. 'I've never had anything like it!'

Gad glanced at Thérèse with a glint in his eye.

'And it's a stimulant too,' said Thérèse slyly, coming out of her reverie. 'You know it's really a kind of drug?'

'Well, don't tell Father Martin, will you? Then I can come here whenever I want some more!'

'No, really, it is,' said Gad, trading on the young man's innocence. 'Believe her, she knows!'

Oh! We're playing on the same side then, thought Thérèse. It was exhilarating. But under this lightness was a touch of panic. Her father had taught her that people who practised Catholicism were misguided if not downright superstitious, and that she should never put herself into the power of priests. Yet here was a priest, in her fiancé's kitchen, come to 'instruct' her. What would her father make of that? And, worse, what did it say about Gad?

Gad took the young priest firmly by the arm now, suggesting more soberly, 'Well, Father, hadn't we better find somewhere to sit down? I should explain that we've very little furniture just now…'

'Yes, sure, I noticed so.'

'You see, we'll get our own later – we wanted rid of the old, lumpy stuff.'

'So…' Fr Diarmid looked around him, raising his eyebrows, which made comical arcs above his dark blue eyes.

'So we'll talk in the bedroom.' Diarmid's eyebrows climbed still higher. 'This way.' Gad led the way along the corridor. Thérèse followed, her step light.

In the bedroom, with its subterranean half-light, there was only a tall paraffin stove, the ancient double bed soon to go, and opposite it the tomb-like mahogany wardrobe with its long mirror. They sat in a row on the bed, first Thérèse, then Fr Diarmid, then Gad. There was a stink of paraffin. Thérèse looked at their reflection and giggled.

'Yes.' And the young priest, catching her mood, began to sing: 'Here we sit like birds in the wilderness,

'Birds in the wilderness' they joined in, laughing – 'Birds in the wilderness,

'Here we sit like birds in the wilderness,

'Tra la la la laa-ah.'

Nobody could remember the last line, though Gad contributed a growling bass.

★

'Well, so,' Diarmid began at last.

'Yes?' she managed, a rising question. The term 'Father' stuck in her head, well before it could reach her mouth. She could not utter it. She could see, in the mirror, Gad settling himself comfortably to listen.

'So you're thinking of marrying this reprobate of ours?'

Why this oblique criticism? Wasn't he the respected organist of St Xavier's?

'It seems so.' She gently touched her new diamonds.

'And you are not a baptised person?'

Thérèse tensed. 'No, my parents did not have me baptised.'

'Ah well,' Diarmid said easily. 'So, now, we have only to make sure that you understand Gad's faith in God and his responsibilities as a Catholic man, and that you will not, so, stand in his way.'

'Of course.' It all began to sound simple, after all. It was going to be a mild and friendly business, this 'instruction'. Then the first bombshell: 'We will get the bishop to allow the marriage, won't we, Gad?' said Diarmid, laying his hand on Gad's shoulder.

Gad started, but answered, 'Yes, fine,' nodding his head as if willing to go along with whatever seemed necessary. Thérèse caught the reflection of his eye. As Diarmid turned back, she was pulling a face at the idea that a bishop could have any say in the matter.

164

'Ah no, you need not worry, darlin'. It will all be fine. It's just because you're not baptised. After this visit, he'll give the dispensation.'

Thérèse made no response to this.

'So, what must I allow my – husband – to do?' For a few moments after saying that word, Thérèse was deaf to Diarmid's reply.

When she tuned in again, it was to hear: '... just not getting in the way, you know? He should go to Mass on Days of Obligation...'

'Days of what?'

'Obligation. They're especially good days when we all like to celebrate – so we go to Mass.'

'Oh.' So strange, to live your life by such rules.

'Yes – Gad knows the days.'

She glanced at Gad's reflection, and received a brief nod.

'Then he should keep the faith, follow the teachings of the Holy Catholic Church...'

'But I don't know anything about all that,' she broke in uneasily.

'Yes, but Gad has been brought up to it. He knows the score, and he knows too –' he added, looking sideways at Gad, 'that he should come to Confession – say his Hail Marys?'

She saw Gad duck his head, and wondered if he made a habit of disregarding the rules; still, he did not demur, and seemed to be accepting what Diarmid said as a matter of course.

Then, almost as an afterthought, Diarmid added: 'And, of course, bring up any children you may have in the faith.'

She had known about this, of course; everybody knew the Church demanded it. But to hear it put so baldly, here, sitting on the bed where she and Gad had so recently...

'Yes,' said Gad from the other side of Diarmid's solid body. 'Mmm.'

She could see from his face that all this was totally integral to him; something he did not question nor need to discuss. She began to suspect that his religion, inherited and lived his entire life, was an inseparable part of him. As for herself, caught up in her new love, she nodded dumbly also. Children seemed a long way off.

'So, is there anything you want to ask me just now, darlin'?'

She shook her head, not trusting herself to speak. Her throat was tight and her mouth dry. She had no more questions for this young man who treated 'faith' as a legacy that could be passed from parents to children, in exchange for eternal life. It was not her faith, and they were not her rules. But she wondered, fleetingly, how much of her antipathy to the Church came from her Huguenot father's hatred of its historic cruelty, and realised that she, too, had never bothered to question those convictions.

'Well, you know, any time.' The young priest got to his feet, and lifted his hand to bless each of them in turn. Gad stood and bowed his head to receive the benediction. In her mind, Thérèse resisted. The fear that she might one day be pressed to convert hung in the air, like some nebulous cloud of unknowing; an immense, risky universe that would take you outside common sense and beyond logic.

'Thank you, Father,' said Gad, holding out his hand. Diarmid took it and they shook vigorously.

'Goodbye, and thank you,' repeated Thérèse and then, on an unexpected impulse, 'Come and see us again.'

'Sure I will, and thank you. I know where there's a welcome,' he replied, and got himself swiftly out of the flat. They stood by the door to see him go.

CHAPTER 27

February 1955

Thérèse wrote to her parents. She worded the letter carefully, because she knew how her announcement would sound, arriving completely out of the blue.

Dear Maman and Papa,

she began formally, and then, after her New Year wishes and enquiries about everybody's health:

> *You know I have not written to you for a month or so, and perhaps wonder why. The reason is that I have some very exciting news, and I hope you will be as happy about it as I am. I am in love with a good man; he loves me and since I came back here after Noël we have decided to be married! You will find it very strange that he is neither French nor English, but I hope that when you get to know him you too will appreciate his good heart and his hard-working character.*
>
> *His name is Garrard d'Silva, he is Catholic, from Burma, of Portuguese-Indian father (an accountant) and Scottish-Burmese mother.*

She thought she had better get this bit over straight away, at the same time wondering if they would understand the implications: that Gad was dark-skinned – 'black', as they would say.

He was brought up in the capital, Rangoon, and came to London on a scholarship two years ago, to study music. He is very talented, and I know he will make a good career as a pianist. We will be staying in London, as his family is far away, and there will be better work for him here.

I hope very much you will come here for the wedding, if only you can find somebody to help on the farm while you are away. He has already given me a beautiful diamond ring, and we want to get married in London without ceremony early in April, but of course you must meet him before that. Could you make a little trip here? You could take the ferry to Southampton and then the train. Garrard's mother will not be here, but some of his family live in London.

I am so excited, and can't wait for you to meet him. Write soon.

Your loving daughter
Thérèse

Thérèse pictured her parents reading this, together at the big kitchen table. Grandmère Bettine, rough old stone dressed in black bombazine, would be standing with her back to the wall, as always, hands folded on her stomach, part of the family yet separated by her years.

What would they make of it? She had been deliberately vague about Gad's appearance, though in some ways this felt like a betrayal – as if she were ashamed of him. But she thought they would never understand someone so far from their own experience, and wanted to bring them into the picture gently. She remembered trying to explain to her mother about her early fascination with Breton history – or rather, prehistory – the pursed lips that met her attempts to convey her excitement when Mlle Grenier, her teacher, first took her to see the wonderful *menhirs*.

'Great rocks getting in the way of the plough,' her mother

had grumbled, closing her lips tightly. 'Just something more for farmers to work around!'

So practical. This was what her upbringing and hard life had brought her to. Her father had said nothing, not contradicting his wife. Thérèse thought that she might have been able to interest him in her newfound enthusiasms, but she had not tried. She and her Pappi understood each other instinctively, never finding much need for words.

She waited, hoping that she had made it clear that she would marry Gad, come what may; that she wanted but did not need their approval. If there was going to be a fuss, let it be now, let it soon be behind them. She did not want to cause an emotional confrontation, but she needed to establish her position from the outset; why did it feel like an act of defiance?

★

It was a week or two before Gad found time to write home with the news. He knew his family would be preoccupied with settling into their new home, did not want them to be distracted by any other concerns, and wanted to tell them in a way they would understand. He got busy with the formalities stemming from his birth overseas.

★

To her surprise and secret satisfaction, Thérèse found that the priest at Gad's church made it his business to check all the parishes where Gad had ever been registered, for any record of a previous marriage. There must have been cases of bigamy amongst foreign students, Thérèse supposed. Presumably, if Gad had contracted a civil marriage, that would not count at all in the eyes of the Church. The fact of Thérèse's foreign origin was irrelevant, since she was not Catholic. There was another issue: the Catholic Church was not the official Church of England, so there had to be a civil registrar at the ceremony.

Amidst all this fuss they turned their minds towards trousseaux, and together visited an Oxford Street store, where they went off in separate directions to emerge later with their trove in paper carriers: three new sets of underwear each. They were hard up; they planned to look splendid on the day itself; what else did they need?

A week later Thérèse got back to her room after yet another visit to the registry office, to find a letter from home lying on the doormat. She picked it up absentmindedly, her head still whirling with bureaucracy; she had had to provide proof of all sorts of facts about herself that she had always taken for granted.

She made some coffee and sipped it gratefully, wishing the whole thing was over and done with, and she could just go to earth with Gad – she rather dreaded the curious scrutiny to which the event would expose them. Then her name on the white envelope jumped out at her, and she realised that it was in her father's careful handwriting.

Unlike Gad, she had received few letters from home since leaving, and it was usually her mother who wrote, keeping her in touch with news of their health, and of the farm's progress. She had little else to say to her daughter. But her father had written this time: it must be so very important to him.

She opened the envelope and read: (trans.)

My dear Thérèse

Your letter has come as a great surprise to us both, for you have not told us until now anything about this young man Garrard, even when you were here for Noël. I wonder when you met him, and how well you know him.

Thérèse remembered that she had not even mentioned him when she was there so recently, not knowing how much to say. She also saw that the emphasis was on how long she had known Gad – did her father think she had only just met him, after Christmas?

You say his mother is on the other side of the world, the letter continued, *and would not be able to come to England. Perhaps his father could do so?*

Had she not mentioned that Gad's father had died some years before?

When two people plan to marry it is usual for the families to know each other beforehand, even to be asked for their permission. Of course, I know that you young people have more freedom now, and that you, my Thérèse, have already travelled far from us in pursuit of your ambitions. We already know that you could not be happy living here with us, but of course we still care about you and what sort of future you make for yourself. There are many questions in our minds: do you dream of children, how you could raise a family of your own in a city surrounded by strangers? With Garrard a foreigner, what place could you find for yourselves? How would your children (our grandchildren) be regarded? I cannot imagine such a thing. It pains me to think how our neighbours here would look at you.

So that was it, then – how would the neighbours regard it?

I cannot say more; I know that you are well over the age of consent but I beg you to think again. Please bring Garrard to see us very soon. If you have so little time, come on the ferry and your mother and I will take the train to meet you in Cherbourg. Come soon.

Your loving
Pappi

PS Your mother insists I ask whether there is any special reason for your wanting to marry so quickly.

★

'My parents have written to say they can't wait to meet you,' said Thérèse. 'Do you think we could go over on the ferry one day soon? It wouldn't cost very much.'

'Of course,' said Gad readily. 'Of course they want to meet me, and if that's the best way of doing it, I'm in. When shall we go?'

'Oh Gad, what an angel you are!' Thérèse hugged him, filled with love and relief. There had been tension in her request – she was not used to asking for something for herself, and this was a big one, with much hanging on it.

'Is this how it is done in Burma?' she asked, holding on to him. He seemed so at home with the idea of what was owed to families.

'Well, there would be no end of sisters and brothers, and aunties and cousins – it would all happen without anybody thinking twice about it.' He smiled at her. 'The family are always meeting together – Christmases, birthdays, engagements, weddings, funerals, you name it – any excuse for a party!'

She laughed, letting go. 'It sounds like a lot of effort?'

'Not really, when everybody shares the cooking – and the cost.'

Thérèse was not satisfied – something still disturbed her. 'But don't they have other things to do?'

'Nothing more important.'

She suddenly felt a bit bleak about her own family situation.

★

This conversation had made Gad realise just how remiss he had been in not writing already to his own family; he made haste to put this right.

5 February 1955

Dear Mummy, Wilma, Veena and all at home, he wrote.

This is going to be a very happy letter, because I heard from you that you are all safely arrived in America and that you have already found friends and a home in sunny California. This is fantastic news. I have been so worried about you, especially since there were weeks on end when I did not even know where you were. I kept thinking about you and feeling frustrated because I could do nothing to help.

I am sending this to the address of your new house – hope you have moved in already and are feeling comfortable. Please tell me if there is anything you need from here, and if any of our family or friends will be visiting over here any time soon. If you can, please send me a photo of the house and yourselves, so that I can picture you there.

Now, I also have happy news for you – happy for me, but a little sad because I expect you will not be able to be here for the ceremony – I am talking about a wedding! I have told you a bit about my 'good friend' Thérèse, who has now become much more than that. In fact, I love her very much and I know she loves me too. There is no reason to delay getting married, so we are planning to do so at the beginning of April. We shall shortly be going over to France so that I can meet her parents, and after that will let you know all arrangements. I hope that Victor and Joyce and others of the clan will come, and as you know, we have many good friends here who will be able to help.

★

They set off for France the following Saturday, catching the early boat train to Southampton. At the docks, they moved through a set of drab buildings and sleepy formalities, up the passenger gangway to the oily-smelling ferry. One or two cars were lifted on board by cranes, their owners watching anxiously as the loaded nets dangled drunkenly in mid-air before the precious catch was deposited straight into the hold.

Thérèse had already made this crossing once or twice, and quickly found a place on deck out of the worst of the wind, so that they could watch the mainland, and then the Isle of Wight disappear slowly astern. The vessel began to pick up the movement of the Channel seas, and leaning together over the rail, they realised that it was going to be choppy for the eight-hour passage.

They had brought sandwiches, but soon found they had no appetite: anxiety and the early morning start made them cold and nervous.

'Let's look for a warmer spot – below decks,' Thérèse suggested. They lasted ten minutes in the warm reek, made up of tobacco smoke, vomit, food and the odour of many bodies pressed tight, and spent the rest of the trip switching between that and the deck with the bitter salt wind hurtling at them straight down the Channel. Thérèse turned pale and Gad listless; both were silent. When Cherbourg loomed up, Gad bent over her with concern. Thérèse took one hand out of her coat pocket to stroke his frozen face, smiling wanly and exclaiming, 'I bet your last sea voyage wasn't like this – you're so cold!'

'So are you,' Gad responded, blowing gently on her cheeks to warm them. 'But I didn't have my trusty duffel coat in those days!' He pulled her to him, opening the coat to share what warmth he had, wrapping the rough cloth tightly around her, and hugging her hard. 'Not worried, are you?'

'Never!' she said stoutly, as they stood feeling their bulky vessel slide smoothly into Cherbourg harbour.

Thérèse had sent a telegram to let her parents know the time of arrival, and they were waiting on the dock to see the ferry come in. From the customs shed, Thérèse and Gad could see them through the dirty frosted glass of the swing doors. They looked small and lost in the grey light.

'Right then,' said Gad, with his big smile, taking her firmly by the arm and making for the doors. Then he did what she had not yet come to terms with, though she knew it was the polite custom in Burma: he went through the doors first, and without looking back left her to follow. So what her parents saw at this important moment was a short black man in a shabby duffel coat, pushing ahead of their daughter in what, to Western eyes, was a thoroughly unmannerly way. Thérèse only had time to think that this needed explaining, before she came up with him, and together they approached the older couple, standing side by side in the twilight, shock registering on their faces. For an instant Thérèse felt sorry for them all. She kissed her mother, seeing at close quarters the tired lines of her face and the silver threads in her dark hair; then embraced her father, feeling the stiffness of his best clothes beneath her fingers.

'Oh Pappi, Maman, it is good of you to come. How have you managed it?' She could not afford to feel pity for her mother just now.

M Kutanguay, impatiently: 'It's fine – everything can wait until tomorrow.'

Releasing her father, Thérèse turned to Gad, a watchful presence beside her, and taking his elbow, smilingly said to her parents, 'Well, here we are. This is Garrard.'

Mme Kutanguay recovered first, to hold out her hand with a polite, '*Bonjour*, M d'Silva.'

Thérèse saw Gad's beautiful bare hand meet her mother's glove for a brief moment, as he bent his head with a respectful: 'Mme Kutanguay.' Then he turned to her father, who gave a little, formal bow before holding out his own roughened hand in a strong but brief handclasp. The first contact was made, though you could not say the ice was broken. She took Gad's arm again and they fell in behind her parents as they mounted stone steps to the quayside. There were a couple of hours before the return crossing, and they were to have a small meal in a nearby restaurant at this odd time of day. Thérèse squeezed Gad's arm. He was behaving with perfect self-possession, as if knowing his own worth but respectful of the concerns others might be feeling.

It was a tense meeting, both sides away from home, nothing familiar to support them or bridge the gaps. Thérèse had the difficult role of interpreter, and conversation over their meal was slow and stilted.

'Your studies are going well?' M Kutanguay enquired of Gad.

'Quite well, thank you, and I have had some engagements.'

She wondered whether her parents noticed Gad's merry brown eyes, his dark curly hair and his expressive features.

Mme Kutanguay wanted to know, 'I understand your family may move away from – Burma?'

'*Oui, Madame.*' Gad had learned this much. 'They are already in the USA.'

Thérèse's parents managed politeness – too much was at stake for it to be otherwise – but they never talked about how they felt about anything since Alain died, and were inarticulate now with shock and fear.

Nothing significant was said until afterwards, when Maman firmly led Thérèse away to the stinking *cabinet*, keeping her there long enough to take a good look and say, with country directness: 'You are not pregnant?'

'No, no. Nothing like that. We will wait to have children.'

'You already look like a couple.'

'We are, *Maman*. That is why we want to be married.'

'Of course. Your father does not like it.'

'But he will come and give me away?'

'I don't know. I will see if I can persuade him, but I cannot promise anything.'

'And you, *Maman*? What about you?'

'Thérèse, you will do as you like; you always do. I can live with it.'

'I am so sorry I am not Alain,' was all Thérèse could answer.

And her mother managed, 'It is a beautiful ring.'

They re-joined the men, who both looked strained, Gad in particular. Something must have passed between them, but Gad never told her until her father died. She went to *Pappi* now and put her arms round him, whispering, 'You will love him in the end, I promise.'

It was time to go. Nothing was resolved, but perhaps the worst was over.

CHAPTER 28

March 1955

Back in London, the days rushed by. Gad told Thérèse that he had ordered a new suit on the never-never – not from the Fifty Shilling Tailors this time, but from Austin Reed in Regent Street. He would have to stay the same size, at least until he had paid it off.

Thérèse asked him again and again whether he had heard from his mother or sisters, to which he replied, lightly, 'They may not have got my letter yet. Don't worry, they will be delighted. My cousins will be at the wedding, anyway, and you'll see.'

Tony was to be best man, one of his chief responsibilities being to look after M and Mme Kutanguay – if they actually decided to come, that is. Thérèse worried until the eve of the wedding, when she actually saw them get off the train at Waterloo. Maman had written to say what time they would be arriving, and Thérèse was left to assume that this meant Pappi would give her away in time-honoured fashion. She knew in her heart that whatever his objections, he would go on loving her as he always had. She also knew that if he had decided he could not do it, he would tell her so directly. She felt optimistic about his silence.

Maman, who was always so reticent, was a different matter. With Maman, she could never be quite sure, especially since Alain.

*

Thérèse had asked Louise to be her bridesmaid. She was a giraffe of a girl, model size ten, and would tower over the bride but, as Thérèse expected, she was thrilled to be asked and immediately entered into the spirit of things. Together they hatched a plan for dresses that would blend together – 'Not white,' stipulated Thérèse – and bought lengths of beautiful wild silk. Louise said she could find fellow students who would make it up, and some catering chums to provide refreshments for the guests in Thérèse's room.

Thérèse was still trying to keep up with her work. It took her mind off the wedding, about which she felt so ambivalent. Left to herself, she would have liked to slide off to the nearest registry office. Living together would be the interesting part, not the wedding – and Thérèse had never been very good at social gatherings, anyway.

However, she did not feel strongly enough about her own preferences to oppose Gad on this: he was Catholic and for him no other ceremony would do. St Xavier's was a second home to him, especially in the absence of his close family – a link with Burma. As she was beginning to realise, he loved surrounding himself with friends, though he had promised to limit the number of guests. Last but not least, he had no intention of having a 'hole in the corner' affair – it had to be as public and celebratory as possible.

★

At Cecil Sharp House one day she encountered her gardener friend 'Duggie' Dugdale.

'You're looking very pleased with yourself,' he commented, an appreciative glance at her face.

'Yes! I'm getting married!' She showed him her ring.

'Married? You never told me! Who's the lucky lad?'

'Gad – you remember me telling you about him – the pianist – from Burma?'

'Ah, so it's him, is it? What do your parents say about that?'

'Well – they'll come round. I'm not asking them to contribute, so it's going to be a small do. I'm so excited.'

'And so you should be. And listen, I'm doing your flowers – no, no argument. I can, you know – you needn't worry. Just tell me what you want for the bouquet – and for your hair as well. There's plenty here, so it'll be my wedding present.'

'Oh Duggie, that is good of you – are you sure?'

'Sure I'm sure,' he said, kissing her hand gallantly. 'Don't give it another thought.'

★

Father Martin offered to provide decorations for the church, in honour of Gad's service as organist, but there was one awkward fact: for the wedding, there would be no organ. Unfortunately, it would be out of use, having a major overhaul to all the pipes and stops. Gad would not only have to find a deputy keyboard player, but one who could officiate on a small borrowed harmonium – not the kind of musical accompaniment that Gad would have liked. Thérèse had jokingly suggested importing some of her Breton singers and pipers, but since they were not Catholic nor even churchgoers, this idea was soon scotched. Gad would have to sort it out himself.

They had planned a small reception, and invited 'only a handful' of guests – Elspeth and Robert, of course, plus Tony, Mary, Sanjay and Estelle from the House (Sam was abroad); her parents and Louise; Gad's cousins Joyce and Victor, with Victor's sisters Violet and Dorothy, with their husbands Desmond and Michael, who had heard about the event and would naturally attend; Pyotr, Gad's Russian violinist friend; there were Frs Martin, Peter and Diarmid, and fellow student Christopher, the harmonium player; Mrs Woodward (singer and Mary's mother) who was lending them her cottage near Cambridge; Thérèse's landlord Don and his wife Alice; and not forgetting Valerie, who had got wind of the wedding and invited herself. And then there were the helpers who had created the whole occasion out of nothing – a 'chauffeur', the self-appointed 'florist' from Cecil Sharp House, and friendly dressmakers and caterers. There would be no toast-racks, most of the gifts being given in kind. Gad and Tony ordered a small amount of sparkling wine with glasses, and actually paid for it in cash saved from funeral fees – 'ash cash'.

Somehow, everything began to fall into place. They were astonished at the goodwill that people showered on them. It almost seemed as though they were some special case, perhaps deserving of generous treatment. They could even look forward to a week's honeymoon in that remote village in the Fens.

*

April 1955

On the eve of the wedding Thérèse stood on the long platform, Gad's arm around her shoulders, feeling the vibration in the soles of her feet as the boat train slid to a halt, the engine releasing a hiss of steam.

'It's All Fools' Day!' she said suddenly.

'So it is. Trust us!'

There was no time for more, as she caught sight of her parents, Pappi descending first and handing Maman down, and ran along the platform to hug them both. Gad shook them by the hands and picked up the luggage: they had very little, just two small cases. As usual, a bus took them to the House, where Elspeth had reserved them a two-bedded room.

After supper, Thérèse went upstairs with her mother to talk privately, to try and bridge the gulf between them before it was too late. If only Maman would open up, would voice her concern, even her fears. She sat down on one of the beds, patting the coverlet beside her to invite her mother there. Maman, however, turned to the open suitcase on the other bed, directing her attention to the print dress she would wear for the wedding, shaking it out, hanging it carefully in the small wardrobe.

Thérèse's hand went back to her lap.

'If only Alain could have been here,' she began.

So much of her life had revolved around Alain – Alain living, Alain dead. Maman and Pappi mourning Alain; longing for the son they no longer had; wishing there was someone to take on the farm; their gaze still upon him, never focussing entirely on Thérèse.

'If only.' Maman turned back to the suitcase.

'He would have looked so handsome – and he would have looked after you and Pappi.' She meant during the wedding, but it came out wrong.

'He's the only one who would.' Maman sighed, picking up on the meaning that lay below the words.

With an effort, Thérèse tried to bring the conversation round to herself and Gad.

'Well, at least you don't have to worry about me – I have Gad now.' She put her hand to her mouth, realising that this was exactly the wrong thing to say.

'Not worry? About you and – Garrard?' Maman stood and faced her daughter now, her cheeks flushed with suppressed anger. 'Thérèse, you have no idea. Just wait till you have children of your own! You must have known we would be against this marriage – you left it so late to tell us.'

Thérèse winced at the truth of it. But surely her mother could give her just a little word of encouragement all the same? Show a little generosity of spirit?

'Well – you will have to get to know Gad better, and then perhaps you will change your minds. I hope you sleep well,' she said, gave her mother a kiss on the cheek and went out, things unsaid still hanging in the air.

CHAPTER 29

AIR MAIL
20 March 1955

Dear Garrard

How happy we are to hear of your engagement and intention to marry Thérèse, who I am sure we will love when we have a chance to meet her. But we wonder whether you could not delay the wedding for a little until we are more settled here and one or two of us might be able to go over to England? Why in such a rush? Weddings take time to arrange – there are the dresses, bridesmaids, food and flowers, as well as the service and the music for it. Then you must send out invitations in good time, so that people can make their arrangements. Of course, too, none of us has met Thérèse, and will she really feel she is joining our family if we are all so far away?

I do not mean to make you unhappy by saying all this, Son, but you know, marriage is for life and not something to be undertaken in a hurry. We are just beginning to set up home here after the years of exile, first in Simla and then again when the Burmese government took a dangerous turn, and this news has taken us all by surprise. Why don't you try to bring Thérèse over here to meet us, or wait until we can see her in England? Please think again, Son, and see if you could perhaps rearrange things, and let us know what your plans will be?

I pray for you, Son, and hope you are not making a hasty mistake. Believe me, I only want the best for you, and know

that you need a partner, but all in good time – surely your music comes first? I have had such ambitions for you.
    With a big God Bless,
    Your loving Mother

Part III

CHAPTER 30

April 1955

Spirals of ribbons circled in the cloudless sky, yellow, red and blue, and Thérèse flung her arms out in her sleep.

Gad! she thought, luxuriating in the moment, picturing his face brilliant with joy. She came to with a start. *It's today!*

And then, of her parents, *They're here, too, Maman and Pappi – surely they won't do anything to spoil it for us?*

She prodded Louise, who was asleep on her floor. 'Wake up! It's today!'

*

Several hours later, Thérèse looked into the mirror at a young woman she didn't recognise: sleek hairdo with a luxuriant circlet of gardenias, warm-coloured make-up, a short, violet-coloured silk dress with satin shoes dyed to match. The image in the glass gazed back at her, nothing like her usual reflection; more like a touched-up version, just when she needed to be most herself. It seemed strange to be living through this rigmarole, when all she wanted was to be alone with Gad, to discover what it would be like to live together.

'*Que tu es belle!*' sighed Louise, smoothing a last strand of Thérèse's hair.

'*Oui, vraiment.*' Thérèse felt herself relax. Gad would be waiting. Louise was there for her. They had so many good friends. All would be well.

★

Tony arrived from the House by taxi, and yes! Pappi and Maman were with him, in full regalia – when was the last time Thérèse had seen Maman in a hat? This was not the funeral one, she noticed with relief; it was dark blue, but it had a little flourish of cream ribbon on one side, to match the flowers on her dress. She looked soberly elegant, with her smooth clutch bag, gloves, and shoes with small heels. Thérèse saw her in a new light, and was suddenly filled with immense pride. *Quelle courage!* she thought, bending through the open car door with the warmest embrace she had managed for a long time.

'Maman, you look so chic! I'll see you at the church. I love you.'

'And I you, *chérie.*' There was even a small smile to offset the tightness around her eyes.

Thérèse stood on the pavement waving goodbye to Maman and Louise as they left with Tony, and then took Pappi upstairs to wait for their car. He was stiff and monosyllabic in his best suit. Thérèse picked a piece of lint from the harsh cloth, letting her hand linger on his shoulder for a moment.

'You are sure about this?' he asked her tenderly. 'I mean, a Catholic *et tout ça?*'

She thought of the raw-boned priest and the principles he laid down, and hoped she would never live to regret her wedding. Her differences of belief from Gad's had never been in the forefront of their partnership.

'*Oui, je sais,*' she said. 'But he makes me happy. I love him and – we will work things out. Just wait and see.'

She smiled contentedly. Linking her arm into her father's, she could think of nothing much but Gad awaiting her in the church, picturing his face when he would see her.

188

Glen, a trade union colleague of Gad's at the LCC, appeared next, his clean car decked with white ribbons and his hands in new chamois leather gloves. Thérèse arranged herself on the back seat with Pappi upright beside her, outwardly proud to be with her on her wedding day.

'Well, my darling,' he said only, 'you must live your own life, not ours. Try to be happy.'

'I will,' she said for the first time that day.

They drove through the sunny, gusty streets, the car with its silent driver a fortress against reality. Thérèse's bubble of happiness included Gad, their many friends old and new and, by the skin of their teeth, her parents. Let everything else wait. Her thoughts jumped here and there, but beneath it all was a steady certainty.

There, not far away, was the church, inviting in the spring sunshine. They mounted the steps towards a small crowd of well-wishers. There was Gad, glowing in his immaculate new suit and his silvery silk tie; the pale sheen of her own dress; the exotic scent of incense and the sweetness of gardenias in her arms and her hair; the anguished look in her father's eyes as he walked her up the aisle, grim but determined to see this mumbo-jumbo through. She turned her head, giving her mother an anxious smile, meeting what she felt was a gleam of understanding. Then she and Gad together, making their vows in the foreign language and the foreign ritual that she had adopted and to him was second nature.

Fr Martin gave them a final blessing, the harmonium launched itself on to its version of the Wedding March and she walked back down the aisle arm-in-arm with Gad, the happy couple in their fine outfits, the deed done, smiles and smiles all the way, and out into the brisk bright air of early April for quick photos.

★

Thérèse and Gad ran up the stairs to her room to be there first, and arrived panting. The waiting air was filled with the scent of Duggie's flowers. They had a moment to themselves before the rest showed up.

'You look just – beautiful!' Gad said, not taking his eyes off Thérèse. 'Look at you – I'm breathless!'

Thérèse laughed with delight, accepting a compliment for once in her life, whilst inwardly thinking that the stairs might have had something to do with the breathlessness.

'I love you too!' she said. 'And you are the most gorgeous man in the world!'

They kissed in a tight clinch, reluctantly breaking apart only when the first guests appeared.

Thérèse's friends had partially cleared the top-floor living space, her papers neatly stacked in one corner. Somebody had set up salmon paste sandwiches and sausage rolls on the desk, and from her small kitchen space there began to issue trays of tall glasses.

As soon as they were all assembled and provided with drinks, Tony stood up on the only chair and clinked a glass to call for silence.

'Time for toasts!' he said, 'and since you'll all be on your feet for some time, I'd better make it snappy!

'First, I'd like to apologise for speaking in English – I just can't help it! Thing is, I can't remember a word of my school French!' (Disbelieving laughter) 'So I'm going to ask Louise to interpret for M and Mme Kutanguay. Thank you' (as Louise moved over smiling, to stand with them, always happy to be part of the action).

'So, Gad has asked me to welcome you all, and to thank you for coming to celebrate their happy nuptials – now there's a word! A word that seems to call for music to embellish it. So isn't it sad that Gad, the Chief Organist of St Xavier's –of course, there is only one organist' (cheers) 'should have to make do with a harmonium for his own wedding? Somehow the Vidor *Toccata* didn't sound quite the same, but anyway, our friend Christopher did marvels – congratulations, Christopher!'

Cheers from friends, and a melodious 'Hear hear!' from Valerie, standing half-crushed against a wall.

'And when our own Chief Organist comes back from honeymoon, and plays the newly refurbished instrument, there will be no stopping him!'

General cheers and cries of 'Attaboy!'

'I won't say any more, except what a good friend Gad has become, and how he and Thérèse are made for each other, and to ask you without further ado to raise your glasses and wish them many years of happiness and good fortune. To Gad and Thérèse!'

'Gad and Thérèse!'

Now it was Gad's turn. Although he was used to the limelight as a performer, Thérèse knew he had dreaded this moment, but fortified with a large gulp of the wine that everyone else was sipping, he planted his feet firmly and took a deep breath.

'Thank you, Tony, for those kind words, and all of you for your good wishes. It's grand to see so many of you here; it's a great send-off for' (turning to Thérèse) 'my WIFE and I' (hearty cheers) 'and you are all welcome to come to see us at my flat – OUR flat! – when we get back.

'We have so many people to thank: first of all, my wife Thérèse's parents,' (raising his glass to them) 'without whom none of this would have happened.' Thérèse could hear Louise translating quietly into their ears.

'Voter santay,' cried Gad, raising his glass to them.

'*Santé!*' echoed the guests.

'And of course my own mother, who is sadly missing here.' He paused, recollecting that he had not heard a word from her since she wrote asking him to postpone the wedding.

Recovering himself, he continued, '… But we do have my cousins Victor and Joyce, Violet and Desmond, and Dorothy and Michael from my family, and I hope you will have a chance to talk to them.'

'To Victor and Joyce, Violet and Desmond, Dorothy and Michael!' cried Valerie, taking a few more large sips from her glass. Gad gave her a sideways look.

'And then my second family, as I call them, Elspeth and Robert and all our friends from the House who have made me so welcome in this country.

'Last but not least, everybody who has helped to create this magnificent celebration for us. Thérèse and I' (cheers) 'never imagined it would be like this. An enormous thank you to Tony, Louise, Christopher and Duggie, not forgetting Glen, and – well, enjoy the rest of the party! To you all!' Thérèse and Gad touched glasses and drank to the guests.

'Whew!' he muttered, and she, 'Well done!' They felt the smooth heat of each other's cheeks as they kissed to seal the accomplishment of duty.

The toasts over, Thérèse and Gad moved round the crowded room, making sure the people in their lives got acquainted, filling in the time until they could be alone together. Their first priority was to introduce Gad's cousins to Thérèse's parents, who were still alone near the window with Louise completing her message. The cousins were standing quietly together, sleekly dressed and composed, not knowing anyone in the rooms (for the party had now spread from the living-room onto the landing), and patiently waiting to be greeted. Gad picked out Victor and Joyce, who were nearest, and amidst their congratulatory kisses was able to manoeuvre them towards Madame, with: 'Madame, Monsieur, may I introduce my cousins Joyce and Victor García – Thérèse has already met them. Joyce, Victor, these are Thérèse's parents, Mr and Mrs Kutanguay.'

There was an awkward moment when Joyce moved slightly forward as for a formal embrace, at the same time as the older woman extended her hand. Recovering herself quickly, Joyce met the proffered hand with hers, and with a polite smile shook it. Rugged M Kutanguay and tall Victor followed suit before standing in nervous silence, soon broken by Joyce in her cooing voice: 'So pretty, your daughter. What a lovely dress! And the ring too – beautiful! I'm sure they will be very happy. We are so enjoying the party and – everything.' She was so pleasant, so inconsequential in her fluting voice, as she turned her attention from one face to another with a flutter of her hands, that everyone relaxed and although little more was said, the meeting seemed like a success.

'You must meet my other cousins, too,' said Gad, waving over the heads of the people round him, and he eased the Kutanguays through the crowd to meet Violet and Desmond, sleek as Lamborghinis, intimidatingly good-looking. It was easier this time round, however, and soon Thérèse and he were able to leave them to a laughing bilingual conversation, with Louise doing her best to help.

Gad introduced Pyotr the violinist first to Thérèse, and then to Mrs Woodward with her daughter Mary, and brought Tony over to help Louise. Thérèse was watchful, saw that Duggie came to speak to her father, whom she kept well away from Fr Martin; instead, she introduced him to Elspeth, another down-to-earth character.

*

But they had a train to catch, and suddenly it was time for Thérèse to change into another silk dress, a pale coat with a detachable fur collar and the prettiest shoes she had ever owned.

Alone in the shared bathroom with Louise, Thérèse breathed, 'Thank you, thank you. How can I ever repay you?'

'Just wait,' said Louise. 'I shan't get married until you are rich and famous, then I'll call the debt in!' They hugged awkwardly, Thérèse taking a deep breath before facing the crowd again to say her goodbyes.

She heard Gad's cousin Joyce remark to her sister-in-law: 'She is a lovely girl, and Garrard needs somebody' before, searching out her parents, she saw them in halting conversation with Elspeth and Rob. She heard Maman speaking urgently to Elspeth in her own language, and Elspeth's reply, in her rather basic French, '*Oui Madame*, I did see it coming, and I advised against it, but no one can forbid such a thing.' She heard Rob intervene – a thing he rarely did – to say, man to man to her father, with Louise translating, 'They will be all right, I think. We will keep a watchful eye on them.'

This was not bad, but unfortunately she was too late to prevent her landlord Don, a man who knew none of them very well, put his oar in: 'You have to accept it, you know. This is London, and they are in love; anyone can see that.'

Stuffing his fists safely into his pockets, her father said, as if it were wrenched out of him, '*Mais c'est le sang que me preoccupe.*'

She could bear no more and emerged, looking for Gad, preparing for their departure, ridiculously happy to see him again through the crowd. It was then that she heard Valerie, rather tipsy by this time, remark offhandedly to Gad's cousins Michael and Dorothy, 'She's such a skinny little thing, isn't she? And that headdress! Huge flowers – a wonder they don't topple off!' Thérèse could hardly believe her ears. The cousins looked too embarrassed to answer, so without thinking twice she waded in with, 'I'm so glad you approve. I cannot think how I forgot to ask your advice sooner!' and hurried on to re-join Gad before Valerie could respond.

The pair went their final rounds, repeating their excited goodbyes and thanks, led the crowd down the stairs, paused at the car door for photographs and to send her rather large bouquet flying in the general direction of Louise. Gad nudged Thérèse to look at Duggie, who had evidently drunk more than his share of the fizz and was determined to have the last word: 'These two will grow together,' he said oratorically from the top step of the house, 'like vines!'

With laughter ringing in their ears, they drove off, leaving Tony and Louise to look after the Kutanguays and wrap up the party.

★

The honeymoon house was in the flatlands outside Cambridge; it turned out to be an ancient cottage, crooked with age, but with the addition of a TV and the surprise of a sound-proofed music room at the bottom of the garden.

As soon as they arrived they lit the wood fire, and in that cold April kept it burning every day. The walls of the house held them in a friendly embrace. Nothing threatened or disturbed. There was a pent-up depth of passion in Gad's lovemaking that made Thérèse wonder if he would ever slow down and attend properly to her.

On the first morning, Gad stood drying his shiny self after the bath they had shared, saying, 'What's for breakfast, then?' It was a joke, but she soon learned that he liked something different each day, whether he or she prepared it: the English bacon and eggs that he had learned to appreciate at the House; tinned peaches with cream newly ordered by the pair from a surprised milkman; home-made hoppers, the pancakes that the Christian Brothers had so enjoyed in their Burmese hill stations, with maple syrup discovered with delight in an odd-shaped cupboard; fresh rolls with butter, spicy vegetables; and always – coffee.

One night, exhausted from lovemaking, they watched a play about a kidnapped child and wept in each other's arms for their own yet to be conceived. In the slow awakening after that, for the first time Thérèse sensed Gad 'listening' to her body, adjusting his to hers.

This marriage is not going to be at all like my parents', she thought happily.

CHAPTER 31

April 1955

At the end of the week, Thérèse and Gad came home very pleased with themselves. They walked from the nearest bus stop, Thérèse with an armful of early lilac to brighten the dimly lit flat, Gad carrying their shared suitcase. There were no letters on the doormat, but a pile on a table in the sitting-room, including thank-you notes addressed to 'Mr and Mrs d'Silva', as they really were now. They could see that their neighbour Carmen had been carrying out her promise to see to things.

Thérèse went straight into the kitchen to fill a jug with bright blossoms, glorious echoes of the spring sunshine that lit up London at this time of year. It would be the last of her extravagances. From now on, she was going to be thrifty.

'Never mind,' Thérèse had said as they discussed their finances on the train home, sitting together in a state of sleepy indolence. 'As long as we can have some good things – real butter and proper coffee – we'll be fine.'

'What about smokes?' Gad had enquired, already deferring to her as household manager. 'We must have cigarettes.'

'Oh, ciggies too, definitely.'

'You've become so English!'

'So have you!' They laughed, complicit as chameleons.

Gad went into the bedroom with their suitcase.

'Hey!' she heard, as he stuck his head out of the doorway. 'Where's the bed? I thought Carmen was going to see it in?'

She ran to look. Nothing – no bed – nothing new at all.

'She was,' Thérèse exclaimed. 'I wonder what happened. Come on,' and she headed up the stone staircase to the flat above, banging loudly on the door. Gad caught up with her just as Carmen opened it, an olive-skinned woman with smooth black hair fastened in a bun, pins sticking out of her mouth. Beyond her they could see brightly patterned cloth hanging from the treadle sewing machine that whirred with its stop-start rhythm for such long hours that they no longer noticed it.

'*Olá!*' said Carmen in her harsh voice, surveying the newlyweds whilst removing the pins. 'You go good? Ees good. You want keys?'

'Yes please,' said Thérèse boldly. 'And we want our bed!' With Carmen, you had to come straight to the point, or she would be lost.

'Ah, your bed!' Was there a glint in her eye? 'Of course. But your bed, he has not come.' Her guttural H's sounded alien.

'You're sure you would hear their knock?' Thérèse insisted.

'Oh yes. I leesten for eet. Ees important, *sí*?' Her black eyes regarded Gad speculatively.

'Yes, it's very important,' said Thérèse with emphasis. 'Never mind; I will find out when it can come. Thank you for seeing to things. *Au 'voir.*'

'*De nada.* I hope you have *placer* een eet.' She withdrew, shutting the door, and Thérèse turned back to Gad.

'She works so hard,' she said, remembering the incessant sound of the treadle machine upstairs, 'and all alone too.'

She put her arms around him in the darkness of the landing, resting her body on his for the sheer pleasure of it as he leaned against the banister, finally releasing him with a quick kiss.

★

That night they made themselves at home on the old mattress, amongst Gad's rough bed linen, and turned to each other, lying comfortable and easy. Thérèse took a deep breath of contentment, stroking the back of Gad's head with its springy curls that made a V shape at the nape of his neck. He had big ears, she noticed for the first time, smiling to herself, and wondered if they went with musical talent. She felt her own ears – they seemed quite small. His beard grew quickly, so at this end of the day his cheek rasped on hers. In the morning, he would shave cleanly till his face was smooth to her touch.

They were warm, the blankets lay heavy on them, and soon their bodies came alive, Thérèse beginning to open herself to Gad, losing herself in anticipated pleasure – only to be cut short by a sudden violent sneeze that made her double up and away from him.

'Oh – *merde!*' she gasped helplessly, fumbling for a handkerchief; but just as she began to turn back, another uncontrollable sneeze convulsed her; and another.

Wanting her, Gad rolled over with a groan, but Thérèse was in no state to respond. She got herself out of bed and fled to the kitchen, where she crouched, pinching her nose to make the fit stop. *How ridiculous!* she thought. Not romantic at all! They must be too close to the dust of the bare boards. She would sweep up in the morning and then scrub the floor. She supposed it a wife's job, though she did not relish the prospect.

She went back to bed after a while, but the mood was broken, and they slept fitfully, the sneezing starting again every time she turned over, as though the dust particles, disturbed, were taking their revenge. Meanwhile, Gad seemed to fall in and out of sleep easily, simply going with the flow.

At last Thérèse too slept, and had a mysterious dream of being *in a room that is completely stuffed with garbage. It is filled nearly up to the ceiling solid with coffee grounds, newspapers, empty toilet rolls, screwed up paper bags, food wrappings, used envelopes, rotting potato and apple peelings, spent cigarette ends and crumpled packets – and dust. She tries to get to the top of the pile and manages somehow to climb into the narrow gap between rubbish and ceiling where there is room only to lie flat. She cannot move nor even breathe.*

She woke up sweating and sneezing. There was something thoroughly unreasonable about this dream, Thérèse thought, but she couldn't quite work out what it meant.

★

One of the pleasant things they had discovered on honeymoon was that they both liked to look at the night sky from their bed, and to see the morning light as soon as they opened their eyes. They decided then that they would never draw the curtains at night, even in London where street lights and neon advertisements caused the stars to disappear.

So, woken by the dawn, Thérèse struggled into wakefulness to find Gad already up and about, smoking a cigarette outside the kitchen door and gazing up at the patch of pale blue far above. He reached for her and held her with his free arm, intoning, 'The weather forecast is good.'

She stayed, sharing his cigarette and shivering slightly in the morning chill. The dark brick walls loomed around them, presenting impassive faces. Staring up at the clear sky, the two of them stood in the hollow of a shell, protected, peering out through its narrow opening.

★

It was Gad who urged Thérèse into action later that morning, though she was inclined to linger in the flat, arranging her few possessions.

'Come on, woman,' cried Gad, grabbing her round the

middle. 'Look, it's sunny out there – too good to waste!' He planted a firm kiss on her cheek, trying to erase the frustrations of the night.

They emerged from the cramped streets of their enclave to walk hand-in-hand up Tottenham Court Road towards the bed shop, Heals. Thérèse had only been in there once, but for Gad it was an old friend – in his quiet evenings alone he had often made a detour on his way to and from St Xavier's, to linger over the sleek objects in the brightly-lit windows. There was nothing like it in Rangoon.

That morning the pavements were crowded. As they walked, Gad noticed a well-built matron approaching; she gave the couple a hard stare, and bearing down relentlessly, forced them into the road without deviating an inch from her path. Gad caught Thérèse as she stumbled, holding her tightly, trying to shield her, casting a furious glare behind – pointless, of course.

He had met such rudeness often enough when he was alone, but now, with Thérèse, he felt a flush of shame. He had brought this on them: it was his skin that offended. He had grown a protective shell for his own defence, but now, newly exposed, he had lost it. Everything was different. Alone, he had proved he could survive. Now, with Thérèse to look after, it was all to do again – and there would be worse, because they were now a conspicuous couple.

'Sorry about that,' he said as they stepped back onto the pavement, searching her face for signs of disquiet.

'Why should you be sorry?' she said, smiling. 'They'll get used to us.'

His heart leapt and he stopped in his tracks. 'You know, don't you?' he said.

'Of course I know,' she said. 'Stop worrying. Come on, we've got things to do.'

'Sure!' he said. 'Let's give them hell!'

They pressed on, Gad on edge now, holding Thérèse tightly by the elbow, wondering if the sort of thing they had just experienced would wear her down, and if so, what it would do to them. But they arrived at the store without further incident. He relaxed, and they dawdled along the window displays. Here there was nothing offensive at all: instead, they were looking at clean lines in beautiful, plain wood; bold-patterned fabrics; glass objects in which water glistened; shining ceramic vases where flowers stood naturally; and jugs you could be sure would pour without a drip.

'This is almost more fun than actually spending money,' said Thérèse contentedly. 'You can change your mind as often as you like – or if you can't make up your mind, you can have it all!'

'Aren't you a cheap date, then?' mocked Gad. 'You're not really saying you want an empty house, are you?'

'No – but all in good time.' She smiled at him. It felt good to be thinking of the future.

A small boy was busy breathing steam on the plate-glass window so that he could draw in it; carelessly, Gad banged into him, eliciting a scowl and a cry of protest.

'So sorry,' said Gad to the mother politely, pulling back, at the same moment as he heard Thérèse ask, laughing, 'Shall we have six of those?'

'It's fine,' the woman smiled, taking hold of the boy's arm to move him out of their way.

Gad looked sharply at Thérèse, caught unawares, taking her joke as a serious question.

'What? You're way ahead, aren't you?'

'Actually, no!' she said soberly. 'We could start any day – don't you realise? I could be pregnant now!'

'Ah!' He felt something like panic. The idea of discussing such a thing – of course he assumed they would have a young family round them, just like the one he came from – but not so soon! He stared blankly at the goods in the window.

'Well, wouldn't you be pleased?' she pressed. 'I think you want children?'

'I do! I do. But – perhaps not just yet.' He tried to edge out of his corner, turning to face her. 'I want to have you to myself for a bit first. Don't you think so?'

'Hold on.' She stood still. 'This isn't the best place…'

'No – in here.' And he took her into a staff doorway. *This is very unsettling,* he thought.

They stood close together in the shadows, hands gripped, looking over their shoulders to make sure they were not overheard. 'Well, obviously – we should wait for a bit,' he said. 'Can you organise something? Please? Just for a while?' *This is how things are done in my family: wives deal with personal things, husbands make decisions. Surely she doesn't want to spoil everything?* He held her gaze, looking intently into her eyes, waiting for her decision. *Either she will arrange it, or we shall just have to let things take their course. It's in her hands. I shall have to trust her.*

'Yes, I could do it. But I'm not sure I want to.'

Why not? What is she worried about? He took her by the elbows, bent towards her like a supplicant, remaining silent.

'Surely your church does not allow?' she continued.

He breathed again, did not intend to let this rule his life. 'Let me worry about that. When the time comes…'

'Yes, when?'

'We'll have our family, and it will be wonderful. Let's get settled first.'

★

Having made sure the bed would be delivered later that day, they arrived at the entrance to the park, meaning to stroll in the spring sunshine, nobody bothering them on this weekday morning. There they were, a 'black' man and a 'white' girl holding hands, and not a soul was objecting. They could relax and enjoy the free day, before the claims of work and study took over again. Friends and family had had their say, and yet they were together. Only now, Thérèse was raising other issues. *How well do I really know her?*

'Happy?' he asked her tentatively, aware that it was a hackneyed question, but not knowing how else to start.

'Oh yes,' she said. 'We got that sorted out.'

There's my practical girl, he thought. *But is she sure?*

They had reached a footbridge over the ornamental lake, and stopped to watch the ducks making white trails in the water below, flapping and squawking in their seasonal rhythm of flight and pursuit.

'Listen,' he said, turning his back on the commotion and feeling that he needed to reassure her. 'It will be all right, you know. If you do get pregnant, I will look after you. I have broad shoulders. We will manage somehow.'

'Yes, I know, but… you would rather not have to?' There was an anxious note in her voice.

'Does that make a difference?'

'Of course it does, idiot!' she said passionately. 'I'm longing to have children with you! But you must want it too. You have no idea what I have been through…' She broke off suddenly, catching her bottom lip in her teeth and shutting her mouth firmly.

'What do you mean? Is there something I don't know?' She had hinted at it earlier, but he hadn't wanted to pry.

'Nothing,' she said quickly. 'I didn't mean anything. It's just – everyone was so against us – against all this.' She looked down at her rings. 'And we don't have much…'

'That's just the point!' he said. *Can't she see?*

'But we can make a family.' She confronted him directly. 'I want a baby soon!'

It was out. They stood, searching each other's faces. He felt winded. She seemed implacable. It could not be left. 'If we were to start a family now,' he said soberly, feeling his way, watching her set expression, 'it would be such hard going, especially for you. I mean, till I've made a bit of a name for myself. Be reasonable.' He saw her flinch. 'Of course I will always look after you.' He nodded vigorously, trying to convince her. 'But we need somewhere better than the flat – somewhere with some green space…'

She flung her hands out. 'What's wrong with here? It's always been your "back garden"!'

'… and I need to be sure of some work,' he added hastily, feeling that this was a much stronger argument than the garden one.

'We should have thought about all this before! Why couldn't we have talked about it? We were so concerned with other people's opinions about us getting married at all, we never thought beyond that! I thought you were like me, and wanted a proper family!'

'I do! Of course I do. Just not yet!' Deadlock. He realised he had been shouting, desperate to make her understand. He found in her face a kind of animal obstinacy that he had never seen before. She turned on her heel, leaving him standing. He was too exasperated to follow, but watched her retreating back until she disappeared round a corner.

Heart still thudding, he gripped the cold metal railing, staring at the water below, in turmoil with rival drakes clashing as they thrashed around, wings and feet flailing, water splashing and feathers colliding, a duck dithering off in panic and always a drake or two on her tail, as if a string were stretched tight between them – she veering to the side, and he immediately following.

It brought him back to himself. Of course, he must follow Thérèse, find her, make it right between them – bring her to reality. Filled with new energy, he set off at an awkward run, remembering how fast she could walk. He knew that the way she had taken led in a wide circle that would bring her back to their starting point; not wanting to miss her by taking a short cut, he kept to the same path. Quite soon he spotted her, not far ahead, slowing down, and called to her: 'Hey! Thérèse!' waving vigorously. She did not look round. She must be really upset.

It was then that a couple walking ahead of him turned and glared, and the man, shirt-sleeved and bulky with his belly bulging over his waistband, stepped into his path. 'Oy!' he said to Gad, hooking his thumbs into his braces. 'Are you following 'er?' And he indicated Thérèse with a nod of his head.

'No, no, it's all right,' said Gad unemphatically, desperate to catch up with his wife.

'D'you know 'er, then?' said the man, accusingly.

'Yes – yes.' Gad tried to step round him. He moved to stand in Gad's way.

'Yeah, I bet 'e does!' said the girl then, leaning against her man. 'These darkies, they're always sniffin' round the likes of 'er. They've tried it on with me too!'

At this, the man's face reddened and he stared down at his whey-faced girl, with the straggly blonde hair.

'Tried it with you, 'as 'e?'

'Not 'im. They. Do. Think they're God's gift.'

It was a good moment for Gad to make his escape, sideways across the grass. *Not again!* he thought. *And always when you least expect it!*

'Oy!' shouted the man again. 'Don't think you can mess with 'er – I've got my eye on yer!'

'Piggin' darky!' screamed the girl. 'Jest let 'im catch yer on a dark night!'

Breathing hard, Gad blocked them out, hoping against hope that Thérèse had not heard, doubly anxious now to catch up with her. She was out of sight, though. Had it been cowardly of him not to say that she was his wife? But then, what was the point of inflaming the idiot further? Had she heard? Luckily the couple were too idle, or too busy with their own jealousies to bother them again; it could have been much worse, and he doubted whether anybody would have come to his rescue if the man had turned violent.

CHAPTER 32

April 1955

Missing Thérèse in the park, Gad went straight home, but she was not there. He hoped she was all right. The place seemed dead without her. He wandered around restlessly, smoking a cigarette, fighting the sense that it was somehow his fault, trying to convince himself that some people were just mindless. If Thérèse had heard... What would she make of it?

They had barely had time to unpack, but her hairbrush lay on the chair beside a small oval mirror, their backs made of some dark wood – ebony? Black – *like that hair of hers,* he thought, thinking of the quick strokes with which she brushed it at night, and held it in his hand for a while before putting it down again. He opened one of the wardrobe doors, and saw on a narrow shelf one or two small bottles, and a gilt lipstick case; was it the very one she had dropped on the staircase that day, when he had first asked her for a date? Or another? How often did you buy a lipstick?

He put it back and shut the door. Yet, still drawn to it, he went again to the wardrobe, opened it and looked at the few clothes she had hanging there: a brightly-patterned skirt, a jacket and a raincoat. He leaned in, burying his face in their folds, inhaling the mingled smells locked into the enclosed space: her own elusive scent through the salty London grime. She was definitely here to stay then, merging with his life. He thought about them walking round the same rooms every day, washing in the same kitchen, eating together, sleeping in the same bed. Would he be enough for Thérèse? She loved him, he knew, and that was that. But she had walked off in the park.

So, where was she? She had already been gone an hour.

★

Hearing the angry altercation behind her, Thérèse paused. She wanted to turn back and stand with Gad, but was afraid of making things worse. *Barbarians!* she thought. *Such pointless spite!* And wondered if he had to put up with much of this sort of thing. She stood and listened until the shouting stopped, then spun round, only to see that Gad had gone, leaving that wretched couple on their own. Frustrated, she also thought it was probably for the best. At least there had been no violence. She hesitated, fuming, then walked slowly on, wondering what to do.

Where was Gad, anyway? Perhaps he had gone home to wait for her – and the bed. She heard herself saying out loud, 'Who do they think they are?' Perhaps he wouldn't want to talk to her just yet. She would leave him for a while, as if she had heard nothing. They had so many other things to sort out, what had just happened might only confuse the issue. They both needed to calm down.

Cretins! She was still seething with fury. How dare they, in broad daylight, in Regent's Park? Maybe it made Gad wish he had never come to England? What if the question should come up: should they go east to be with his family? Surely that could never happen. But what if it did?

★

Seized with restless energy, Gad took an airmail form and sat down to write to his mother. He needed to think before putting pen to paper. It was a pity that the last message from

209

her had been reproachful, that he had rushed ahead with the wedding. But how long would they have had to wait?

Dear Mummy and All at home, he wrote,

This is just to let you know about our wedding – a very happy day, except that all of you were too far away to attend. I am indeed sorry about that, but I must explain that by the time I got your letter everything was organised and would have been difficult to change in any way. I knew you would wish us well, in any case, and I thought of you many times during the day.

You will be glad to hear that Thérèse's parents, Monsieur and Madame Kutanguay, came over from France and of course there were Victor and Joyce and their family as well as Robert and Elspeth and several others from the House – about thirty in all, squashed into Thérèse's little place.

As you know, we are not well off, but you would have been amazed to see what a fine wedding we had. We had so much help from everyone (Thérèse's French friend Louise was bridesmaid, and I had Tony as my best man), for the girls' dresses, the flowers, the catering, the music – everything! We are so lucky in our friends. Here in London many people are away from home and so they help each other out, whereas at home, we would rely on family. Of course, I will send photos as soon as I can get them processed, and then you will see how elegant we were.

Thérèse and I had a week in a cottage near the university town of Cambridge. It was cold there, but we lit fires and had a grand time. Now we are back at the flat and settling down as an old married couple. We are happy to be together and to be making plans for our future. It is such a relief that you are safely in the US, and that the children can continue their schooling there. I hope that Don finds a good job soon.

The next important thing for me is to work for the Diploma exams, which are in a couple of months' time, and you can imagine that I have plenty of practice to do still. We both need to get qualified, so that when we start to look for jobs we will be in a good position to impress people. Here, everyone has to have something to show before they can get through the interviews.

So, we are all in the middle of change, but I am sure it will all work out well and we shall all be fine.

With love from my wife and I,
Your loving son
Garrard

★

Abruptly, Thérèse veered away from the main path, suddenly wanting to touch base at the quiet library in Cecil Sharp House. She needed a break, somewhere cool and dim. She had been on the track of a new reference, a book about hobby horses that would link the old Cornish dances with a figure in the Breton story; you couldn't get further away from present-day London than that, she thought with a wry grin.

The disagreement with Gad still stuck in her mind, though, like a piece of half-chewed gum, neither pleasant nor soluble. The sun shone. Birds were still singing their spring song. She felt guilty about not being with him in the crisis, but thought he must have had practice in dealing with such morons. She would ask him about it when the time was right.

She saw a little girl trying to skip, her rope tangling with the grass. Her mother lay on the ground, idly watching her while she tried, and tried again. Calmer now, Thérèse began to wonder how, indeed, they could look after a child if she were to become pregnant soon. There was the money, of course, but children needed your time more than anything. Did she really want to give up something she had chosen to do, something she loved? She was not at all sure she was ready to abandon that yet. She smiled at the little girl before pressing on.

The tall gates at Cecil Sharp House were open as always, and she went up the steps with a sense of anticipation, but feeling also slightly queasy, so before settling down in the library she went into the Ladies to get a drink of water. And then she discovered that there would not, after all, be a baby yet. *Oh! the disappointment.* And then the relief, and the old sadness. Still, she thought, it's only this month; there's plenty of time.

In the library she tried, resolutely, to do a little reading, but found that she could not concentrate. All she wanted was to be at home with Gad, and to tell him the news. They would have the chance now to make proper decisions. And maybe he would want to talk too.

★

Thérèse turned the key in the lock and entered the flat to the sound of voices: Gad was not alone. She went straight into the living-room, and saw him with an elderly man, rumpled, with an air of abstraction about him, as if he were not quite there.

Giving Thérèse a quick kiss, Gad squeezed her arm and said, 'Murray, have you met my wife, Thérèse?'

Murray stuck a hand into his rough white hair. She remembered him then – Murray Mackenzie, Gad's tutor.

'Yes. I have. Charming. We spoke at the Easter concert. Do you remember, my dear?' He held out his hand.

'Of course I do. How are you?' They shook.

'Fine, fine. Is this wretch treating you well? How long is it?'

'Well, only a week,' she said politely, her thumb touching

her rings. 'So far, so good.' She sneaked a questioning glance at Gad, whose eyes met hers with a steady gaze.

'Goo-ood.' Thérèse caught Murray regarding her with enjoyment, hot and breathless as she was. Finally, 'Well, anyway –' he tore his attention away, and turned back to Gad 'to business. Are you going to accept the offer?'

'I need a quick word with Thérèse first,' said Gad.

Murray flung a hand out, raising his eyebrows. 'Of course.' He waited, and so did Thérèse, as Gad drew her aside. She could see the eagerness in his face.

'Listen to this,' he said. 'Murray is arranging for me to get a piano...'

'What? Another one?' She was startled, remembering his earlier experiences with dud pianos that people had offloaded on to him.

'Yes, I know.' She could see he wanted her to be excited too. 'But a decent one at last; that I can actually use.'

'I see,' she said cautiously.

Gad grabbed her firmly by the shoulders. 'Listen, if Murray says it's a good one, it will be – I promise. We're not going to be trying out any more pianos after this!'

'I hope not!'

'But the thing is, it's a grand – not a concert grand, of course,' he added hastily, and before she could protest, put a finger on her lips, 'but still, it's going to take up rather a lot of room.'

'Most of the sitting-room, I should think,' Thérèse said, an edge to her voice. 'Do you think we'll have room to sit round it – on little stools, or something?' The absurdity of the prospect caught her fancy. 'Or shall we stand, to make room for your piano?'

'Now you're just being silly,' he said with some impatience, giving her a little shake.

She didn't mind too much; the piano was plainly a prize

worth having, and they could surely work round it. The point was, a piano was essential for Gad. He could not be without one. But the previous two had been disasters – even after tuning, they had apparently sounded horrible. How big was this one?

She longed to bring the business to a conclusion, anxious to talk to Gad, to tell him her news, to go over the events in the park if he was willing.

'What kind is it?' she asked.

'A Broadwood; a boudoir grand, they call it.'

'Goodness – how big is that?'

'Just over seven feet long – and a keyboard wide.'

This was a novel method of estimating. They examined the space where it would go, and she saw that it was adequate – just.

'Well, fine then', she said, and turned to Murray, conscious that his effort in coming round in person was exceptional – if only it wasn't just now. Of course, without a phone... 'How very kind of you. I'm sure Garrard appreciates this.'

'He does, my dear. He does – and he deserves it,' he said, giving Gad a pat on the arm.

Before she could say more, Gad intervened.

'Well, sir,' he said. 'I think I'd better come with you now – strike while the iron is hot, isn't it?' and turning to Thérèse, 'You'll be all right for awhile? Did you see the bed has been delivered? I'll be back before long. It's just that...'

'Yes, yes, you go,' said Thérèse. 'I'll sort things out here.' And she turned away, deflated, leaving them to it, looking blankly out of the window at the empty yard. The room behind her seemed already over-populated. She knew she was being ungracious. When the piano arrived, Gad would have thoughts for nothing else. Her news would have to wait.

'See you later,' called Gad, and Murray, 'Goodbye, my dear.'

The front door closed.

Left alone, she reached for a cigarette from her bag, and smoked slowly while the silence took over. This was the first time she had been on her own in the flat. It echoed. Soon the piano, that great hulk of a piece of furniture, would be installed. She looked around, trying to visualise it, to imagine where they would be able to sit comfortably, and failing. It was never going to work – but it had to. The bed, on the other hand, sat just right in their bedroom, and she went to get out what clean linen they had, wanting it to look beautiful before Gad's return.

The second post rattled through the letter box and she picked up an airmail letter for Gad from America, and a short note from her mother:

Ma chère Thérèse,

This is to greet you when you arrive back from your holiday. I hope you are both well, and that you will soon be settled in your new home.
Write to us soon.
Maman

PS You looked beautiful in your dress.

CHAPTER 33

April 1955

It was all arranged in an hour. Gad walked with Murray to his office in college, and they entered the little room that he seldom left except to teach, the faded chair cushion always holding his imprint. Easing himself behind the desk with a sigh of relief as he took the weight off his feet, Murray opened the top drawer and pulled out an envelope containing a single sheet of paper.

'There!' he said, passing it to Gad. 'Read this!'

Gad stood reading the note, handwritten, though formally laid out, whilst Murray made the necessary calls.

It was from a retired concert pianist, who had left instructions before moving away: *My piano is to go to a promising student of limited means,* it read. *He or she is to play it regularly, to keep it tuned and otherwise to maintain it as well as he or she can afford. On this occasion I will pay for transport. If he or she should lose interest in the piano, he or she is to pass it on, without profit, to a similar student under the same conditions. I wish the recipient joy in playing the instrument, and a fair measure of good fortune in his or her future career.* Signed: *Letty Hardwood*

He looked at the letterhead: a street near the college. How sad she must be, this old woman, and how gallant. She must have lived her life to the background of students practising in college practice rooms. He imagined her sitting at her desk, finally licking the envelope and sticking it down with satisfaction. Her handwriting was still elegant, although a little irregular. She had made her wishes clear before abandoning her home; she was still in charge, and he admired that. Excitement ran through him – what a lucky break for him!

'That's wonderful, sir,' he said finally. 'I can't thank you enough for thinking of me.'

'I've watched you, you see, my boy,' said Murray. Somehow, Gad didn't mind the diminutive from Murray.

★

Following Murray's directions, Gad walked to Miss Hardwood's flat in Welbeck Street, glad that the day was fine. There was a dark green removal van already stationed outside. A man emerged from the building, carrying a bundle of piano legs under his arm. He stowed these, neatly wrapped in hessian, before turning to Gad, who stood on the pavement with his hands in his pockets, watching keenly with a mixture of excitement and trepidation – would this one fulfil its promise?

'Afternoon, sir.'

'Good afternoon.'

'We're going to your place, are we?'

'We are. It's quite close – a bit awkward getting in, though.'

'It always is,' said the man, stretching his back. 'That's our job – every day, more awkward corners.' He grinned then, showing nicotine-stained teeth. There was a pencil stuck behind his ear, though there was little to anchor it there. 'Better get on,' added the man now. 'The guv'nor don't like to wait.'

He disappeared into the house, and in a few minutes Gad saw the body of the piano appear, in its shoe, edges protected with hessian. He watched while three men manipulated it gingerly out of the front door and down the steps, shuffled across the pavement, and manhandled it into the waiting van, settling it tenderly and making sure it was held quite steady.

Gad's eyes followed anxiously, wondering how it would sound, how that polished wooden case would respond as the strings were struck. His hands already seemed to feel the touch of the keys.

Mistaking Gad's interest for fascination with their work, 'Same for three miles as three hundred,' said the man who seemed to be the boss.

The others stayed silent.

'Well,' he said to his crew. 'Look sharp, now. Let's get moving.' He motioned them into the house, from which they presently appeared carrying the front board, the music rest and other small pieces.

'That's it then, sir,' said the boss as the tailgate banged shut. 'We'll be at your place in a jiffy.'

'Fine. You know it's a one-way street?'

The boss man gave him a look.

Gad set off for home on foot, seats in the van being needed for the crew. He took the back ways that he knew so well, anxious to be there first to open up.

The flat was empty – Thérèse was probably out shopping – and seeing the airmail letter on the table, he stuffed it into his pocket to read later. He looked round the living-room, nervous about the bulky new arrival and its effect on their space, then went to the bedroom to watch from the window, and soon heard the van inching its way along the narrow, enclosed street, one of the men peering out at the house numbers.

'Right, here we go,' he said aloud, hitching up his belted slacks and hurrying out to meet them.

The next half hour was like trying to get a ship into a bottle: the piano would only make its awkward progress down into the flat from one particular angle, and it took a while and a few experiments for the men to find it. Gad left them to it, went into the kitchen to make tea and found himself trapped until they had finally manoeuvred the instrument into his sitting-room. He waited until they had hoisted it onto its legs, and then went to look. It was at that moment that the full height and solidity of the thing was revealed, black and imposing in the small room with its low ceiling.

'Fills it up nicely, don't it?' said Gad's man, showing his darkened teeth again.

'Is tea all right?' Gad asked the crew in general, longing for them to be out of the way, not wanting to exchange pleasantries while his piano stood waiting.

They drank, looking over the ill-furnished place with disfavour; they were plainly used to better things. Finally they were gone, Gad's thrifty tip snug in the boss's hand.

With a sigh of relief, Gad took the one upright chair over to the piano, where there was just room to place it a barely adequate distance from the keyboard. This was the moment. He lifted the lid and stretched his hands over the keys, dropping a soft chord or two. The chair was too high, and the angle of his foot on the pedals uncomfortable. He shifted his position, trying in vain to move further back, then decided that for the moment it would have to do. He began to improvise, feeling the weight of the keys, hearing the sound the Broadwood gave back. He would get it tuned soon, though it wasn't at all bad even now. With an exuberant flourish, he broke into a piece of Liszt that stretched his hands to their limit and sent a shower of notes to fill the enclosed space. With the window shut, the walls seemed to bulge outwards under the pressure – the music filled the room and had nowhere else to go. He opened the window and played again, hearing the sound echo up the well.

He stopped, and heard Carmen's machine whirring steadily above him.

★

At the click of the front door, Gad jumped up and went to meet Thérèse, holding the flat door wide open as she came in, arms heavy with bags of provisions – straight into the living-room, where she stood surveying the scene. Gad waited for her reaction.

'Well – what do you think?' he asked.

'It's – big!' she said, looking round. 'But that curve – it gives a bit of space – lets you into the room, at least.' She considered, head on one side. 'I think if we have a small round table in the corner, with chairs either side – and one upright chair for the desk – we'll be all right for the time being. Not much room for friends, though.'

That's my practical girl, thought Gad, breathing again and throwing his arms around her, feeling her smallness and warmth. He could feel his whole face smiling, and her smiling back.

Then, holding him off. 'But wait a minute, how is it?' Her eyes were saying: *Please let it be all right this time*.

'Magnificent!' he exclaimed. 'Come and listen!' He seized the bags and dumped them on the floor, grasping her hand to pull her towards the keyboard. He sat, and drew her close as she stood beside him, paused, then played her the Bach *Gigue* that he usually kept as an encore. He felt his hands light over the keys as his fingers struck them precisely, confident with the familiar notes. This time the music danced delicately in the room, for the Broadwood gave an instant response to his touch, the strings answering directly with the special virtue of good pianos; nothing like his old ones or the stubborn organ he played on Sundays, when you always had to think ahead, to play a note half a second before you wanted to hear it, and then play the next before the first was done. This piano voiced sweetly just when he wanted it; he and the instrument in immediate sympathy with each other. Thérèse leaned against his shoulder, her hand on the back of his neck. He stopped, turning to her, and she bent to kiss him, her mouth gentle and warm.

They made a dish of spaghetti Bolognese with a touch of grated cheddar and ate straight away, sitting cross-legged on their new mattress, wishing Parmesan were not so expensive. Gad peeled an orange and they shared it messily before licking the juice from each other's hands.

He saw Thérèse take a deep breath, as if about to tell him something important. It was too disturbing. Gad's head was still full of the music of his piano, and he felt an impulse to avoid being diverted. He had his excuse: 'Hang on a second,' he said, and taking the crumpled airmail letter out of his pocket, he took a knife to slit carefully along the folds – you had to be careful with a mother like his, her plump script always reaching to the very edges of the paper. Noticing at last that this was in Wilma's handwriting, his heart began to thump. She only wrote when there was some drama.

The thin paper crackled in his fingers as he began to read…

The words made no sense. This had nothing to do with him – could not have. He had a mother three thousand miles away. The letter said that she was dead. Not possible. Silently present behind his shoulder. Of course it made no sense. Standing erect. Watching. White plait neatly coiled round her head like a queen. Must have meant a neighbour. Roundly packed bosom close to him. His mother, dead? No, Wilma could not be telling him that.

He turned to the letter again.

8th April 1955

Dear Garrard, Wilma had written.

I am sorry to write you this very sad news. I am afraid Big Mummy passed away… (never one to waste words,

Wilma. Dead? She died?) *She had a very big heart attack;*
you know she always had a weak heart... (Well, she said
she had when I proposed leaving home)*... and she had*
a bad pain in her chest, so we called Dr Harris and he said to
call an ambulance to take her to the hospital. He didn't come
so we did, but they said they would try but could do nothing,
and she passed away on the way to the hospital. Oh Garrard,
if only our house was nearer to the hospital, but you know, up
in the hills. They took long to get here, and Veena went with
her in the ambulance, and I followed in my car, and I went to
find a space and then I went to the emergency department and
then a young doctor told me.

Oh Garrard, one minute she was smiling and then she
had this terrible attack, and they will keep her in the hospital
until they check the cause of death, and then we will stay with
her in the funeral parlour, and then we will go with her to St
Theresa's in a few days, and I will let you know when the
funeral will be. It was at 3pm this afternoon. (Oh – when
she died, you mean? Wilma must have written straight
away.)

Well, Garrard, no more room, so God bless,
Your sister Wilma

There was no doubt then. But he could not take it in. Dumbly
he held out the letter to Thérèse. There was an aching pain in
his chest. The distance from his mother had always seemed
bridgeable. Her letters had held her voice. The fact that he had
left her behind never mattered; he could always go back to her.

He walked slowly along the corridor and sank onto the
kitchen stool. Thérèse, following, put her arms around him
and said, 'I'm so sorry, Gad. I'm so sorry.'

He hardly felt it; he needed to be alone.

'I must send them a telegram,' he said, getting to his feet
with sudden urgency. 'What's the date?'

'The tenth.'

'Good Lord, this was posted on the eighth, the day – it happened. When we were away.' His voice roughened. He could not yet say that she had died. 'Why didn't they wire me? The funeral must be any day soon.' He paced restlessly up and down the room, thinking. Thérèse watched him, her face full of concern. 'And then I must phone Victor – do you have any change?'

She gave him what she had, while he rummaged in the desk for his address book. 'I suppose you will go to the funeral?' she said.

'I don't know – I've got to think. I'll see you soon,' and he took off for the post office, realising a minute later that of course at this time in the evening it would be closed. If only he had read the letter earlier, instead of thinking about the piano... But at least he could telephone his cousins – except that, like him, they had no phone... His brain seemed to be malfunctioning. He walked faster, trying to pull himself together, to think clearly about what he must do. By force of habit he made for the International House.

But at the last minute, he turned away and headed towards Lincoln's Inn, away from the parts he knew well, hoping that walking would help to calm him, ease the pain of his guilt. There was no getting away from it – he was her youngest son, and he had not been near when she died. Under the great plane trees of Lincoln's Inn Fields where there was nobody who knew him, he stood and wiped his face, but tears kept coming. She had never really wanted him to leave the family, though she had finally sent him away; but that was exactly what he had done. In a kind of fury he emerged into the streets again and finally into St Xavier's, never locked, with the light burning steadily before the altar. Here he knelt down. He had no words. Remembering how Mummy had pulled him through childhood illnesses by sheer force of will, praying for him like a good Catholic and pledging her diamond earrings to the Church; how to make doubly sure his spirit would return to him, she had tied cotton threads round his wrist in the old Burmese fashion. He had felt embarrassed about that, later...

It had all worked, too, and here he was, in the West, while she died thousands of miles away from him.

CHAPTER 34

April 1955

It got to be late. Gad was still out. Eventually Thérèse went to bed, knowing she would not sleep. So as not to lie awake worrying, she took a notebook and pencil and began to make lists – essentials for the flat: small round table, and chairs for the living-room. She asked herself how she would manage to do her own work, once Gad began to practise for his Diploma in earnest, and decided she would move the desk into the bedroom. She felt so unsettled that she was tempted to get out of bed and move it there and then. Where was Gad? If he could not contact anyone, wherever would he have gone? She wanted him back. She had been shocked to see the effect of the letter on him; that lost look, his gaze turned inward with a kind of absence. It didn't seem like ordinary sorrow (if there was such a thing). Then she was back in the time after Alain's death; Alain, who had died whilst racing her across a field in blinding sunlight. Had she ever felt she was to blame? Had she been so? It was an accident, pure and simple – wasn't it? That old guilt pierced her and hot tears sprang to her eyes. 'No!' she said fiercely aloud, and thought, this was Gad's business, not hers. It was not the same. He didn't want her now – but he would.

She fetched a glass of water and took a book back to bed, staring at it as she lay, trying to lose herself in something ordinary, not turning a page, alert for Gad's step. When it finally came, she threw back the bedclothes and jumped up to meet him. He looked washed out, and all she could do was put her arms around him and get him into their warm bed. By the time she came back with a mug of hot tea, he was asleep; Thérèse too, at last.

★

Sunlight fell warm across their faces as they woke to face the day. There was so much Thérèse still wanted to say, but most of it would have to wait, at least until Gad had contacted his family and made his arrangements to travel to the West Coast.

She went to prepare breakfast. Gad came into the kitchen, rubbing his hands over his face but looking resolved.

'I'm not going, you know,' he said at once, leaning in the doorway.

'Not going?' she said in amazement, turning to face him.

'That's right. We can't afford it. And it's only four weeks to the Diploma.'

Thérèse looked at him sharply. It sounded inadequate – completely out of key with the misery of the night before. But she saw his resolute expression.

'Oh surely – you must!' She could not understand it, in a family so apparently devoted.

'No!'

She ran the cold water and filled the coffee pot, mustering her arguments as she did so. There was something wrong about this.

'But, surely the family will expect it – your sisters will need you there.'

'They have my brothers. They never thought I was any use.'

Impasse. And his answers came too pat. He must have been thinking about this all night. She put the coffee pot down and went up to him, putting a hand on his arm, looking into his face. She couldn't make out what he was thinking – his expression was set, his lips firm. She turned back to spoon coffee grounds, and tried a less direct approach.

'Are those the only reasons?' she asked, cautiously, her back turned.

'That's it,' he said, his mouth tight, and then she felt his quick kiss on her cheek.

She knew he was lying, but seeing his stubborn face, thought better of pressing him. Only, in a moment, she suggested tentatively, 'If it's a question of money, I don't need to go?'

'I'm not going without you,' he said. 'They don't need me anyway.' And he turned away.

She thought that it must run deep. Her instinct said that he was refusing to acknowledge something important, and would regret his decision. Keeping an eye on the coffee to make sure it didn't boil dry, she wondered how much else he suppressed; his account of his early years had been so breezy, so – entertaining. He had made such a story out of it. Was he doing it again? She poured the cups and watched Gad gulp his, black as he always took it in the mornings, and go into the living-room, to check addresses, perhaps.

But then – Thérèse made toast and munched it thoughtfully – if complicated feelings were safely put to bed in your memory, why would you want to awaken them? Would you really long to relive them – she never deliberately revisited the subject of Alain's death, but still; she couldn't help that image flashing onto the screen in her head. Perhaps it was the same for Gad? Perhaps suppressing his feelings had become a habit.

This was something else, though. Surely he could grieve naturally for his own mother. She shook her head, feeling out of her depth, and it made her impatient. She thought of one way to break the deadlock.

'Look,' she said, going to find Gad, 'it's so sad that I never even met your mother. Come on, let's both go – we can take out a bank loan – you've done it before – and we can pay it back over time. There isn't going to be a baby this time anyway.'

'There isn't?' he asked. She saw relief flickering behind his eyes.

'No, not yet,' she said, looking for a sympathetic hug, for some sign that he minded as much as she did.

Instead, 'Well, perhaps it's as well, just now,' he said. 'This – has happened. I have to do things. I can't go to the funeral. I just can't. I'm going out now to do the telegrams and phone calls.' He left without another word, excluding Thérèse. She watched him go.

★

As soon as he had disappeared round the corner, Thérèse went out too, unable to stand being on her own with her disappointment any longer, and made a beeline for International House where she was sure to find company. Elspeth would want to hear the news of Gad's mother, and would perhaps be able to explain his reaction.

She walked in on a rumpus; there was nobody in the office, but hearing loud bumps and scrapings and the sound of disgruntled voices from upstairs she ran up to find both secretaries in one of the bedrooms, hurriedly throwing a motley collection of exotic clothes into a black tin trunk. A young visitor from the Gold Coast, called Grace Imara, had apparently left without warning the day before, and had just telephoned to say that she was sending a taxi for her belongings, if the staff would kindly pack them up for her.

'She really knows how to do it,' said the energetic Estelle, hurling a pile of brilliantly patterned cloth in the general direction of the open trunk. 'She hates to pack – I hate packing, too!'

'As long as it all fits…' said Mary, stuffing the trailing ends in and squashing the pile as flat as it would go.

'Shall I help you?' enquired Thérèse.

Mary sat back on her heels, and both looked up in surprise.

'Oh, hullo,' said Estelle without stopping. 'What brings you here? Yes, do, come on, the more the merrier.'

Thérèse began the task of handing over the contents of drawers: thick socks, scarves and cardigans, most likely bought against the English climate. It felt good to be busy.

'Just stuff them in the corners,' urged Estelle. 'Only hurry up, the taxi will be here any minute, and we've still got to get this thing downstairs.'

With everything packed, the two of them sat on the lid, and Thérèse fastened the catch and locked the big padlock. They bumped the trunk downstairs while Thérèse watched for the cab. It amused her to find this sort of makeshift arrangement so normal at the House. 'People are always the first priority,' Elspeth said, and that was how she ran the House.

Standing by the front door, Thérèse asked, 'Where's Elspeth?'

'Out shopping – why?'

'I thought I'd better tell her – Gad just heard that his mother died suddenly. He was really upset; but he says he's not going over for the funeral.'

'Not going – why ever not?' asked Mary in astonishment.

'He wouldn't say. He's gone out to send telegrams. He'll be back soon. I just wanted to tell you.'

'Yes, well, thanks.' Then, seeing Thérèse's downcast face, 'There isn't a problem, is there?'

'Not really. He's desperately sad, but he won't talk to me about it.'

'Oh, don't worry – he's always like that,' said Mary sympathetically. 'I've seen it before. He can be quite moody sometimes – don't take it personally. Let it go and he'll talk to you when he's ready.'

'Yes, but it's difficult.' Thérèse found she could hardly speak.

'Just give him time.'

'What do I do then – just wait?'

'Yes,' said Estelle. 'But you'd better get back home. Come on, we'll come too. We're not expecting anyone this morning. We can say how sorry we are, then scarper so you two can talk.'

'I'm not doing very well. I don't know how to get through to him. I never met his mother, you know – I don't know why I'm upset.'

'Come on, you're all over the place. Here, take a hanky. Buck up – there's the taxi – let's go to the flat. He'll be in a call box phoning his family, and the lines to California are usually terrible, and his timing's all wrong, too.'

This practical sense was exactly what Thérèse needed – for somebody else to be logical and down-to-earth for a change. The three young women crossed into the bright square and filed through the iron gate under the trees, at the back of the statue of Gandhi. And there was Gad, standing in front of Gandhi, hands in his pockets as usual, gazing sadly at the ascetic face.

As soon as she caught sight of him, Thérèse felt a rush of love, knowing she would hold this picture for years to come: the dark figure standing disconsolately in the sunshine in this London square, facing the image of the holy man from India, Hindu not Catholic like his mother, but still – a link of sorts.

CHAPTER 35

30 April 1955

Gad said to Thérèse, 'I've got to write to them all, and I don't know what to say. I feel like I'm cut off from all of them. Before, it was like talking to my mother.' *Now*, he thought, *the circuit is broken.*

'I know, my darling. You'll just have to do your best. It will get easier.'

He sat at the desk, the blue airmail paper before him, staring at it blindly. There were no natural words. This event was too unnatural. The world had changed.

Dear Wilma, he wrote,

Well, the funeral is over now, and you must all be feeling very sad. I hope you got the flowers we sent by Interflora. I know Big Mummy always said lilies or chrysanthemums were right for funerals, but I've always hated them, and anyway, they said there would be plenty of pink roses – please let me know if they made a good bouquet for her, and what else they put in with the roses, and of course, whether they got to you in time.

Who came to the funeral? Did you have plenty of help? Please tell me everything. On that day I had to work, but I couldn't concentrate well. How are you and Veena? And the boys? Julian especially will badly miss her. But Veena mustn't wear herself out looking after him. And the children? How much do you think they are feeling it?

Honestly, Wilma, when I think of those days in Burma – all our fears when the Japs invaded, and the chaotic days when Billy and I didn't know where any of you were, and then you finding me and getting me up to Simla to join the others – she was all skin and bone when I saw her again – I was shocked – and she did some weird things (do you remember the cigarette packets in the curry?!) and Daddy was ill too, remember? It was a wonder she survived, but that's her. She was a survivor. Who would have thought she would get you all to America? I will write again soon.

Well, Wilma, I must get on with my practice – the Diploma is only three weeks away now. Write soon, and tell me everything.

With love to all of you, and a big God Bless,
Garrard

★

2 May 1955

Dear Garrard,

I am writing to tell you about the funeral. It was very fine, with Fr O'Malley who has known Mummy ever since we arrived in California. The organist at St Theresa's played and the choir sang well, but they did not make the music sound the way you do. But anyway, your flowers looked fine – pink roses that were scented, with stephanotis and some feathery leaves – I don't know what they were. You could smell the flowers and the earth at the burial. Everybody was there – all the family of course helped when we went back to the house afterwards, and the nuns too, who had been to stay, and some of the neighbours too. She was a very loved lady.
PS Thank you for your letter, just arrived. Yes, of course you must think of the Diploma now. Your future depends on it.

And Big Mummy sent you to England with her prayers, because she knew you would do so well. She missed you very much, you know, but never said so. She used to read your letters three times and hold them to her face. She missed your music, too – I wish you had sent a recording. I expect you were too busy. No more room – love from us all, and good luck in the Diploma.

    Your sister
    Wilma

It was agony for Gad to read this. Nobody had ever told him this before. His mother had led the world in hiding her own pain, giving it no attention unless she did so privately in church, sharing it with her God.

Religion would not sustain Gad in the same way. Nor, it seemed, in this cold London, were people required to keep things to themselves. Thérèse had told him all about Alain, and Elspeth had been open about her own early courtship days. Still, he had no intention of making a complete break with family tradition. He would remain reticent about his wartime experiences, but perhaps later he would learn to open up.

CHAPTER 36

May 1955

In the days and weeks that followed, Thérèse seemed to hear a new note in Gad's playing: a melancholy that she had always sensed in him, but that seldom found its way into the music. Whereas his natural instincts had always been to express himself with playful exuberance – to reach out, as it were – now he seemed only to be listening inwardly, bending his head over the keys as if they held secrets, things he could hear but scarcely catch.

He worked obsessively. When she sat down to her little portable typewriter, or left at eight o'clock for one of her libraries, he would already be riffling through the pile of music that lay on the piano, deciding which of his Diploma pieces to work on first, or running scales up and down the full range of the keyboard, trying for the perfect evenness that was demanded, and that would be the rock solid foundation for his music.

Thérèse would call out 'Well then...', or 'So long!' as she left with her books, and had to be content with a cheery 'See ya!' from the sitting-room.

She found that her routine had not changed much. Her nightmare had been unfounded. Against the music, she could not have used a hoover even if she wanted to. All she had to do was plan their meal, and in the evening one of them would go out to shop while the other tidied their rooms. They were lucky enough to live in a working district, where German delicatessens were well-established and open till late, selling delicious food – *matjes* herrings, *apfelstrudel, liverwurst* and *pumpernickel* that did not require cooking. Some of these were too foreign for Gad; failing the spicy rice dishes of home, he preferred even English food. Their gas stove had no oven, so French casserole dishes were in any case out of the question.

His concentration was fierce; he stretched his back and arms only every hour or so, drinking black coffee and smoking. But by midday on the eve of the Diploma he had finished. Closing the lid of the Broadwood decisively, he went into the bedroom and lay down on his back, enjoying the springy new bed, his face relaxing gradually. She turned from her books, leaning her arm on the back of her chair.

'Well?' she said. 'You're ready?'

'Ready as I'll ever be. Do you want to come out for a bit?'

'Of course. Where?'

'Let's go to Kew!' he exclaimed, jumping up energetically. 'I'll row you down the river!'

'Can you row?' She really didn't know; such a thing had never cropped up before.

'There's always a first time! It'll be fine.'

They walked to Oxford Circus, caught the Underground to Kew, and paid their penny at the turnstile to enter the gardens. The sun glittered on the magnificent palm house, and drew them in to wander among the heavy green smells, the huge-leaved plants and snaking creepers, Thérèse marvelling and Gad at home in the hot drench. You could not hurry in this greenhouse atmosphere, were forced to linger, drawing the almost liquid air into your lungs with difficulty, feeling your skin become clammy from sweat that would not evaporate. Outside, a row of great blue agapanthus stood sentinel, watching as they left and strolled towards the river in the sudden chill of a light breeze.

Said Thérèse, 'That must have been like Burma.'

He smiled at her. 'Well, not quite like Rangoon. A bit like

the hotel gardens and the parks, perhaps. I've never been in proper jungle – but the smell was good.' He flared his nostrils, remembering.

They found their way to the broad, slow-flowing river, where there was a boatyard with a few skiffs remaining for hire. They watched as a young couple clambered into one of the boats, Gad attentive to its tilt as they took their places and the young man settled the oars in the rowlocks. Thérèse thought how deft Gad was in handling solid objects, and felt confident about trusting herself to him: they might get carried away by a current, she felt, but he would never fumble nor let go of the oars.

They made their way along a floating walkway towards the owner, a 'Ben Hodson' according to a printed board heading the wooden boathouse.

'Good afternoon,' said Gad, jingling the money in his pocket.

The man grunted. *Oh no*, said Thérèse to herself. *He's going to be awkward.*

'Can we take a boat, please? For an hour.'

The man looked him over. 'Don't think I've got a boat,' he said, bluntly.

Thérèse's heart sank.

'Looks like you have?' said Gad, gesturing towards the two or three remaining.

'Nah, they're unbalanced ones.'

'Unbalanced? What do you mean?'

'Unbalanced. Lopsided. Will tip you over,' said the man. 'You don't want that, do you?' he added, looking speculatively at Thérèse.

'They look just the same as the others,' Gad protested, not giving up easily.

'That's just where you're wrong, then,' said Ben Hodson. 'Have you ever rowed a boat before?'

'No, but it can't be difficult.'

'That's just where you're wrong,' repeated the man. 'Sorry.' His voice was final; his face was a picture of scepticism. He had been polite – just – but was not about to let them have one of his boats. He might let a novice Englishman have one, but how could he have confidence in this foreigner? He was a man who knew his rights.

Gad turned back to Thérèse. 'Do you want to wait till one of the others comes back?'

Hiding her disappointment, Thérèse looked at him with an ironic grin. 'Don't think that would do much good, do you?'

They understood each other. They could see what the situation was. You just never knew when this adamant blankness would show up.

Thérèse turned back along the walkway, and sensed Gad reluctantly following. The water lapped gently at their feet. She felt Gad had been on the verge of making a scene, and didn't want it to come to that. They would not win. Reaching solid ground, she waited for him, and linked her arm in his.

'That stupid man,' she said. 'I tell you something, we should come back another day with some of the others, and see if he still refuses to give us a boat.'

Gad only grunted, clearly frustrated and angry.

'Let's walk the long way back to the station,' she said. 'Nobody can stop us enjoying the river, at least. And then, we'll be back in plenty of time, too.'

Disengaging himself, he remained a silent figure at her side, hands in pockets; she sensed his scowl though his head was down. It was the first time she had seen him so disconcerted. This time, she saw that he was really angry, and didn't mind showing it. There must be a limit to the number of times a man could be humiliated.

At home, he played one last set of arpeggios before bedtime. Thérèse heard fury in them.

★

The day of the Diploma. Gad spent some time dressing, fastidious about easing trousers on hips, jacket on shoulders and slicking back his hair till it was just so. He checked the Diploma pieces into his music case, though she knew he would be playing from memory. He seemed calm, preoccupied as she kissed him at the door.

The morning dragged as she waited, unable to settle, preparing to make quantities of scrambled egg and toast for lunch. She tried not to shadow him in her mind, feeling it might bring bad luck. She was to attend the evening concert that would follow, and would hear him then in reality.

★

She heard Gad's key in the lock just before one, and stood rigid with tension, waiting to see how he would look – surely not downcast?

He bounded down the stairs, flinging his music case into the corner and throwing his arms around her. Before she could ask: 'I gave them hell, *wunchi*,' he cried. 'You should have heard me!' He stood back, arms wide. 'I don't know what got into me – I just took off!' His delighted grin split his face in two and his eyes sparked fire. 'Those scales – I ripped them off! And their questions – I was answering them before they'd finished asking! Right or wrong – I don't know – but that was me at last – don't care what they made of it! Anyway, it's done now – Murray shook my hand...'

'And the others?'

'The others? Who knows? They'll either love me or not. Is there anything to eat? I'm starving!'

He ate ravenously, and drank coffee as fast as Thérèse could pour it, until at last he sat back, satisfied but still full of energy.

'Let's walk along the river,' he said, pulling her to her feet. 'Leave all this!' as she started to clear the plates.

They left the flat and marched arm-in-arm, skirting the busy shopping streets on their way towards the Embankment. They knew by now how to navigate London on foot: always take the downward slope to reach the river, and then follow it up or downstream to steer west or east. Thérèse could feel the spring in Gad's step, enjoying his sudden spirit of gaiety.

'Why do you love the river so much?' she asked, squeezing his arm as they walked.

'I don't know – the Thames,' (he pronounced the 'Th'… as in 'themes') 'we always heard about it. It's so huge – bigger than the Salween, much – and it never hurries.' He sounded pleased about that. 'I always wonder why people don't use it more, these days. They used to. The streets are crammed full, yet there's all that space…'

It was typical of him, she thought, to be interested in such a thing when this was the very day that so much of their real life depended on: he was right in the middle of his baptism of fire. She tried a direct question.

'How are you feeling?'

He looked at her quizzically. 'Fine, just fine. How are you feeling?'

As a matter of fact, she was feeling bitterly disappointed. Another month had gone by: no baby. But it was not the moment. She managed a smile.

'Que tu es bête!'

They leaned on the parapet, watching the mass of water find its own way through the arches of two of the great bridges of London town: the smooth grey curves of Waterloo to their right, and downstream, Blackfriars, with its weight of brightly painted wrought iron reflected erratically in the choppy water. They could hear little waves slapping against the wall below, sending up the sour dank smell of river mud. Below Blackfriars they could just see picture postcard Tower Bridge before the river broadened, winding its bridgeless way to the sea.

'Do you think there will ever be more crossings?' Below Tower Bridge, people had to burrow underneath like moles, at Rotherhithe or Blackwall, or take a ferry at Woolwich. Beyond was foreign country – docks and lonely marshes that were home only to criminals and migrating birds; islands and an ancient castle; dangerous sandbanks.

'Maybe,' he replied. 'I hope so. As usual, the LCC has plans but too little money.'

There must be boatmen, she thought, who knew these lower reaches as she and Gad knew the city streets, who would know exactly which way to turn for the Far East. She hoped this was not in Gad's mind, felt again the fear that he might one day wish to return home.

'Do you ever think about the voyage over here from Burma?' she asked.

Gad turned to look at her, propping his elbows on the parapet behind.

'Yes, I do, as a matter of fact. Perhaps it's why I like the river: all the same water system, isn't it – rivers, seas – England, France, Burma, America? All joined up in the end.'

'M-m-m.' She pictured the map.

'You know, I was thinking,' said Gad suddenly. 'Why don't we look for a place to buy?'

'To buy? But – how could we?'

'Well – we must. We've got to have a stake.'

'*Mon dieu* – this is sudden! Why now? This really isn't

the moment. Look, it's time we got back – you must eat, and change for the concert.'

'Yes, I know – but think about it, will you? I've had the idea for some time. Whatever happens, I'm sure we need this.'

*

Thérèse sat in Row F in the college auditorium, the idea of buying a permanent home dancing at the back of her mind, waiting for Gad to make his appearance. He was third on the programme of four piano students.

The second performer left the platform to polite applause, and there was a pause while the three examiners made notes, positioned behind a long table near Thérèse's seat. She strained her ears, but couldn't hear any comments; each was keeping his thoughts to himself.

After a few moments the applause began again, as Gad's neat figure stepped onto the stage, walking straight towards the open Steinway without looking at the audience. Thérèse's heart missed a beat, but in his own good time he turned, touching the piano with one hand, surveyed the audience briefly and bowed deep, before taking his seat with a practised flick of his coat tails. He took a moment to adjust the height of the stool and its angle. Thérèse saw how burnished his skin looked in the stage lights, how his face and hands shone against his white shirt collar and cuffs, and how well the black tailoring set off his compact frame. She set herself to listen to the music. Although she had heard it running through the days and weeks before, the backdrop to her everyday life, it sounded utterly different here, in this large space, framed, as it were, by the formalities of dress and distance and audience. The lights were bright over the platform and the people sat still, in the miraculous way that a good audience can, all attention focussed with critical goodwill on the performer. Thérèse found herself listening in a different way too, following the cool threads of sound as Gad wove his way through Bach's *Italian Concerto*. Knowing little about this period, she felt an energy in the playing that she thought must come from the particular tempi he had chosen – neither over-emphatic nor rushed, but with a living pulse.

Her impressions were confirmed by warm applause, acknowledged with another bow and a smile, before Gad embarked on his central piece, Robert Schumann's *Carnaval*, with its gallery of vivid characters, supposedly masked revellers at a ball. One section followed swiftly on another with rapid changes of mood, from the passionate *Florestan* to the dreamy *Eusebio*, from genial *Valse Noble* to lyrical *Estrella*. Thérèse saw Gad's fingers flying over the keys with unerring exactitude, nursing the notes as he bent to his work, absorbed in the musical world he was recreating. And the audience rose to it, cheering with excitement after the complex counter-melodies of the *Marche des Davidsbundler contre les Philistines* flew off the keys as Gad emphatically brought the work to its conclusion and rose to acknowledge the acclaim.

Thérèse saw from the programme that Gad's last choice was entitled *Five Piano Pieces: Trees op. 75* by Sibelius – a group of atmospheric, rather spare pieces with little to offer the pianist in terms of technical gymnastics. Hearing them at home without knowing much about them, Thérèse had wondered whether this was a wise choice. When he performed them in the concert hall she saw that they were perfect: cool and contained, they forced the performer to create colours from a very limited palette. The piece cleansed the senses after all the razzle-dazzle of *Carnaval*.

CHAPTER 37

After the Diploma, Gad found time to write to his younger sister Veena, who had cared for their mother for so long. Remembering took him back to 'Burma days', as the expats called them, and which he had not chosen to recall recently.

June 1955

Dear Veena

I am very sorry to think how you must be feeling, so bad without Big Mummy, I am sure. You looked after her for a long time, and I am sorry to think I was not able to help you with her. At least she did not suffer a long or painful illness.

But I cannot imagine her not being alive anymore. When something like this happens, it makes everything else seem small. She was the steely heart of our family – got us all out of Rangoon to India, and then together again in Rangoon, and then all of you to Borneo and then to where you are now in sunny California. What a woman. I often wonder about her and our father – were they happy while he lived, do you think? He did not seem to me very strong, although he was clever all right. I don't remember that he spoke to me very often. He used to be nice when he was singing, but with all the gambling? It must have been hard for her to keep our household going, and yet she still managed to look after Henry and Amy when they needed it. I look at the old photos of her and she is never smiling. Do you have the picture of her with the red car with a smart handbag over her arm? And the big house with the

veranda behind her? Was that taken in Borneo? Our house in
Rangoon was never so big. She isn't smiling then either, but
she looks lovely – quite proud in her way of standing.

Well, I have taken the Diploma exam and played in the
Diploma concert. I think it went well, but I must wait now for
the result. I will write again when I know.

I am so sorry you had such a shock with her sudden heart
attack, which she did not survive. I cannot quite believe any of
it.

With love to you all, and a big God Bless,
Garrard

PS How are the children taking it?

Gad thought of his family now, laying 'Big Mummy's' small
body to rest in the earth of a Californian hillside under blue
skies and sunshine, near the church where she attended Mass.
It was good of his sisters to understand his absence from the
funeral, leaving him to prepare for his Diploma in peace. Now
it was he who regretted the necessity. If only he could have
played for her one more time.

CHAPTER 38

June 1955

They relaxed into a new routine, Thérèse to work on and Gad to dream, returning always to his loss. There had been an exchange of telegrams and other letters telling of Big Mummy's funeral, with all the American family present. There were no reproaches from his sisters. In the aftermath, he had no consecutive thoughts at all – felt that limbo must be like this.

He waited to know the result.

★

August 1955

It was early in August. At a loose end, Gad peered up into the street. Spears of rain were driving across the window. He remembered another rainy day, in a twisty street in Kensington.

'Are you going to walk through the park in this?' he asked Thérèse.

'Of course. What else?'

Her hair would get plastered to her face again. 'I'll come with you.'

'You hate the rain!'

'I know, but...' There was something about rain that loosened things up, made things happen. The monsoon... 'I'll carry your books, miss!' he said.

Outside it felt cold to Gad, even though he had on his

trusty duffle coat. Thérèse put on her short mac and tied a scarf round her hair, the red one that he liked. Her shoes were flimsy. She wrapped the notebooks in a piece of Gad's Burmese cloth and he tucked the bundle under his arm. It felt solid and workmanlike, and comfortable.

One day we'll have a car, he thought, but said only: 'So, is it going well?'

'Not altogether. I've got so many unresolved questions. And everyone's away on holiday.'

'So, shouldn't you take a break, too?'

'I can't. I'm behind schedule, what with the wedding, and our lovely honeymoon.' She hugged him as they walked.

'You're not having regrets?'

'Of course not, stupid! It's just that…' she frowned, 'the more I uncover, the more there is to know.'

'But you still have a year to go.'

'That's not long, you know – the time goes fast.'

'And you're still keen to do this?' It was selfish, he knew, but it would be satisfying to have Thérèse to himself, at least until his career took off – or until they started a family.

She seemed to hesitate slightly, and her answer lacked conviction. 'Yes, *bien sur*. It's why I came to England.'

★

Gad made a habit of walking with Thérèse across the park and back each day, but they found they were attracting sour comments. Once a bedraggled young girl, huddled in a doorway, spat out at Thérèse: 'You're only with him for his money!' – a comment that was so inappropriate she burst out laughing. The girl was looking at the carrier bag dangling from Gad's finger. In it were two sleek wine glasses wrapped in tissue paper and the name on the bag was Heals. He planned to buy more when they could afford to – these were only so they could celebrate properly if he passed the Diploma. But the girl perhaps had nothing. Gad's finger tightened on Thérèse's arm in acknowledgement of the barb, but he neither slowed down nor turned his head.

'Don't you get tired of this sort of thing?' Thérèse asked. 'Doesn't it make you feel unwelcome?'

'Unwelcome?' He tried to imagine why she thought that. 'No. Why should I worry what she says?'

'That's true. But why does she bother? What's it to her?'

'That's what I wonder. She's just a girl.' He always felt sorry for girls, knowing what could happen to them – had often happened in Burma during the Japanese occupation.

'So why, do you think?' she insisted.

Gad rather wished she would let the matter drop – it did no good to dwell on the negative side of things. 'Well,' he said, 'the other lot – in the park that day – that was just about a threat to his women, of course! Suspicion of the rogue male!'

'I suppose so. But how can you ignore it?'

'The thing is – they all have their reasons. Even the wretched boatman. I'm used to it, you know. Burma was no paradise, even in the old days!' He thought of how, as a matter of course, the British expected deference from Anglo-Burmese families like his own, despite the fact that accountants like his father were enabling the Railway Company to keep the vital lines of communication going, without which the country would have been ungovernable anyway.

'Meaning?'

'Well...' he tried to define something that was second nature to him, 'the British were incredibly clannish out there – expats clinging together.' A memory of Robert's snake man flashed across his mind – the instant rapport between those two tall white men and the way they had automatically ignored him. 'Not all of them were people to be respected, either, though of course they all had the upper hand. Some were. I'd stick with my own countrymen too, if only there were more of us here! You watch the Indians and the Africans, especially the Nigerians. Oh yes – we non-whites,' – he gave her a questioning glance – 'we have our cliques too! I've got no more in common with the Windrush lot than I have with Haile Selassie or the Queen!'

'That's some thought.'

The idea seemed new to her. He felt uncertain about explaining things – after all, English was not her native language as it was his. It didn't make conversation easy. And really, such things had to be experienced before they could be understood. Better to keep things light.

'Always patriotic, that's me!' he laughed.

'And royalist too, a true son of the Raj! Do you think we'll ever go to Burma? I have little idea what it is like there, you know?'

'When it's so derelict now? Falling into rack and ruin, while the generals line their own pockets?' His face tightened. 'I'd love to take you – it's a beautiful country – but not to see how it is now. I never want you to see that. You'd get completely the wrong idea. They wouldn't even let us travel up-country – I have a British passport, you know, so I'd be suspect.'

'Oh. I thought because you were born there…'

'No, no. The thing is, when Burma became independent, we were allowed to choose between British or Burmese passports. I was already in England, and I was advised then to naturalise as a British citizen, which I did – I'll tell you the story some time. It was hilarious.'

There it was again – everything became a joke.

'Some of my family still have Burmese passports – some probably American by now – but I am considered an outsider because I threw my lot in with the British – and I'm glad I did. The Burmese government has become dictatorial and secretive – no such thing as a free press – and nobody wants to risk overstaying their welcome; Insein Gaol is no joke! To think we lived in Insein when it was a nice suburb!'

'But French would not be a problem?' At the same time she wondered about his family in America, and why he preferred to stay in England.

'No.'

Thérèse went on. 'But to stay here – with all this hate?'

He wanted her to stop. 'England is a wonderful country, don't let's forget. They open their doors to everyone. It's not really hate – only fear for their own position. It's just that they feel naturally superior to everyone – it can be irritating. You just have to shut your eyes and ears to the rubbish and look for the opportunities.'

'It's the politicians who let everyone in,' she said. 'They don't ask the people whether they want us or not!'

★

One humid afternoon a week later the news came by hand: Gad had been awarded a Starred Distinction in the Diploma. The formal announcement came with a curt note from Murray: 'There you are, my boy! Well done! Murray.'

Gad stared at the piece of paper, disbelieving. Privately, he had dared to hope for a Distinction, but a Starred Distinction? In the past, perhaps one student a year had got a star; often nobody. It was, in fact, a rare honour. He wondered what it was that had given his work a special appeal to the judges, what it was that had made him feel so liberated on that particular evening.

He said nothing to Thérèse, but put an arm across her shoulders as she sat leafing through the books on her desk, and gently put the notice on top of them. She glanced up at him, taking a moment to refocus. Then: 'Gad! Oh Gad! Oh my darling, how marvellous!' She jumped up and threw her arms round him, delivering several hearty kisses on various parts of his face.

'I told you they would love you. Oh Gad, you must be thrilled!'

Gad supposed he must be. He needed time.

Thérèse linked her arm through his, and drew him into the sitting-room, where it was fresher.

'Are you always like that in performance?' She sat down with him.

'No, no – it's unusual. I've always been tense, you know, worried about "doing well". This time I felt free as air. I know I keep saying this – but it actually felt like flying… The wind under my wings – that sort of thing. Pretentious, yes?'

'No – even I could hear that. It sounded as if you could do anything you liked with that piano!'

'Yes – almost like having a little violin tucked under my chin. It was small and I was a giant!'

'A giant! You?' She laughed, squeezing his hand.

'Well – I can always dream.' Experimentally, he took a few steps on tiptoe, and smiled to see her giggle.

'You were magnificent. I was so proud!'

Immediately he sat down again, retreating into himself.

'No, don't be proud,' he said, emphasising the word in suppressed anger.

'What?'

'Can't you just enjoy it? A good performance, yes – but it was their judgement I wanted.'

'I know – not mine.' He saw her wince, but she swallowed and went on, 'They'd be mad not to love you.'

'Maybe. But remember, they say a performer is only as good as his last performance. You have to keep on proving yourself. Anyway – I don't want you as judge, you understand?'

'Whatever do you mean?'

'Too many of them in my life already, at home.'

She tilted her chin at him, quizzically.

'The family let me come to England, but for that I had to be the best in the world – for my mother, at least,' he explained. 'The irony is that she wasn't really all that musical, herself; never listened to music for pleasure, except when I played, or when my father used to sing on Sunday afternoons. Only one of my sisters – that's Wilma – really loved music. I hope she's going to lots of concerts in America. She'll really enjoy that. The others – well, if I wasn't going to play football with them, I had to be a genius to make up for it!' For Gad, this was a long speech.

'Oh, you're making too much of all that,' she said impatiently. 'OK, OK, I'll admit – I don't know much about the piano classics, so you might say I have no right to judge; well, I don't want to do that anyway. I just felt proud to see you up there, so handsome, dominating the hall, so absolutely gorgeous – can't you understand?'

Her eyes were on his, insisting on her right to – what?

'Now you're talking! Keep going!' He fell back on humour.

'Oh, you – come on now, *ne pas le lait!*'

'Well, you're my wife, don't forget – not my mother or my teacher.'

But she was not going to give up, he saw.

'And you still feel the pressure from home,' she said, 'even now that your mother is – now that your mother has passed on?' Her voice faltered.

He flinched. Even the weasel words hurt. Again he tried, hesitantly, to explain. 'That's the amazing thing. I did, but then again I didn't.' He reflected. 'In a way she was there, looking over my shoulder like she used to – but there was something else: a current of electricity; something that made me play for my life.' He gestured impatiently. 'I'm not explaining very well.'

'Go on,' she prompted.

'For once, I was not afraid of making mistakes, of making a

fool of myself. All those anxieties – I seemed not to have them anymore. Do you get it?'

★

There was a party at International House at the weekend, to celebrate Gad's success. They strolled through the streets, Gad in a clean shirt and slacks, Thérèse in a new dress she and Louise had concocted for the occasion. It was brilliant jade green with a puffball skirt held up inside by long threads from hem to waist, and looked a little insecure, but suitably celebratory. Gad caught her checking to make sure the fragile threads had not broken.

The party was raucous and cheerful, with much shouting and laughter, though there was no alcohol. The staff had known Gad ever since he had arrived in England, and the visitors seemed glad to find a cause for excitement in this strange chilly country.

Gad sat at the piano as usual, preferring music to conversation, running through his repertoire of wartime hits – they had reached Simla through the BBC World Service, which was heard playing in every household in that very British town as the war wound its way to a conclusion.

At the end of one session, he went out of the room for a moment to reappear in unexpected guise, his shirt unbuttoned deep down his chest, the collar turned up, and round his neck a gold chain with a large medallion fashioned from gilded butter paper. He wore his white tuxedo, the lapels covered with silver milk bottle tops that glittered like huge sequins. In his hand was a clumsy improvised candelabrum with white grocer's candles, which he lit with a cigarette lighter before setting the whole construction carefully on the lid of the old Blüthner grand. There was no need, but before sitting down Gad propped a piece of card against it, saying simply *GADERACE'S HALF-HOUR*. Flashing an ingratiating grin at the astonished revellers he sat down to play – sloppily, flashily, turning always to smirk and nod at the audience, who by now were leaning all over the piano. He played any popular classics he had ever heard, fielding requests with aplomb, raising a hand now and again to wave to 'Mother' (Elspeth, hovering on the outskirts), plundering the repertoire for tuneful numbers. It was outrageous.

He had seen a short film of the real Wladziu Valentino Liberace, and read: 'When it is too difficult, he simplifies it. When it is too simple, he complicates it'. He thought it would be fun to put the classics through the same process in an outbreak of joyous vulgarity, from *Jesu Joy of Man's Desiring* through the *Blue Danube* waltz to the Liszt *Liebestraum nocturne*, relishing the sudden release from discipline and good taste, from strict fidelity to composers' intentions. His teachers had always complained that if he forgot a bar or missed a phrase, he could easily improvise another. He had formed the habit in early years of poor or non-existent guidance, using sheet music which sometimes had pages missing. In Burma, this had not mattered. In the concert hall, it certainly did. Here, he reveled in returning to his bad old ways to amuse his friends, who cheered and hollered, clapping him painfully on the back when he finally rose and extinguished the candles.

The pair were lighthearted as they walked back home, went to bed late and loving. Thérèse fell asleep immediately afterwards, but Gad was wakeful. Finally he got out of bed and went through to the living-room, lighting a cigarette as he leaned against the window frame, peering up at the night sky.

What was I doing, to play like that? he thought. *It was a mistake.* He felt slightly sick. He remembered the times he had played for his mother's friends, showing off so as to earn their applause. They were much more impressed with the young player than with the music itself. But he would not be young forever. He thought of playing for school assemblies in Simla, improvising freely to spin out the sound while the masters entered and reached the front of the hall. He thought of weddings and funerals. He thought of his rough nights in the Green Parrot, the whores leaning over the piano to show him their breasts, their hands plucking at him invitingly. He thought of the white grand in the ballroom of the Strand Hotel on Rangoon's waterfront, with the whiskey sours and chasers under the slow-turning fans, while his head gradually grew fuddled though his fingers still found the notes. Popular, that was what he had been – popular, he had made sure of that, and therefore successful. He was in demand and had made good money.

He had no money now, though – only a Starred Distinction to his name. How far would that get him in London?

★

At the weekend Gad raised again the subject of buying a property.

'It needn't be big,' he said firmly, 'but it must be in a good area.' He wanted to be away from tenement houses crammed together as they were in his street.

'But that's going to be so expensive...'

'It's important, though. Did you see how your parents looked at this place – as if they couldn't believe their eyes?'

'Well, they don't have to live in it!'

'I know, but – we should start as we mean to go on. People judge you by these things. If we have children...' He cocked an eyebrow at Thérèse; she shook her head with a forlorn moue that seemed to touch him, so that he stopped, tilting her chin up, murmuring to comfort her, 'It's all right, you know. It'll be all right.'

★

They started the house-hunt that day – first with a good look at the A to Z, eliminating some areas they disliked for whatever reason – like Croydon because of its name, or Bloomsbury because there were few places to buy, or Chigwell because of its reputation for pretentiousness, or Stoke Newington because there was no tube station nearby, or Kilburn because it was too Irish – and others that they thought too pricey, like the whole of Hampstead east of the Finchley Road. They decided to begin with West Hampstead, knowing that they would be able to afford only a tiny flat at best, but longing to be within reach of the Heath.

Thérèse wondered, who was to say everything would be all right? That business in Paris: Gad still knew nothing about all that. It seemed so long ago – another life – but could it be affecting her chances of having a baby now? Or was there something in Gad's history that made conception problematic – what about those bouts of malaria, for instance? At least she knew, though he did not, that she had conceived once before. She was going to have to tell him about that some time, but not yet.

CHAPTER 39

August 1955

Gad wrote at once to his family, though desolated that it was too late now for his mother to share his exciting news. She was the one person in the world who would have been entirely jubilant to hear it, and would have foreseen a golden future for her son. Nevertheless, his sisters deserved a letter.

Dear Wilma, Veena and all at home, he wrote.

You will not believe this good news – they gave me a Starred Distinction in the Diploma – a Starred Distinction! They hardly ever give this! I am walking on air. My biggest regret is that Big Mummy did not live to see it. She always had faith in me, and made me practise, and found teachers for me even though it turns out they were not very good. It's a shame she did not understand why I had to come away to learn at a higher level. To her, I suppose I was always that little boy playing for her friends, with my own programme on Burma Radio. Nobody here has even heard of Burma, let alone Burma Radio. How I play now is very different! I have to say, though, that competing with European pianists here is not easy, and I am beginning to wonder whether I need to find a more informal way of performing.

But enough about me. Thérèse is fine, working hard on her thesis. I want to start looking for a place of our own, to raise our family. Houses here are incredibly expensive though, and I worry about getting a mortgage, since neither of us is in steady work. *I have increased my hours at the LCC for the summer, but in the autumn I shall need to start trying to build my musical career.*

When all this settles down, and we have the money, we will come over to visit you all. Are you planning to stay in the same place? Keep me in the picture.

Write and tell me how you are.

My love to everyone, and a big God Bless,

Your brother,

Garrard

CHAPTER 40

August 1955

House-hunting became Gad's preoccupation.

'Let's make a start today,' he said to Thérèse one morning as they got dressed.

'Trouble is, darling, I've simply got to do some work first.' She waved a hand at the untidy scatter of notebooks and papers on her desk. 'My tutor will be back soon, and I must have my list of queries ready – it means sorting out everything I've done so far – if I don't I will be wasting his time, and he doesn't like that.'

'Well, I wish you could, but anyway – I suppose if I find anything promising, you could take time out to view it with me?'

'Of course, yes. But there's no hurry, is there? We can't actually buy anything, or take out a mortgage, until you decide what you want to do.' She worried, thinking how little Gad had immersed himself in music since the Diploma – he neither played nor listened. 'Aren't you busy looking for an agent or something?'

He frowned, looking away. 'I'm having a little break. Nothing's going to happen in August – everybody is on holiday. Time enough for all that in September.'

He was looking forward to the hunt. It was a change of pace – a release. The idea of a proper home for them – 'an Englishman's castle', as it figured in his imagination – had taken hold, and he bent his energies to making the thing possible.

Of course, money was the biggest problem: who would give them a mortgage, and why?

He had done the obvious thing, and stepped up his days with the LCC. He aimed to build up his record so that when they needed it, he could claim a regular salary there. If it came to a choice between working full-time to support Thérèse or pursuing a music career and living in squalor, he was beginning to realise which he would choose.

He decided, too, that the property would be in their joint names, and this meant the mortgage offer would be more generous, as his wife would be jointly responsible for the repayments. Certainly, Thérèse was not employed now, and might not be able to work if they had a young family, but mortgage companies looked favourably on well-educated partners without caring too much whether they had studied Breton folklore or international finance.

*

All this was going through Gad's mind as he took the train to West Hampstead on his first free day. He had thought of consulting Rob and Elspeth at the House, but they were living 'over the shop' rent-free, and the birds of passage who also lived there had, in the main, families to return to, and were not yet looking to buy properties. Nobody at the House ever talked about money. He was on his own.

Turning out of the station, his head bent against the unseasonal gusts of wind that had sprung up, he saw that there were several estate agencies nearby, and stopped to look in the windows of the nearest. It was a shock: the descriptions were mostly of beautiful, large, high-ceilinged rooms that would easily accommodate a piano and its sound, but the prices for a two-bedroom flat were twice the amount he had in mind. Perhaps, he thought, this agency handled the high end of the market, although its shabby shop front hardly suggested such a thing.

He walked on, and looked in a second window. It was the same story. Not yet discouraged, he went on to a third, and this time he went in, determined to make his requirements known directly. Perhaps those chosen for display were untypical. There might be details of others hidden away inside.

The girl was polite, at least. 'I'm afraid there is very little here in your price range, sir. In fact, we have nothing at the moment. Perhaps further down the hill...'

'In Kilburn?' Gad interrupted. 'Thanks, but we're not thinking of Kilburn.'

'I'm sorry, then; I'm afraid I can't help you today. Perhaps if you would fill in one of these cards?'

'Is it worth it, do you think?'

'Oh yes, sir, in this business you never know.'

Feeling that he had nothing to lose, he filled in the card.

He stepped out of the office again, the wind blowing grit into his eyes, and walked straight into a woman who was busy trying to control several light scarves as they tried to fly off her shoulders. He pulled up short, prepared to apologise, and realised that it was none other than Valerie – Valerie dressed all in black, dishevelled and flustered, but with the familiar bright cheeks and bold eyes.

'Good Lord! Valerie!' he exclaimed, holding his hands out to her.

'Gad! Hello! What are you doing up here?'

'Oh – business,' he said vaguely. 'And you? You're looking great. I haven't seen you since the end of term – how did it go?'

'I live here, remember?' Lilies and an elegant curving staircase sprang to Gad's mind.

'Of course, sorry.'

'And yes, it went well – I got a Merit.' She gave a modest smile. 'And you – I bet you did really well? Did you get your Distinction?'

'Congratulations! And yes, I did OK,' he said, with reserve.

'Well – what?'

'You'll never guess: a Starred Distinction – for what it's worth.' The gloss had already worn off, for him. Who would care, except Thérèse and his closest friends?

'For what it's worth!'

They seemed to be talking in exclamations. He recalled the circumstances of their last parting: how she had tried to push him into an unwanted dependence on her father and his patronage; how her father had attempted to recruit him for some role not clearly defined.

'Well, you know, I'm married now. I need an income,' he said prosaically.

'Yes, of course. Well, tremendous congrats, anyway. How are things with you and – Thérèse?' She hesitated and flushed a little, as if finding it a struggle to remember the name.

'Oh, really fine,' he said. 'She's working on her thesis, trying to make up for lost time. Her grant won't last forever.'

'I'd love to see her again.'

It was nothing but a polite remark. Gad looked at her sharply. He didn't think Valerie liked Thérèse much.

'Would you?' he said doubtfully. 'Well, why don't you come down and see us one day? We're still in our same place, and there are always people dropping in.'

'I might do that. Actually,' she said in a conspiratorial tone, glancing up and down the street, 'there is something I'd like to talk to you about. Have you got a few moments?'

'Yes, I suppose.' He was loath to postpone the house-hunting, but decided that a few minutes' delay would do no harm. 'We could have a coffee – there's a place.'

Directly opposite was a small café, 'Sid's' according to the name over the door, which was convenient for their conversation. On the counter were buns and a tacky bottle of Camp coffee. Gad raised an eyebrow, decided to play safe and ordered two teas and two sticky buns. Valerie liked sticky buns.

Then, 'Well?' he asked.

'Well – I thought I'd tell you. I've decided to leave home.'

'What?' This was a big surprise. Valerie was so well looked after there.

'Yes.' Valerie gave no word of explanation.

'So – have you fallen out with your parents?' he asked hesitantly, not wanting to pry.

'No – not yet.' She put a hand over her eyes.

'Not yet?' Gad felt stupid; she was not giving him much to go on, and her reserve was uncharacteristic.

'No. Things are fine at the moment. They're pleased about my results. Daddy is getting busy with plans for me…'

Gad winced as he recalled the force behind Bernard's handshake, his booming voice that would stand for no opposition. The only escape was to break free, as he had done.

'But you don't want to go along with them?' he asked, gently. She seemed different – wounded, almost.

Valerie concentrated on picking the currants out of her bun, then crumbling the soft dough between her fingers, not meeting Gad's eye. 'It's not exactly that,' she said.

'Well – are you going to tell me?'

'I suppose I must,' said Valerie finally, seeming to drag her gaze away from her littered plate. 'I'm pregnant,' she said flatly.

The café door rattled violently in the wind. Taken aback, Gad stammered on a rising inflection, 'Well – congratulations?'

In a rush: 'Not really. I don't want to be.'

'Oh – so, who…?'

'That's the problem. Mummy and Daddy would hate it.' She hugged herself, as if to protect her body.

'Well – it's a bit soon, but that's not unusual – you'll get married?'

'No, we won't, and it's really hard to explain to you.'

'What, you mean he won't? But your father can…' – 'make him marry you', he was about to say, but stopped short of suggesting a shotgun wedding. Bernard would be perfectly capable of managing the situation.

'Oh, he could do it all right,' Valerie interrupted, 'but he won't. I absolutely know he won't.'

There was anger in her voice, and Gad looked at her full face and realised she was crying, fat tears rolling down her cheeks and her mouth twisted with tension. He took her hands in his and held them hard, pressing with his thumbs to lend her strength.

'Valerie! Valerie! Listen – it can't be that bad. Who is the – father, anyway?'

'That's just it. That's why it's so hard to tell you! It's Sanjay – Sanjay!'

'Sanjay?' repeated Gad idiotically. 'What Sanjay?'

'Sanjay – your Sanjay! I wish I'd never met him!' she cried.

'But, how did you? Meet him, I mean?'

'This is hard,' Valerie said again, visibly pulling herself together. She drew a handkerchief out of her pocket and blew her nose. 'I had a kind of crush on you, did you know?' She gave a little laugh, but gave him a look that was serious.

Gad tried to ignore the quickening of his heartbeat.

'Well, I did, and I kind of haunted International House for a while, hoping to bump into you there. I never did, but I met Sanjay instead – I'd met him at your wedding and – well…' Her voice trailed away.

'But – where did you go?' was all that Gad could think to say. The House was far too public a place.

'Sanjay had friends, you know – other Indian students, who were sharing a room in Euston. We used to go there. It was stupid; I knew Sanjay was careless – a "take what you want and move on" sort of chap. Not the steady kind.' She glanced at Gad. 'And anyway, he'll go back to India when he's got his law degree.'

'Yes, I know. Sanjay does whatever he needs. Oh Lord, Valerie, what a mess! Why on earth did you…?' He bit his lip, remembering how it was with himself and Thérèse. But that was totally different, he thought.

'For heaven's sake, don't you start!' Valerie exclaimed, half standing up, holding on to the table's edge. 'As if I haven't thought… I can't stand it! I can't stand it!' She collapsed onto her creaking chair again, spreading her arms over the table and dropping her head on them, weeping bitterly. Dust blew across the floor in gusts, stinging Gad's eyes as he watched her helplessly.

Valerie seemed to have no resilience at all, no self-respect. He did feel sorry for her, but something in her made his skin crawl. Confusion made him speechless. Had he still been single, he might easily have told her to come and stay at the flat, such was his instinct for hospitality, for saving people – just like his mother and her adopted children, Henry and Amy. Now, he was not going to take that step over the precipice. He sat back and folded his arms tightly across his chest. He would get Thérèse to help.

'I must be getting back,' he said. They had been in the café for an hour or so. 'I can't leave you like this. Come and have lunch with us, and we can all talk.'

CHAPTER 41

August 1955

As she worked her way through her notes, Thérèse realised the end was in sight. It was just as well: it was already halfway through Thursday, and her tutor would be back at the weekend. She couldn't wait to hear his take on her queries; not that he would answer them – far from it. She had never met with anything but challenges from him. That was what she relished about his supervision. But she felt she had got as far as she could on her own, and needed to find some perspective on her work.

She sighed, pushing her hair back impatiently from her face, and stacked the notebooks on her desk, placing careful markers as she did so. The flat was quiet with Gad out, and the wind was rattling the ill-fitting windows. She stretched and wandered from room to room, relishing the silence. Every room had been painted plain white, to reflect as much light from the distant sky as possible. She looked at the curtains in the living-room, which Gad had bought from Heals to make the place look welcoming for her. They were of Swedish linen, with a geometric pattern of dark greens and blues to complement the blue carpet, and were more austere than she would have chosen, but still, she appreciated his intention. Laying a hand on the piano as she left, she went back into the bedroom, and thought that they really should have curtains for this room when they could afford them. This time, she would choose. The piles of books and papers on the floor of the bedroom were beginning to irritate her; it was time to bring some order into them. She would put together some lunch; sit down with Gad to hear about the house-hunting; go for a walk, maybe; then settle down for another session.

At the sound of his key in the lock, she hurriedly straightened the remaining materials. She was a little curious to hear voices, though it was not unusual for Gad to bring a friend home unexpectedly – who was this, and how long would they stay? Pulling her sleeves down, she went to the bedroom door. Valerie! Damn! Gad was close behind. He looked worried.

'Thérèse! Just say if you're busy,' said Valerie, glancing into the bedroom, and seeing the piles of paper.

Trust her to butt in straight away, before anyone else could speak. Thérèse looked enquiringly at Gad, who was closing the front door after the visitor.

'I ran into Valerie in Hampstead,' he explained, coming forward to kiss Thérèse, his face lingering against hers, his hand on the small of her back. 'She's got a big problem. She needs to talk to someone, so I brought her back here. Is that all right?'

His eyes searched her face, and she could see his need for reassurance. She gave him the nod he was looking for, but she was disappointed all the same. There would be much to discuss after Gad's first stab at house-hunting; she felt that he had rushed into it without much forethought, and she wanted to talk it over with him. Valerie was an intrusion. She knew by now, though, how Gad's mind worked, what his priorities were.

Actually, she quite liked Valerie, appreciated her exuberance, her enthusiasm – but found it not so much contagious as overwhelming.

'No, no. I've finished for the time being,' she said with belated politeness, leading her into the sitting-room, with its cramped living space.

Valerie halted in the doorway, astonished by the acreage given to the piano, with so little space left for anything else. 'Gosh! That's some piano!' she exclaimed.

In the light, Thérèse could see Valerie's face as she spoke and realised she had been crying.

'Exactly the same size as yours,' Gad was saying with some pride. 'It's just that our room is so much smaller. Come, sit down.' He indicated a small easy chair near the window. 'Thérèse and I will make some sandwiches, and we can all talk while you eat – keep your strength up, you know!'

His attempt at a joke was met with blank silence.

Thérèse felt herself hustled into the kitchen. 'What's up?' she whispered.

'She's pregnant.'

'*Mon dieu* – really? So, is she getting married?'

'It's worse than that. It's Sanjay. Her father will go crazy.'

'*Zut!*' said Thérèse. She sat down suddenly on the edge of the bath. Sanjay had always been an unknown quantity to her, secretive in his ways, but she knew Gad and he used to talk together at the House. 'What idiots!'

'Yep. But Sanjay can be very persuasive. I've seen it before.'

'Have you?' She looked at him for a moment, wondering what he had known. For the first time in months, she thought of Paris. Then she saw Gad was watching for her reaction. If she were honest with herself, she didn't quite know how to respond. Past events seemed to be flooding her mind, drowning out everything else. She knew she wanted to hide all that from Gad, though. She would tell him one day soon – she would. But not now – not when it would be all mixed up with Valerie's problems.

To take her mind off herself, she began looking in the cupboard to find something to put in sandwiches, saying to Gad, 'Why don't you do the coffee?'

They busied themselves in thoughtful silence, the clatter

of plates and knives sounding loud; water hissed into the coffee pot, cupboard doors opened and shut. Valerie would have to have an abortion, like Thérèse herself. That was a bleak idea – and where would she get the money? Oh, the stupidity of it all! Sanjay certainly had nothing. She buttered bread viciously. At least Guillaume had had plenty of money. She was trying to be sensitive to the situation, but the gears in her mind jammed as she realised the enormity of the secret she had kept from Gad. And she must still keep that secret, at least until they had dealt with Valerie – helped her if possible.

And then, how could Valerie get pregnant without even trying? That made her furious. The ache never quite went away.

Gad was watching the coffee. 'Is something wrong?' he asked, his back to her.

'Oh no, I'm fine.' Thérèse tried to smile, but was not convincing. She lifted a tray loaded with mugs, a plate of cheese sandwiches and a bowl of apples. 'Poor Valerie.' She took the tray through and placed it carefully on the only table in the room, the small round one in the window. Valerie was huddled like a black crow, feathery scarves drifting raggedly from her neck, arms wrapped protectively round her belly. By some strange alchemy her presence had managed to make the room seem dead; the bulk of the closed piano loomed like a cliff over her hunched figure. She said nothing as Thérèse went away to bring the extra chair from the bedroom.

'There now, let's all help ourselves.'

Gad brought the coffee pot in, and they watched him pour with his usual deftness, setting three mugs carefully on the little table before sitting down on the upright chair.

Thérèse sipped for a moment, composing herself before she asked, 'So, what's this all about?'

Valerie was lifting a sandwich to her mouth, but at this her hand froze. 'Hasn't Gad told you?' she said. 'I thought Gad would have told you. Oh please, Gad. Oh, I can't.' She let her hand sink onto her lap and turned her face away. 'I don't want to tell you, Thérèse, when you're so happily married and everything. It's not fair; I don't want to load this on you but – I just don't know what to do!'

Thérèse put in, 'Well, yes, Gad did tell me you're pregnant – and you think Sanjay is the father.'

'Think? Think!' Valerie turned on her, flushing. 'What do you "think" I am? Do you "think" I sleep with every Tom, Dick and Harry? Of course it's Sanjay – and I shan't see him for dust, I don't suppose!' She clutched at her hair. The sandwich fell to the ground. Thérèse would have put her arms round her, but restrained herself in time. This was Valerie.

'Well, won't he help you? Do you want to marry him?'

'He wouldn't marry me, even if I wanted him to. I know he wouldn't.'

'You have told him?'

'Told him? No, because it would never work, anyway. How could I live in India…?'

Unable to sit any longer, Valerie jumped up and began to move around haphazardly in the confined space, hemmed in by window and piano.

'He's going back, then?' Thérèse sat back in her chair, giving her space.

'He made that perfectly clear. This is his last year.' She stood still, her hand over her eyes. 'I wouldn't be surprised if he's got a little wife back home, anyway.'

'Possible, I suppose. Gad?' Thérèse felt her wits deserting her, needed him to help with everything he had brought crashing into her life.

'I don't know, but yes. He might have.'

'But you ought to give him the chance anyway, shouldn't you?' Thérèse insisted, looking up at Valerie.

'What's the point?' Defeated, Valerie sat down again. At least she had calmed down enough to debate things.

'Here, drink this. There's the sugar – take plenty.'

They were quiet.

Then Gad said slowly: 'The problem is, Valerie dreads telling her parents. They won't like it at all.'

'Tell them?' Valerie's voice rose again to a wail. 'Can you imagine what it would be like? All Daddy's plans for me gone to waste! And the shame! Daddy's girl having a black baby…'

'But…' said Gad, then Thérèse saw him shut his mouth. She shot a glance at him, and saw that he would say no more.

'Well,' she declared, beginning to tire of these histrionics. 'I'm really sorry you're in this problem, but you will have to decide. If you cannot marry Sanjay, will you keep the baby or not?'

'Not?' Valerie seemed startled, as if this possibility had not occurred to her.

'You don't have to have it,' Thérèse said briskly. 'Things can be arranged, you know, but you will need money.'

Gad shot her a glance, half admiring but half disgusted, that said, 'practical as ever'. Thérèse knew what Catholics thought.

'You don't mean an abortion? No, I couldn't.' Down went her head.

'Yes, you could. It's not exactly legal, but I am sure there are plenty of doctors – yes, good ones – who will do it privately. There certainly are in Paris…' Thérèse caught herself, biting her lip. Gad gave her another sharp look.

Valerie, in tears again, hiccupped, 'An abortion? God no, it's far too dangerous! People can die! You can get infected! And anyway, the poor little baby…'

'The poor little baby?' Thérèse was running out of patience, and her tone was harsh. 'How far gone are you? Seven or eight weeks? That's not a baby yet – but it soon will be if you don't do anything.' If she had had a glass of water handy she might have thrown it in Valerie's face. 'Get Sanjay to fork out! He'll have to borrow the money somehow – tell him you'll report him to his college if he says no.'

'Oh no, no, I can't...' She sobbed hysterically.

'Well, what are you going to do, then?' She jumped up. 'Bring the baby up alone in some bedsit?' She had to bring Valerie to her senses. 'And what landlady will let you do that? Ask Mummy and Daddy to help?'

'No, no, it would break their hearts!'

Thérèse reached the end of her tether. 'Then get an abortion! I did! It wasn't too bad...' She broke off, and stood in petrified silence, not daring to look at Gad. Her face was stiff with terror. This was not what she had meant to say at all – nor the time to say it. She risked a quick glance. Gad had turned to stone. He was staring at her.

'Excuse me, I need a cigarette,' he said, and left the room.

Thérèse half rose to follow him, but turned back for a second to say hastily, 'You mustn't mind me. It's just – I've been through something like this myself, so I know how it can be done. You have to be realistic. This baby will not go away. An abortion seems like the only solution. I know it's not nice. Look, stay here a moment. I'll be back.'

She went out to the kitchen, leaving the food for Valerie but taking the empty mugs. Gad was at the back door, smoking. Thérèse put the mugs carefully into the sink and stood beside him, saying nothing. Valerie could look after herself for a while; this was too important. She put her hand on Gad's arm without speaking.

'You never told me,' he said, without looking at her.

'I was going to,' she said. It sounded trite. She took away her hand.

'But you didn't.'

271

'No.'

Silence. She could hear the ticking of his watch.

'I don't really know you,' he said.

'Yes you do – really! It was so long ago – in Paris. Long before I knew you, or even came to England.'

'But it still happened. Why?' He stubbed out his cigarette and turned at last to face her.

She looked back, drowning in his hostility, waiting to see gentleness return to these stony eyes. There would be no softening until she had told the story. She took a deep breath. Gad leaned against the doorjamb, watching her. She tried to stand firm and not waver.

'I was at the Sorbonne,' she said. 'It was after Alain was killed. There was this young lawyer – he was two years ahead of me, and he swept me off my feet...'

'Without you knowing it, I suppose.'

'Yes it was, actually,' she said, with a spark of resentment against his sudden sarcasm. 'Paris was new to me, the work was hard, and I had no money. He just – overwhelmed me, I suppose. He made me feel helpless: not like you.' She cut herself short, afraid he might see this as an insult to his pride, rather than the compliment she intended.

'So, what's the story?' He seemed more interested in what had happened to Thérèse than in this other man.

'Well, I got pregnant, obviously...' with a quick glance to gauge Gad's expression, which was unreadable. 'He wasn't serious about me, as it turned out. He had money and the right contacts. He arranged everything, and I turned up at a clinic – there was a shiny brass plate outside – and went through with it, and then he took me in a taxi back to my room. He stayed with me for an hour, and then left me to it. I never saw him again.'

At that Gad looked at her properly.

'No?' He still seemed miles away, though.

'No.'

He moved then, though slowly, and gathered her into his arms. He held her until the tension eased out of her and she relaxed against him. For the moment they were safe. For the moment no more hurtful words were going to be said.

CHAPTER 42

August 1955

As they went back to Valerie in the living-room, Gad heard letters falling through the letterbox, and went to pick them up. He slit the envelopes open mechanically, and saw that one was a letter of congratulation from Murray, another an invitation to play at a women's club in North London – no mention of a fee. A third was from his family. He dropped them on the bed till later.

He stood for a moment in the bedroom, before facing the two women again. Like a drowning man, he saw his family's life in Burma flash on some magic inward screen: his parents, not rich, in their small flat in Rangoon, undefended, fearful of invasion by the Japanese, and then – preserving their lives at all costs – parting from their children to keep them safe, whilst they attempted the long trek to India, struggling over mountains of mud and across raging rivers.

His head was aching; there was a pain in the back of his neck. There was too much going on, and he felt unable to concentrate on any single issue; the way ahead was clouded with disquiet that prevented him from thinking straight. Thérèse in that clinical room – a white-coated figure bending over her – alone… It was unimaginable.

And then, a cold anger at that lover of hers. Not a word of comfort for Thérèse? In Burma nobody would be left to go through such a thing alone. It must have hurt her. And what happened to the unwanted – stuff? He forced himself to feel the reality of it. How could Thérèse speak of it so clinically?

*Then – that is the only way for her to cope with this. I should never
have landed Valerie's situation on her, but I didn't know –* and round
and back to her secrecy.

Valerie had eaten half a sandwich and finished her coffee.

'Good, you've eaten,' said Gad, adding with insistent
Burmese hospitality. 'Have more. Come, come.' And he
pushed the plate towards her, but Valerie turned away, rejecting
both him and the food.

Thérèse was back to her practical self. 'You know there
are other ways? We haven't yet talked of adoption,' she said
tentatively.

'No.' Gad took over. 'But then, you'd have to have the
baby first and your parents would have to know.'

'No, they wouldn't,' said Valerie, waking up at last, her
eyes wide open with new hope. 'I could pretend I was away
on a course, in Paris or somewhere...' Thérèse flinched, not
meeting Gad's eye. '... have the baby, get it adopted and then
come home. They need never know...' She faltered, hearing
the impossibility of this even as she said it: how long the whole
thing would take to arrange; how her parents would want to
know all about the course, or visit her in Paris. They were not
'hands off' parents – never had been. 'No, that couldn't work,'
she said, downcast. 'If only I knew somebody...'

Gad echoed her 'No', not wanting to be the one to point
out that European families might not want a 'half-caste' baby.

'Look,' said Thérèse after a pause. 'Look, this isn't
something to decide in a hurry. You'll have to do something
soon, but you won't be showing for a while yet. Gad could
speak to Sanjay, and find out what his situation is...'

Gad put his hand out in protest, but was ignored.

'... and meantime, Val, you should go home and try
to weigh things up – talk to other friends too, if you can,
without your family finding out. If you like, I'll try and ask
about doctors here.' She never looked at Gad. 'In case you

decide to go ahead, you could stay here for a night or two afterwards.'

'Could I?'

'Bien sur.'

'Oh thank you, Thérèse, you're a star.' She leaned over and gave Thérèse a hug. Gad noted her slight recoil, and wondered about it.

They drew apart, and he could see Valerie bracing herself, ready now to face the world.

'I'll walk you to the bus,' said Gad, and opened the door for her, following her up into the street.

★

Thérèse went through into the bedroom and stood at the window, watching their feet pass. She felt tired to the bone, and at the same time (if that were possible) wound up tight with the tension of it all. She looked longingly at her books, but knew she could not retreat into her work that day. Events were too urgent.

If she could only take it all back! She could think of nothing else. It was the wrong way to do it. Not that there was a right way. Gad was a Catholic. He was sure to think her action wicked. That was the problem – why she had found it so difficult to tell him before. She wondered what a Catholic girl in her predicament – which was now Val's – would do? Go to a convent, probably, and let the child be brought up as a slave? No, probably that was ridiculous – her father's anti-clerical suspicion, not her own.

The question was, would Gad get over it? 'Forgive' was not the word. Not his prerogative. She began to speculate – not for the first time – why she was not pregnant yet herself. She had conceived once before, after all, so why not now when she was hungry for a child? She even allowed herself to think that Gad could be responsible. Well, at least it was out in the open now. She spared a quick thought for Valerie, and was ashamed of her moment of recoil. A hug was what Val had needed, but for Thérèse the physical contact was too much.

Staring up through the dusty window, she saw Gad's feet return, and went to the door eagerly, hating to be at odds with him.

But when he came in, she saw him holding out a letter to her, wanting to tell her something himself.

'Just look at what came just now!' he said indignantly. 'These women – they want me to go up to Willesden to give half an hour of music for their club's AGM; no talk of a fee, or even expenses! Who do they think I am, a schoolboy? I'm not going.'

'I'm sure they don't.' Did she care? At this moment, his dilemma was of no interest to her.

'Well, I did play for free when I was sixteen, for all sorts of things – but in return I was excused fees for my school in Simla, and that was worth a few pennies, I can tell you! I'm not doing it for nothing now!' He paced up and down the bedroom.

'It might help you get started.' She thought Gad would think her uncaring, but he was too angry to notice.

'I got started when I was sixteen!' he exclaimed.

'But I mean here, in London.'

There was no stopping him. 'No! It would set me off on the wrong footing. Why should I do that?'

'Well – how did they hear about you? Maybe Val's father put them on to you...' Gad glared at her. '... or Murray?' At that Gad stopped short. 'You don't want to upset him, do you?'

'That's true. Tell you what, I'll ask Murray, if he's around.' He seemed relieved to think there was something he could do.

'Yes, and if not, perhaps you should just do it anyway. You never know where it may take you.' She had been drawn in, wanted to calm him, to get back to her own preoccupation. Gad acted as if all that was settled – all over – and he was on to the next thing already.

'Yes, I suppose. I'd better write to Murray now – thank him for his letter, and ask him about this.' He made for the door.

'Yes, you do that. But listen –' she held him back.

'Yes?' He was standing with his hand on the doorknob, ready to put his words into action.

'Please. Wait a minute. Don't rush off. Come over here. You can do your letter later on.' She sat down on the bed and made room for him.

'All right then – what do you want?' he asked impatiently. 'You wanted me to get on with things!'

'No – come here. I've got something on my mind.' Her voice was firm. It had to be. Still he stood by the door, alert as a cat, poised to run. She coaxed. 'Please. Just for a minute. It's all right.'

Reluctantly, he let go of the door and moved to sit stiffly beside her. It was not far, but he made it seem like a long journey.

'Well?' he said, his eyes making the question hard.

'I never wanted to hurt you.' It came out as abrupt. 'You do know that?'

'Yes.'

'I wanted to tell you, many times. But there was never a good time, and when I did not say anything, that made it worse. You see that?'

'Yes.'

She tried again. 'Do you understand why I did it?'

A pause. 'That is more difficult.' He stared blindly at the wall.

'Why?' She had to know whether condemnation was his own gut feeling, or whether she could reasonably blame the Pope.

'You cannot just – dispose of a life,' he said with difficulty and great seriousness. She understood that these were not empty words.

'Nobody wants to – but sometimes it is the only option. I hated the idea – really hated it.' The polished brass plate, the pavement, Guillaume beside her, smiling.

'Why do it, then? You're the practical one. Couldn't you have gone home and had the baby? Wouldn't there be somebody who would look after it? My mother did this…'

'Your mother – did she?' She couldn't see her own hardworking mother welcoming an extra baby into her life.

'Sure, so many times. She looked after several babies born during the war – one at least had a Japanese father, and that was not very popular, you can imagine. Our house was always full of children. Were there not wartime babies in France?'

Thérèse was still, thinking back to her war. There had been French girls who had 'fraternised' – that was the word – with German men during the Occupation. Local people had hounded them, shaving their heads for shame. And their babies – there must have been babies. Nobody had asked.

But Thérèse had been ignorant. She never realised that Guillaume was not going to marry her, or even support his child. Her parents would have thought her stupid, and so she had been – oh, it was all impossible.

'I didn't know what to do,' was all she could say.

'Why couldn't you have prevented the pregnancy in the first place?' He didn't understand anything, she thought in frustration. Yes, she could have resisted Guillaume – but she hadn't really wanted to.

'Because I didn't know how', she said, impatient with him now, wanting to move on. 'Anyway, it's done now. I was a different person then. It was long before I met you. We're together now – it's now we have to think about. I so much

279

want us to have our own child, but it's not happening and – how can Valerie be so lucky? It's not fair!'

'Valerie is like you were in Paris. She doesn't want to be pregnant.'

'I know, I know. I wonder what she will decide to do.'

Gad gave her an odd look, which she could not interpret. 'I suppose you want me to talk to Sanjay?'

She was relieved that he had suggested it himself. 'I think you'd better,' she said. 'Surely he's not a bad person.'

'Not bad exactly, no. Careless, I think you'd say.' He got up. 'I'll go now, the sooner the better,' pointing to the letters lying on the bed. 'You might read those, and see what you think.'

CHAPTER 43

AIR MAIL
18th August 1955

Dear Garrard

We are all proud and excited to hear about your great success in the Diploma. I, for one, never doubted that you would achieve a Distinction, but the star on the Distinction means so much more, since it is so rare. Were you (as I believe) the only student to gain such an honour? Congratulations for the results of your natural ability and, on top of all that, your years of hard work. Those practice hours must have been well spent!

My only concern now is that you are able to launch your career in the way you want and deserve. I have already heard the San Francisco Symphony twice, each time with a piano soloist, and I seemed to hear you in the music. But I understand it will take time to build a reputation before such performances will come your way, and now that you have a wife to support, it will not be easy to give proper time and attention to your music. Here there are only the big classical concerts or the jazz, dance or light music events. Perhaps in London there are different paths to take.

When you begin your London career, be sure to let us know how you are doing.

Here we are settling down to life without Big Mummy. Veena and Don are planning to buy their own house soon, probably up in the hills. Julian is about to start work on a newspaper in Oakland, and will find himself a small place there. Now that we are all safe from discrimination in Burma, we can set about establishing ourselves, each household separately, in this beautiful place. California is not yet our true home, but it is our future, which we are looking to as you must to yours.

With love and God Bless from all of us,
Your sister Wilma

Gad's response to this was complex. His first reaction was the physical shock of seeing Wilma's writing in place of his mother's. Then he reread the letter, and thought of Wilma's lifelong love of music, relishing the fact that now she lived near a city where good concerts were available to her.

Lastly, he found a new interest in her opinion, seeing that she understood better than anyone else the challenges that lay ahead for him. She, of all people, single and childless herself, had managed to take a view of life wider than simply family matters. He remembered hearing of Burmese carvings that she had been buying, and hoped that these would keep and maybe increase in value. Like their father, she was also a trained accountant, and would be able to practise this business to keep herself in funds.

CHAPTER 44

August 1955

The steps of the House felt strange to Gad as he ran up them. It seemed an age since he had visited. The old crowd was losing its hold on him, though several of them dropped into the flat from time to time – not Sanjay anymore, he realised.

He went straight into the untidy office. Nothing much had changed. There was the same sense of purposeful chaos, as Elspeth and the duty staff prepared to meet the unpredictable. This evening he was the unpredictable, and there were little screams of joy as the girls greeted him: 'Lovely to see you!' 'Where have you been?' 'How's Thérèse?' and 'What's the news?'

It was six o'clock, and soon everybody would be gathering for the evening meal.

'You'll stay for supper,' they demanded.

'No, no, sorry. Thérèse is expecting me back,' he said. The phrase was strange in his mouth, both exciting and embarrassing. 'I'll just – er – look in upstairs – see who's around…'

He made his escape, taking the stairs two at a time, having adopted a Londoner's sense of urgency.

He stuck his face into the lecture room – nobody. The old Blüthner beckoned, and he couldn't resist playing a phrase or two, but without company there seemed to be little savour in it, so he went on upstairs to Sanjay's room, hoping to find him alone. By good luck he was, his door open. Gad saw his trim figure lying relaxed on one of the beds, in loose orange pyjamas. Smoke rose from the cigarette in his hand.

Gad went in without knocking, shut the door behind him, and at the sound, Sanjay turned his head, waving a languid arm. He made no attempt to get up.

'Gad! What brings you here?' he murmured.

'Guess.' Gad's voice came out uncharacteristically clipped.

'No. I can't. Tell me.'

'It's about Valerie, of course.'

Sanjay took a longer draw on his cigarette. 'Ah! What about her?'

Gad felt his temper rise, and his voice had an edge to it. 'She hasn't told you, then? You don't know she is pregnant?'

Sanjay seemed to be examining the ceiling with some interest. 'That silly girl. These English girls are so ignorant. I am shocked.' With no change of expression, he flicked ash off his cigarette onto the floor beside the bed.

'And you had nothing to do with it?' Gad demanded, tight-lipped.

'Of course I must have been somewhat involved, but naturally I expected her to take care of things. Otherwise, why would she enter into such an arrangement?'

'So you had some sort of arrangement?' Gad folded his arms, his back against the doorpost.

'Oh no, that was just a manner of speaking. It was all quite casual.' He turned his head to look at Gad. 'She should have taken care of herself.'

Gad felt the blood rise in his face. 'So,' he said deliberately, 'you feel you have no responsibility at all? You left it all to chance, or to her?' He shrugged. 'Fine – but perhaps she is ignorant?'

'I don't know. I didn't ask.' Sanjay blew a smoke ring.

'Or perhaps –' Gad began to walk about the room, 'have you thought of this – she trusted you? And now, what about the child?'

'Oh, this is all so tedious.' Sanjay sat up gracefully, swung

284

his legs down and stubbed his cigarette out in an unseen ashtray.

Gad stopped himself from lunging at this figure, sitting there so relaxed. He needed to inflict bodily damage, but what earthly use would that be? Throwing his fists in the air, he turned and shouldered his way out, not bothering to close the door. No wonder so many English people regarded foreign students with suspicion – they would think Sanjay's behaviour typical, and it reflected on him too, however unfairly. It was frustrating, to have tried and failed to persuade Sanjay to face up to his responsibilities – it wasn't going to happen. Sanjay would be a rotten father, anyway.

He left without a word to anybody, stood on the pavement raging, stuffed his hands into his pockets and strode off, not sure where. There was something about Sanjay that completely threw him: that he could simply detach himself. Gad had the feeling that he would soon forget who Valerie was.

He found himself on the broad stretch of Euston Road, opposite the station, and stood indecisively at the pavement's edge as the traffic poured past, busy yet orderly. *To think that such messes come about even in England.* What had happened in wartime Burma was bad enough – the country overrun by foreigners, families scattered, girls assaulted, impregnated, made sick, abandoned; surely here, in England, it shouldn't be happening?

Thérèse had made a terrible choice – had been forced to take it when she was young and isolated. He trusted the Thérèse he knew – must believe what she told him. He was not there.

And now Valerie – what were her options now? And how close could he allow her to get? He knew she liked him; that was obvious. She was so obvious. And dangerous.

Suddenly, he realised what he was going to do. Jay-walking

across the dual carriageway with its iron railings, he dived into the Underground and bought a ticket to Hampstead.

★

In the hallway of Bernard's beautiful house once more Gad waited, no longer intimidated by its clean grace and elegance. His blood was up. Valerie would hate to know he was there. A car purred to a halt in the driveway, and hearing a key in the lock, Gad braced himself to meet Bernard.

The big man came in with his heavy tread, hooded eyes lighting on Gad at once.

'Well, well,' he said. He dropped his car keys on a glass table. 'The wanderer returns!'

So Bernard assumed that he had come back to beg for the patronage he had once rejected? Gad steeled himself. He was not going to be put in the wrong. He would be at a disadvantage until he had explained the real reason for his visit, so he must just get on with it. There in the luxurious hallway he stood his ground.

'Good evening, sir. How are you?' What he had to say would not be welcome. He was doubtful that he would be allowed to stay once the news was broken. But he was the messenger, and he must get to the point – be heard to the end.

'Fine, fine. But I don't suppose you've come to ask that, have you?' Bernard moved towards the drawing-room, perhaps in need of a drink.

'No. Actually, I have something important to tell you, and it's not about me...'

Bernard stopped in his tracks. 'Not? Oh. Really?'

'No. Let me explain.' Gad stood still, regarding the older man steadily.

Bernard was already impatient. 'Do that!' he said.

'It's about Valerie, sir.' Gad felt a little sorry for him, for

286

his present anxiety and for what he would have to understand soon.

'What about her? And what's it got to do with you?' Bernard made to turn away again.

'It's all right, she's safe and sound.'

'What the hell, then?' said Bernard, red-faced. 'What the hell is it?'

'Could we perhaps sit down somewhere?' he asked. 'And your wife – is Adèle at home? Could she join us?'

Oddly, and without willing it, Gad realised that he was in the driving seat.

But Bernard took command again. 'Certainly not. She's out, anyway. You'd better come in here.' And he strode across the hall to a small room opening off it. It was set up as a study in dark wood and leather, though Gad could see that the books were only part of the furnishings, not real. It was a man's room, Bernard's room.

He sat down at the desk in a director's chair with arms, and indicated an armless chair opposite for Gad, who would have preferred to remain standing.

Gad began, feeling his way. 'So, Valerie,' he said slowly. 'She is a good friend of ours, you know…'

Bernard gave a curt nod.

'… and I'm afraid she has a problem. Of course, she doesn't know I'm here.' To his surprise, the right words were coming to him now.

'Why would she talk to you?' Bernard cut in. It was insulting.

'Because she knew – I know – that you are going to be angry.' Gad waited.

'My family never gives me cause for anger.' It was said with authority.

Gad thought this might be part of the problem. Bernard was so very sure of his wife and daughter. They were not

287

expected to make decisions for themselves, so that Valerie had no experience of dealing with real issues.

'Sir, you know Valerie better than we do…'

'Certainly do.'

'Yes. So you know she's impulsive and – loves life. Loves attention, and all that.'

'Nothing wrong in that.' Bernard was on the defensive. His bearlike paw reached for a cigarette from an ivory box and lit it with the matching desk lighter. He did not invite Gad to light up. 'What are you saying?'

'Well – that she might not be willing to wait for your plans for her; she might have sort of – plunged into something on her own.'

'Doesn't sound like my little girl.' Bernard sat back. 'So, you'd better tell me what it is she's "plunged into". Make it short.'

'Fine. In a nutshell, she has – become involved with a young man, but not in the marrying way.' Gad paused.

'You're saying – she's having an affair?'

'Had. And she's pregnant.' It was out.

Bernard drew in his breath, and a vein throbbed in his temple. 'What?'

'I'm afraid so. And…' Gad felt he must throw the whole bombshell at once, 'the young man is a penniless student, and he's from overseas, like me.'

He paused, and Bernard gave him a sharp look.

'He's Indian,' said Gad.

Bernard's face darkened, and he burst out with controlled venom: 'You mean he's black? You're sure this – student – isn't yourself? Or if not, I suppose you introduced them?'

So there it was, exactly as he expected. Well, if Bernard thought any of that, he probably believed that all 'black' people were feckless, must at least know each other, might even be responsible for each other.

Gad sat it out, while Bernard ranted on.

'You people – you all stick together. I'm not having it. I'm not having any of this.' His fist crashed down on the desk, making a paperweight of the Statue of Liberty jump. At the time, it was not funny. 'What the hell did you think you were doing? You think it's a game? My daughter's future? Hah?'

Gad looked at the reddened, furious face, the eyeballs bulging. He tried to judge when it would be time to go on. He made no reply to Bernard's tirade, not wishing to be thrown out before they had got to the point.

'And all the time I was trying to help you!' Bernard raged.

This was too much for Gad. 'It's not about me though, sir, is it?'

More fulminating.

'I didn't actually introduce them, and I think Valerie has been very unwise...'

'Hah? You think so, do you?'

Ignoring the flak, Gad kept trying to make his point, wishing that Adèle could have been here – she would at least have listened.

'But what I'm concerned about, sir, is...' he persisted, 'what is Valerie going to do about it? Now...' He held his hand up firmly before Bernard could get going again. 'I know it's not my place...'

'You can say that again – bloody wog!'

Gad ignored this. '... but I've been to see Sanjay...'

'Sanjay? Good grief!'

'... and it seems he cannot be relied on.'

'Well, he's not English anyway. As if we'd want her to be with him! Let him go back where he came from – anywhere but here!' Again, objects rattled on the desk.

'Yes. So of course we know that good doctors can be found to...' His mind's eye saw the brass plate by that door in Paris.

But Bernard exploded at the mere suggestion. 'What the hell are you suggesting?'

'... but Valerie is simply appalled at the idea.'

'You've spoken to her about it?'

Gad nodded. 'She spoke to me.'

'Good grief! This has gone too far. This is a matter entirely for the family. You've done more than enough – come and told us, got her into it in the first place, no doubt...'

'No.'

'... and now you think you can decide what she should do? Outrageous! It's completely outrageous!'

He sank back in his chair, the wind knocked right out of him. Gad seized the opportunity to finish what he had come to say.

'Sir, all this must be a terrible shock to you, and I'm sorry to have been the one to break it to you. But when you have discussed this with Adèle...'

'My God! How am I going to tell her? None of your business, anyway!'

'When you have – I wondered... You know, my mother back home, when she was a little younger – she looked after several children who were not really legitimate, as you might say...'

'What?!'

'One at least had a Japanese father, and you can imagine how people felt about that.'

'Listen to me, you,' Bernard said, with icy contempt. 'How is that any concern of ours? This is England – we don't behave like that; taking on any little bastard that's going!' And he got to his feet, fury written on his face.

He was throwing Gad out. *So that's it,* Gad thought, the insult to his mother piercing him. *I've tried.* There was really no more to say. At the very least, perhaps he had broken the ice for Valerie. But now what?

CHAPTER 45

August 1955

Resolute, Thérèse went upstairs to see Carmen; who else could she ask? She believed Carmen had lived in the building long enough to know the neighbouring streets. She had been there with her established business and her predictable routine long before the two of them had moved in. She was sure to be able to help.

As she went up the stairs Thérèse could hear the sewing machine whirring, as usual she supposed, although she and Gad had long since blanked out its beat. Today it meant Carmen was in. They had hardly spoken since the delivery of the bed.

After she knocked, there was a small delay: Carmen must be navigating the tricky corner of some garment – a shirt collar, maybe. Then the machine stopped, and Carmen opened the door, pale as ever, with her black hair piled high and smooth. She did not invite Thérèse to go in.

'*Olá?*'

'Carmen, good morning,' Thérèse greeted her with a nervous smile. 'I am sorry to interrupt your work. I would like to ask you –' she hesitated. To her, the question was a profoundly private matter. 'Do you happen to know a good doctor nearby?'

'A doctor? Ah – I see.' Carmen's eyes flicked down to Thérèse's belly. 'A special reason, *sí?*'

'Oh no. I just thought we should sign with a doctor, that is all.' The lying 'we' was a comfort to her, tormented as she was by her childlessness – the irony of her own situation as opposed to Valerie's – and not wanting to think that the problem lay solely with her.

Carmen retreated into her rooms in search of an address, while Thérèse stood on the doorstep trying not to think about Valerie. She never wanted to see the girl again, but the more she tried to forget, the more boldly Valerie marched into her head, full of her own dilemmas, loud and intrusive. Why couldn't Gad see it? His concern should be for her, not for Valerie.

At last Carmen returned with a name and address, and Thérèse managed to thank her coolly and retreat down the stairs. Worry was foremost as she made her way to the doctor's surgery. She didn't want there to be any more secrets, but she had to know whether what had happened to her in Paris had affected her fertility, whether her strong body was finally letting her down.

★

Gad strode at a furious pace down Haverstock Hill, grumbling to himself. *The trouble with Hampstead people is they think they are better than anyone else. Well, perhaps they are,* he conceded. *Well-mannered, with lovely houses. A child would have a good start in life there.* This thought fought with his growing conviction that it would be no place for Sanjay's offspring, that the child would be in some nameless danger there, and that as the years went by the teenager would be a misfit. Sanjay would not be any sort of father.

In any event, Bernard had flatly refused the responsibility – had no heart, or stomach for the task.

It frightened Gad to think of Valerie homeless. She would have a long way to fall; she didn't know how to find lighted doorways on the street, and as far as he knew there was no extended family for her to fall back on.

What do girls do? Young voices from Rangoon spoke urgently into his ears: 'Please help me.' 'He forced me.' 'I didn't mean to do it.' 'Please help.' If Valerie was a Catholic she could find sanctuary, but who was there for her to call on?

He didn't understand how Hampstead worked. He had tried, to no effect. Valerie would be forced to deal with Bernard herself, and Bernard would be obdurate. His prejudices got in the way of helping his own daughter. He was only looking to his family's interests, and in that light, Sanjay was irrelevant, beyond his horizons.

At Belsize Park he shunned the rest of the walk, and took the Underground like any other Londoner.

★

He was back at the flat before he knew it, but was disappointed to find the place empty. Something was brewing in his mind: an idea that lifted his spirits and made his head inflate like a barrage balloon floating up into the light and clarity above the city buildings. He flicked his cigarette out of the window to smoulder in the yard, and paced up and down, impatient for Thérèse to return. When she did not, he went down the corridor to the kitchen and opened the back door wide, taking in deep breaths of the air that was marginally cleaner there than in the street.

Now he must find something else to do, and by habit picked up the coffee percolator which was always to hand, prepared it and set it on the stove to heat, too preoccupied to light the gas. He watched it till he realised his mistake and waited then, doing nothing, listening for Thérèse's step, picturing her face when he broached his big idea.

At last he heard her step, and went eagerly to meet her. She looked at him soberly as she came in, and it struck him that she was rather downcast. Never mind, that would soon change when she heard what he had in mind.

All the same, perhaps the flat was not the best place – somewhere less workaday might be better. Taking Thérèse's elbow to stop her removing her things, he said breathlessly: 'No, come on – let's go out to supper.'

'Out? For supper? Why?'

'Never mind, just come. We deserve a bit of a treat.'

He hurried her out, slamming the door behind them, and along to a small Austrian restaurant nearby, where they had once enjoyed *wiener schnitzel* together. Innocent red-checked tablecloths again; Thérèse disliked them for some reason that she would never tell him – some uncomfortable memory, evidently.

They sat down opposite each other. Their order given to a sullen blond waiter, Gad began at last, unable to contain himself.

'Thérèse, *wunchi*, I've got something to say to you – something exciting and important. Are you ready?'

'Yes – yes. What is it?' He could see her attention returning to him from whatever had been bothering her.

'Well, listen! You and I, we want a family?'

Her face reddened a little. 'Of course we do! You know that and I know that.'

'And so far, we've had no luck?'

She lowered her eyelids. 'No luck,' she said with a sigh.

'No – no,' he said. 'Don't look like that. It will happen – I know it will. It's not long at all.' He put a hand to her cheek; there were little lines of worry at the corners of her mouth.

'We just have to be patient,' she murmured, her eyes on his.

'But that's just it – we need not wait!' he exclaimed triumphantly.

The waiter came between them with their plates.

'And two glasses of red wine, please,' Gad ordered.

'What? What are you talking about?' asked Thérèse with a puzzled frown, twisting her hair back behind one ear.

'Right, listen,' said Gad in a lower tone, picking up his knife and fork but not yet eating a morsel. 'I've been to see Bernard, and he is definitely not in the mood to help Valerie in any way, let alone have her in the house.'

'You told him? Does Valerie know?'

'No, she doesn't. I was trying to make things easier for her.'

'But, behind her back?'

'I know, but he was so angry. It was better for him to be angry with me than with her.'

'Why? Why must you always be into her affairs?' Thérèse looked upset and angry herself. Was there no way to keep everybody calm?

'Well – I did, anyway, and please, just listen,' Gad continued. 'Sanjay is completely useless. Clever, but no principles. And Bernard – well, even if he changed his mind and let her stay to have the baby, he would be so angry, and the baby would be brought up in such a bad atmosphere; I hate to think of it. And they would not understand what it is to be a child of mixed race.'

He saw wariness in Thérèse's eyes, as she said, 'But you – you would understand?'

Had she guessed what was on his mind? Taken aback, he paused in his headlong speech and took a small forkful of meat.

'Yes,' he said quietly. 'Yes, I would. This is a different country, but still it is… the British and the rest, just like everywhere, just like it was at home. I am one of "the rest" – a man with dark skin that I can never change; with an educated British accent, an oddball. A proper "Coringhee pickle" of a man – neither one thing nor another, and disrespected for it. I said "at home", but this is home too. I have two homes, and none. I have to make up my life as I go along. I have never spoken to you about this, but I would understand it, in a child…' he paused, '… would understand this, in Valerie's child.'

He concentrated on his meat, not daring to look at Thérèse, giving her time. There was a long silence. Thérèse crumbled the bread on her side plate.

'You would like us to adopt Valerie's baby,' she said flatly, at last.

'It was an idea I had,' he replied, lamely, then held his breath.

'But what about our own children?'

'Of course we shall have our own children, my darling. And they will come, in time. But just now, there are only the two of us, and there is this baby, who might need us, and – just imagine, sweetheart. What do you think?'

He could see it all: Thérèse with a baby in her arms, the three of them snug in their own home, and by the time others came along, perhaps they would find somewhere bigger, with a garden even. A swing perhaps, like English families had? A pet tortoise that he would put to hibernate, and release in the spring? And a good education for them all, of course.

'Your mother, she would do it, would she not?'

'In a heartbeat!'

Silence.

'Let's go,' said Thérèse, pushing her plate to one side.

'Fine.' Gad took a last gulp of wine, before settling the bill and going after her into the street. Which way would things go? He had no idea; he could only follow Thérèse's lead, and actually, he was not even persuaded of the rightness of his own suggestion. It was his gut instinct that the thing would fit neatly with both Valerie's needs and their own, but it was far from being a plan.

★

Thérèse's back was towards him as he caught up with her. The evening had darkened, large raindrops were falling fast and the pavements were already wet. To his surprise, Thérèse had turned away from home, as though she needed to be in motion.

'You'll get wet,' he said. 'Shall we get into a doorway?'

She shook her head, and he saw strands of hair were already sticking to her forehead, giving her an oddly dissipated air. Without turning, she tucked her arm into his and they fell into step, warmed by the wine though half-blinded by the rain that stung their faces as they walked.

'You see,' she said, 'to me, Valerie is a kind of alien – can I say that? And I have never liked Sanjay very much. They did not make this baby with love, and I am afraid...'

'I know.'

'Could I love it?' Silence, while each thought about this.

'I know. But the baby will need parents.'

'There must be others who want to adopt a baby.'

'One of mixed race?'

It was her turn to say 'I know.'

They zigzagged down through back streets lined with rubbish bags and overflowing bins, the trade entrances of big stores and restaurants, the backside of the West End. Without a word said, both knew where they were heading. It was where they always ended up at times of crisis.

'Is it because you want to be as good as your mother?' she asked suddenly.

Gad took a sharp breath, as after a physical blow to the heart. His mother was suddenly there beside him, walking in the rain, grumbling indignantly to herself about the discomfort he was inflicting on her. Her presence invaded him; how watchful she was of those she loved; how generous in action; how her rounded face could look both disapproving and gentle at the same moment – her mysterious authority. Only she had ambition for him – plans that it was his job to fulfil.

'No,' he said at last. 'Not as good as her – that was not what she wanted. She wanted me to be successful and famous. That was what music meant to her.' He pondered for a moment before, with one of his typical swerves, he went on: 'Did I ever tell you about the diamond earrings?'

'No.'

'You see, I was not strong as a baby, and my mother made a bargain with God: that she would give her diamond earrings to the Church if He would save me. Well, He did, as you see – and you lost the earrings!'

'I?'

'Yes – the earrings were supposed to go to my wife!'

'Oh dear!' said Thérèse in mock dismay. 'Well, I suppose I will have to be satisfied with you only, then!' And she squeezed his hand tight.

Sensing an absence, Gad looked round for his mother, and realised that she was no longer there, walking beside him or even in his head. For a moment, he could not even remember what he used to call her. 'Mother' seemed too formal, 'Mum' too English. 'Big Mummy' – that was it. Everybody called her that. But he could not recall ever saying it directly to her. With every step they took, he felt he was walking away from her, leaving her standing alone in the English rain.

CHAPTER 46

August 1955

It was nearly ten o'clock by the time they came to the river. The rain had stopped. They went by streets leading from Charing Cross Station and down steps to the Embankment, leaving behind the neon bustle and finding only a dim expanse of water faintly lit, the street lights here standing on ornate columns. There was the tide with its reflections that marked out the water's movement. There was the dank smell, coming from way back in the past. And then, the fabulous new building opposite, veiled in rain, built of hope and optimism. It was like no other public place in London, had not yet acquired its patina of London grime.

Thérèse caught her breath at the brilliance. It always stopped her in her tracks, however many times they walked this way – the Festival Hall, pristine, blazingly modern, with light glittering from banks of glass. Other structures, jetties and the like, floated over the water. She never anticipated the shock these pieces of geometry gave her, toy-like objects that looked too fragile to stand up to wind and rain and the passage of many feet. Well, they had already lasted nearly ten years without crumbling. Such magical constructions made everything possible. One day she and Gad would enter, would purchase concert tickets, truly belong to this city that was shaking off the violence of war and starting to grow wings.

They reached the bank and stood side by side, looking around them and smelling the river as it flowed slowly towards the sea.

On sudden impulse she turned to face him. 'Let's do it,' she said.

'My goodness, that was sudden!'

'Yes, I know. It's the thing to do though, isn't it?' She searched his eyes.

'I thought so.' He looked at her, his own gaze thoughtful. 'You must be feeling brave, then. You know it won't be easy?'

'I am, totally. And happy too!'

'Well, that's the best thing of all. Come here!' and he hugged her, resting his chin on her head – just. Thérèse wished for a fleeting moment that he was a tiny bit taller.

'I hope we're allowed to,' he said, releasing her suddenly as if at an unexpected thought.

'What do you mean, "allowed" to?'

'The rules are what I mean. I mean, we actually know Valerie, and I'm not sure if you can officially adopt from somebody you know. We're in England!'

'We'll have to find out then, or else do the whole thing unofficially…'

'No! Definitely not!' Gad stiffened. 'If we adopt, we do it properly! We can't have any arrangement where they could question British citizenship – all the papers have to be absolutely in order.'

Thérèse had seen Gad's treasured passport, locked with hers into a cashbox safely hidden away in his flat. Their marriage certificate was there too. She remembered his shock when, visiting the India Office to check details on behalf of a cousin, he had seen how sketchy the records of births in Burma had been. Gad had told her then, emphatically, 'Always keep your papers in order. You never know – it could be a matter of life or death one day.'

She thought he exaggerated but, 'Of course,' she said vaguely. 'I know.'

Now her thoughts were far away, with the day in Paris that

still haunted her. To adopt a baby would somehow balance that act. If they turned down the chance, she would be repeating the same awful pattern.

Could they afford it? Of course not, but they would manage – people always did.

'I wonder whether it will be a boy or a girl,' she went on. 'Will it matter to you, which one it is?'

'Nope,' said Gad cheerfully. 'A child's a child.'

'Yes, until it grows up!'

'And I won't be a footballing father, whichever it is.' He whistled a few bars of *Honolulu Honey*. 'That was one of my father's favourites. He used to sing on Sunday afternoons.'

'You need a swanee whistle for that – or a sax. It would be good on a swanee whistle!'

'I suppose. Nice and soupy?'

'That's it. Come on, let's walk,' she said.

They began to stroll downstream, past the Inns of Court; it seemed appropriate if they were considering embarking on an important legal arrangement.

'Course it will be a little Valerie or a little Sanjay! Can you stand that?' He pulled a face.

'You have a point. Perhaps we will arrange, do you think?' She always stumbled over her English when she was moved.

'Ye-e-es! Together we can do anything!'

In this mood of optimism, they continued their walk, Gad's arm looped over her shoulder, enjoying together the cool of the night.

'Imagine Christmas,' he said, 'with children in the house! We must have a tree – they will love tinsel and stuff.'

'Yes, just a small tree this year, and each year a bigger one, with more candles.'

'Now you're getting ambitious!' he teased.

Thérèse sighed. 'I do hope we have our own children as well.'

'Yes.' He looked at her gently. 'All in good time, I'm sure we will. We have to be practical too. We have to find ways of making a good living – we do need a home of our own.'

'So the children can have their friends to stay?'

'Of course – a houseful.'

'Yes.' She signed again, contentedly this time.

Each lost in their thoughts, they wandered along quietly.

'What a pity,' she said, 'that your mother did not live to see this.'

'She would have been so far away though,' he said. 'A good Catholic would believe that she is looking down anyway.'

'A good Catholic?'

'I'm not a very good one. And actually, I can't believe she's floating around up there on a cloud. I don't think I've ever worked out what I believe about death. I don't know that I ever will either – let it come and get me, I won't complain.'

'What, whenever it comes?'

'No, no – only when I reach a ripe old age. Of course!'

'I hope we are both lucky. How do you think of your mother, then? You haven't talked to me about her since…'

'Since she died? No, I couldn't. I got choked, just thinking about her. It was very confusing, my feelings about her. Perhaps it's always like that with the one you're closest to. And I hate to think I did leave her behind, even though I was perhaps her favourite. You know?' He stopped, remembering. 'It seems to me that I came to England as if – on her back, on her wings. Does that make any sense? That although I arranged it all, it was her energy, her love and of course her ambition for me that sort of sent me forth! God, that sounds biblical! Or like a second birth!'

'Oh, Gad.' Thérèse leaned against him. 'I think I see what you mean. But now you're here, and she – passed away, and we have our lives to live. What now?'

'What indeed? I don't exactly miss her because I never truly had her. But I grieve – I do – I miss her voice…'

'I know. I can see.'

'I grieve more for lost opportunities than anything else. I could have said more to her…'

'Yes, it was exactly like that with Alain.'

That made him look at her. 'But she's gone now. No use looking back. And I can see that, bit by bit, she will sort of – recede. But not yet.' He smiled suddenly. 'I'd like her to stay at the party for a while longer anyway.'

★

There was the small matter of putting their idea to Valerie, and Gad thought about how it should be managed. They might easily offend her, by implying that they would make a better job of looking after a baby than she would; or insult her father who had spoken so brutally. They would have to persuade her that the two of them could carry such a responsibility, that between them they could earn enough and give enough time and love to a child in their care.

They would have to think hard about their personal ambitions. Might they have to put both studies and music on hold? How could that be possible?

They needed to reach Valerie at her parents' house without even knowing what had happened between them since Gad's unsettling visit. Would she forgive him for interfering? It was quite possible she wouldn't want to speak to them at all.

They found a call box nearby. Thankfully, it was in working order. Valerie answered the phone on the first ring, and Gad asked her to meet them at the coffee bar in Heath Street, so that they could 'see how you are'.

She sounded agitated.

'I can't talk now,' she said, her voice high and tense. 'See you tomorrow at about ten.' And she rang off.

★

As Thérèse came, and came again, Gad was amazed and then appalled to find that her mouth was a rictus of pain, her face wet with tears that ran across her nose and into her ears.

'What is it, sweet pea, what is it?'

She turned away from him and reached for a handkerchief, then turned back with a watery smile.

'I can't explain it,' she said. 'But don't worry, it's good.'

'You mean, when you cry it's good?'

'I don't know, it's never happened before.' Her arms went tight around his neck, and her head rested on his shoulder. 'Just let's enjoy.'

Gad lay still, content in the moment. *How strange women are!* But he saw a serious message in this episode. Perhaps he had underestimated the degree of tension Thérèse had felt at his proposal. The decision she had made – was it only to please him? Or was it to exorcise the loss of her baby in Paris? Or to distract herself from the fact that she was still not pregnant?

That was a disappointment to him too, but he began to imagine, as they lay warmly entwined, what all this might mean to a woman – to Thérèse. *And Thérèse has her work*, he thought. *How much does her thesis mean to her?*

Her tears had told him of many undercurrents. He looked again at this young woman, her hair pushed back from her face, sleeping against him. He was only beginning to understand her.

He saw her dilemma. She had been presented with a golden opportunity to adopt Valerie's baby at a time when she really wanted one of her own. He understood why she had taken the decision she had, and applauded her. Finally,

304

some decisions had to be made by instinct. Her reasons were different from his, and that was fine.

He envisaged his mother, with her houseful of children demanding her love and attention, and wondered if he and Thérèse were capable of as much.

Detaching himself gently from Thérèse, he got out of bed and reached for a cigarette.

Britain was still recovering from the war, he mused, half asleep, aiming smoke out of the window, although it was already more than ten years since it had ended. There was a new young queen, but she had lost India, and Burma too, though few here would even notice that. There were strikes and the creeping threat of communism from Eastern Europe.

Unlike America, Britain had managed to resist without resorting to witch hunts, and they continued to welcome Commonwealth citizens to settle in their country. It was up to him – him and the others – to make the most of it.

And then there was the Bomb, thought of which sent him back to his warm bed; impossible to contemplate such mindboggling reality when he was so thoroughly embroiled in his own small struggles.

CHAPTER 47

September 1955

Ten o'clock came in the coffee bar. It was rather a smart one, well ventilated, without the cosiness of their usual haunts. They waited; there was no Valerie, but within a few minutes she blew in, bringing with her a gust of fresh air.

At once Gad noticed a difference in her: a kind of clarity he had never seen before. Gone were the fluttering scarves and loose shawls she used to love; here she was, in sweater and slim skirt, hands in the pockets of a warm, stylish jacket. It was a transformation that left him, and Thérèse too, speechless, and they sat staring at her for a moment like surprised children.

Valerie sat down at their table, saying nothing except to call for her cup of black coffee.

Then, 'So,' she said, looking Gad in the eye, 'you went to see my father.'

It was a full broadside.

Gad was on the defensive at once. 'I did, yes, but...'

'I know exactly why you went,' said Valerie. 'Did it do any good?'

'Well, perhaps not,' said Gad, 'but at least...'

'At least nothing! All you did was rub him up the wrong way! I arrived home later that day, and he was so furious that I went straight out again!'

'I'm sorry. I was only trying to break the news to him so that...'

'So that he could work himself up into a frenzy before

I opened my mouth? Thank you very much!' She looked at him accusingly.

'Look – what can I say? I thought you were dreading having to tell him.'

'So I was! It doesn't mean I couldn't tell him! Anyway...' she went on, cutting off both Gad as he opened his mouth to try again, and Thérèse, as she too started with, 'Give him a chance, he was only trying to help!'

'It wasn't for you to do it,' Valerie snapped. She was truly her father's daughter. 'Anyway, it's all water under the bridge now. He's had his say and I've had mine, and so has my mother, and guess what?'

Giving up their protests, the couple lifted their heads to listen.

'I've made some decisions,' she said, putting her hands flat on the table. 'It's taken me ages. I've been going out of my head with worry; couldn't see any way ahead. I had terrible dreams about all the bad things that could happen to me whatever I did – what people might do to me. I might be completely alone in the world – everybody could turn their back on me in disgust.'

Such dramatics were typical of her. Gad heard her, amazed. Thérèse had never given him the least hint of any feelings like these.

'I might even hate myself; I could simply starve to death!'

Nobody spoke, but in the silence the Gaggia machine hissed and a good-looking young man brought her coffee over.

'But the other day I woke up and thought, well, I simply don't care. I'm pregnant. He's just a baby, and I really want him. If Sanjay can live here – and you too, Gad – so can the baby. He'll be born here...'

'He?' Thérèse put in.

'Yes, it's a boy. I just know. He'll be born here and speak

beautiful English, and go to school here, and – everybody will get used to him. He will be a success, no doubt of that. I will make sure of it!'

Mothers! thought Gad, with admiration and pain. He hardly dared to look at Thérèse, but sneaked a covert glance and saw that, like him, she was trying to hide her astonishment. People could be very strange, he thought, in the way they made decisions.

'So what made you change your mind?' he asked curiously.

'Actually, it was something you said, Thérèse.'

Thérèse blinked.

'You know, when I was at your flat?'

'Yes?'

'You said: "We haven't yet talked of adoption." I hadn't even thought of that. But it made me consider it. Well, I realised then that it was not the point, at all – no – to go through all that and then give the baby away? I could never do it in a million years.'

'I see,' said Thérèse, as if that was the end of it.

Gad couldn't let it go so easily. 'Not even if the adopters were friends?'

Valerie looked shocked. 'What? Do you mean anyone in particular?'

'What about us?'

There was a startled silence, and then Valerie threw back her head and let out a yell of laughter. 'You two? That would be the last straw! What a hoot!' And she cackled with hilarity again. 'Good Lord, whatever put that idea into your heads? That is crazy!' She chuckled to herself, scarcely listening to anything Gad might say.

Gad felt his back stiffen. 'What have you got to laugh about?' he demanded. 'What on earth are you going to do?'

'Well, have the baby at home, of course. Mummy and Daddy will help. It'll be fine.'

What kind of reasoning was that? What did she have for a brain?

He saw that Thérèse could hardly contain her feelings as she burst out, 'But they won't! You said so yourself! We had that big argument – don't you remember?'

'Oh, I was a bit upset,' laughed Valerie. 'Of course they will help – I know they will.'

'But they haven't said so yet? You're sure of it?'

'No, they haven't said so yet, but I'll soon get round them, don't worry. I always can – I just have to let Daddy calm down, then he always sees sense.'

'Sees things your way, you mean,' said Thérèse.

Gad said carefully, 'It wasn't a joke, you know. Thérèse and I talked about this for a long time, and thought we would have the understanding – and the experience – to be good parents to your child. We hoped you would be pleased for us to help you out of a difficulty. It was not a joke.'

He waited.

Valerie fiddled with her cup, the chink of the spoon chafing at Gad's nerves.

She sighed then and said, 'Well, I'm sorry I laughed. It just seemed so preposterous.' A smile lurked again. 'After all, you don't have any money! And anyway, how could my parents let go of a grandchild that is half theirs to a mixed couple like you? It would make matters much worse.' Gad felt he could not deal with the craziness of this reasoning.

'But the child…'

'… will be well looked after.'

'But how can you really understand him?' Gad was surprised to find that he felt a personal interest in the baby's welfare. Was it that he, somehow, identified himself with the unborn child – could see ahead of time the dangers that might lie in wait for it? And then, to have invested so much of themselves in making this offer, only to have it ridiculed! He had had enough.

'Come on, Thérèse, let's go!' he exclaimed, pulling her to her feet. 'Sorry, Valerie, we've got things to do. All the best. I hope it goes well.'

'Bye, Valerie,' cried Thérèse, but her final words – 'Keep in touch, won't you?' – were lost in the slam of the door.

Two steps down the street: 'What was the rush?' she asked, freeing her arm, while Gad raged on.

'That woman! She's outrageous!'

'Well, she always was, wasn't she?' Thérèse raised her eyebrows into quizzical arcs.

'She's unbelievable! She lies! She forgets what she last said! And she uses people!'

'Well, to be honest, we didn't need to get involved!' said Thérèse. 'She didn't ask us to do anything!'

'That's what makes it so maddening! We offered of our own free will – actually, we didn't even get as far as making the offer before...'

'There you are, you see? You inflicted this on yourself!'

'Well, I had the best intentions.' He felt sulky.

'Yes.'

Gad looked into her face, saw humour and knowledge there, and caught himself up. 'OK,' he said, letting out his breath. He started to laugh. 'Oh, why the hell do I take myself so seriously? What a good thing I have you around.'

CHAPTER 48

Wednesday and Thursday were quiet days. They heard nothing from Valerie, and were content to let things lie.

Thérèse busied herself with following up her tutor's suggestions.

Gad practised every day, but with no performance in prospect he chose pieces at random, easily lost concentration and would leave the flat to walk aimlessly through the familiar streets. He would go northwards towards the park – his 'back garden' – and on at a measured pace, aware only of changes in the atmosphere: bright sunshine; or grey light that pressed down on him like a shroud; or the whisper of morning mist on his skin; or a blustery wind that wakened all his senses.

Day after day music ran through his head. He would walk alert and relaxed like a cat, sometimes reaching his hand out to the cold touch of iron railing or the friendly roughness of brick, with tunes and rhythms ricocheting round his brain. He was not 'thinking' exactly. He was simply there, as were the pavements hard under his feet, the noisy buses and vans and taxis and cars that rushed so close as to make the air beat against his ears, and the crowds weaving their choreography around him. Released from his aborted promise to Valerie, he felt strangely happy.

One day, in his wandering, he came upon a middle-aged man who stopped him with his hand held out.

'You don't remember me, do you?' He was tall, mid-brown and handsome, with a clarity of voice unusual in African Americans, as his accent revealed him to be.

Gad hesitated, trying to remember – he had met the man

before, at the House, soon after his arrival, when he was too green and bewildered to focus on individuals.

'I'm sorry, I don't...'

'Think nothing of it. I'm James Wilby – from Pennsylvania? I sang and you played – at the House?'

'Yes – yes, of course! I remember now. Trouble is, I do that for so many people. I'm always meeting people – mostly in the kitchen department at John Lewis...' He realised he was babbling. 'I've moved away now – I'm in my own place. Are you staying at the House?'

'Sure. Come and see me there.' The tone was casual, but the stranger's eyes were intent.

'I'm not sure about that. I'm newly married.'

'Married? I'm impressed.' Wilby stepped back a pace. 'And she's a black girl?'

'Actually, no.'

'Big mistake, man. Bi-i-ig mistake. It won't last.' He turned away, and they moved on, falling naturally into step.

'You're wrong.' Gad felt strong in this assertion. He and Thérèse had already been tested. What did this guy know?

'You married?' he asked.

'No. Not the marrying kind.' James gave him a half smile.

They had reached Tavistock Square and as they passed under its massive plane trees James indicated a vacant bench. 'Shall we sit and talk? Smoke?' He offered an unfamiliar soft pack of Camel regulars.

'Thanks.'

They lit up and sat watching the smoke of their cigarettes spiral towards the lowest branches.

'Ah, this is good,' said James, stretching his legs out before him.

'So, what are you doing these days?' asked Gad. 'Can I ask, who is "we"?'

'Yes, well – I'm only here to pick up some stuff.'

312

'Stuff?' Gad looked at him, eyes big in alarm.

'Yeah. You can pick up old stuff here that people will kill for back home – broken bits of carved stone off country churches, that sort of thing. I'm on the hunt to raise funds.'

Gad breathed again, though he felt indignant on behalf of the little pillaged churches.

'So – funds for your campaigns?' he said, remembering now how James had been involved in civil rights activities in America.

'Right.'

'Didn't you get on the side of the Japanese living in America?'

'Sure – had to get them out of the internment camps.'

'The Japanese were not victims when they invaded Burma,' Gad protested with feeling. 'Far from it.'

'Maybe, but these are different – they are country people, fruit farmers. Nothing to do with invasions, or Burma either, for that matter. It's all about human rights, isn't it? If we can get things settled peacefully, let's do it.' He flicked ash into the earth. 'The violence against blacks in the South is another matter.' His eyes were on the distance. 'We have to be vigorous there – we're really up against it.' His voice took on a practised tone. 'It's going to take mass action to change things, but it has to be peaceful, or we lose everything. We can never achieve justice by violence. The time is coming for change, and we are the ones who will make it happen.'

Gad let his words fall to the ground, before asking, 'Do many people think as you do?'

'No, unfortunately. There's Malcolm X calling for a separate black nation, and – don't you know anything over here? Don't you people read?'

'Of course, but how much of it can we believe? I'm not a political animal.'

'Yes, you are! You can't help it. You're in it, up to your neck. A black man, trying to make it in a white system – you've got to be political!'

'I don't see it that way,' Gad said. 'Things are different here. See that bus?' A number sixty-eight bus rumbled towards them. 'I can get on that bus any day, sit anywhere I want, up or down, back or front. I don't have to ask anyone. I can sit next to whoever I like on that bus. I can go up to Euston or down to Waterloo, get on a train and go anywhere I want – or anywhere I can afford, at least.'

'Ah! That's the point – what can you afford? Are they gonna hand you a job with a fat pay cheque and say, "Here you are, little black man. We are happy you are in our country, and we would love you to be a boss over some of our lazy white workers?" Well, are they?'

That made Gad stop and think.

'Maybe not, but listen: this country lets me stay when my own country is wrecked. Do you think the generals back in Rangoon would welcome me, a mixture of races, a Western classical musician, if I went back there? In Insein Prison, maybe!

'And how many Burma people do you think there are here, anyway? A handful – hardly a mass movement. The Caribbeans may campaign together if they want to, but they wouldn't have me alongside them; I'm not one of them.'

'You're all black – got to have solidarity.' James tapped Gad's knee.

'My God, not you too! It's not like that here.' Gad sprang to his feet and stood looking down at James. 'I'm not part of any mass movement. You talk as if blacks are all made from the same mould. Soon you'll be saying, "You all look alike to me!" I'm here on my own; going to make the best of it.' He blew out a great plume of smoke. 'And it's not bad, either – a bit uphill sometimes. Maybe it will get better, but it bothers me to see such numbers of people coming here en masse – sometimes I think they demand too much, and they certainly frighten the Brits. Perhaps it will get worse, but I hope not. It's got to get better in the long run, because anything else is too stupid for words.'

'The Brits had it their own way in those countries for long enough,' James reminded him. 'And anyway, the immigrants were invited here – Britain needed their labour; look at the British Nationality Act 1948…'

'You have been doing your reading! Most Americans hardly know where the UK is!'

'It's my job. It's my life.'

'Fair enough, if you don't have a family to look after. Thérèse is a good girl. We're really together, and that's how we're going to stay.' With some impatience Gad ground his cigarette stub into the ground. 'I have to go,' he said. 'It's been good meeting you again. You've made me think.'

James stood too and, leaning over Gad, planted a kiss on his cheek before he could object. 'You're sweet – and you're clever too. You'll make it. Take care. I'm off tomorrow, so goodbye,' and he strolled off, whistling *Yankee Doodle Dandy* as he went.

★

With a small package in her hand, Thérèse came out of Boots the Chemist and made for the flat, trying to overcome the queasiness that was afflicting her, her stomach jolting every time her foot hit the pavement.

She shut the door behind her with a sigh of relief, kicked off her shoes and made for the kettle. She was not much of a tea drinker, but today her body craved hot tea; coffee didn't feel like an option.

She had not yet mentioned her suspicions to Gad, in case

they were unfounded and he was disappointed. But if – if she should be pregnant, then it was remarkable timing. She could not have faced the prospect of bringing up an adopted child and a child of their own side by side; though she had to admit to feeling deflated, resentful almost, at Valerie's reaction to their offer. What a self-centred woman she was! Clearly she had had no idea how the couple had agonised over their offer.

The more Thérèse thought about it, the clearer it became that it had never been a good scheme. There was something about Valerie that had drawn Gad to her like an unwilling magnet – her energy, perhaps. The fact that he always came out of any involvement full of criticisms did not stop it happening again. The last thing they needed was the ineradicable bond of a child. However the thing was set up, they would never again be able to keep Valerie out of their lives; lucky she had refused, or she would always have been the bull in the china shop, the elephant in the room. Now it was herself and Gad, face to face.

CHAPTER 49

September 1955

It was a touch chilly at this hour of the morning: summer had come to an end. Gad pulled on his grey jumper, the thick cable knit, tugging the cuffs well down over his hands in the way habitual to him; he had long abandoned the gloves his solicitous mother had urged on him.

As he left, he picked up the note that had arrived the night before: *Please come and see me as soon as you have time. I have something to discuss with you.* It was signed *Rob*.

He stuffed it into his pocket and walked briskly down the street.

★

The House was buzzing with activity. In the office there were several overseas visitors settling their bills and saying their goodbyes. Elspeth, presiding with her usual busy benevolence, waved to him as he appeared at the door, but he was content to pass by with a nod, impatient to find out what business Rob had with him.

He could see him seated at his desk in the little alcove that served as his headquarters – it was barely a room, since once inside, there was never enough free space for a person to open or shut the door.

For form's sake, Gad reached round to knock on the door, but hesitated when he saw that Rob was distractedly hunting for something on his cluttered desk, his long arms reaching everywhere but his hands finding nothing.

'Can I help?' Gad asked. It was a phrase he had uttered a thousand times here, but this time it felt unfamiliar on his tongue.

'Oh – Gad!' Robert exclaimed, glancing up. 'Good to see you. I just can't find – oh well, never mind. It can wait.' His big features relaxed into a broad smile as he reached over the desk to grasp Gad's hand.

'Are you sure?'

'Sure – sure,' he said, releasing Gad at last. 'We haven't seen you in so long. We've missed you. Have you spoken to Elspeth?'

'No. I thought I'd see her afterwards.'

'Good – good.' He sat back, smiling. 'Well, how are you?'

'I'm fine, as you can see.' Had Robert forgotten his summons?

'Yes. And Thérèse?'

'She's fine too – working hard.' He gave a nod for emphasis, and to move the conversation on.

'Ah yes, her thesis.'

Mary stuck her head in to say, 'Adeola's staying another night.'

'Ah – so I'll talk to her at supper.'

The head disappeared.

To Gad Robert said, 'So, what brings you here today?'

Gad smiled inwardly. 'You said you wanted to see me about something.'

'Oh – yes. I'm sorry, I wasn't thinking. I sent you a note, did I? Well now, sit down, sit down.'

Gad moved his eyes around carefully, and identified an upright chair stacked with files. He put them down on a small bit of floor space that happened to be vacant, and dragged the chair over, raising dust that drifted in the gloom. 'Thanks,' he said. Feet ran up the stairs above them.

Robert settled in his chair as if he had all the time in the world, crossing his long legs in their greenish thorn-proof trousers. Now he was focussed.

'Didn't you do brilliantly in the Diploma, Garrard?' His deep-set eyes glowed.

'Thank you. I was pleased – and surprised,' he said.

'I suppose you've got a heavy schedule lined up for the autumn?' Rob continued.

'Not too heavy.' He thought of the women's club in Colliers Wood, and winced. He still had the invitation in his pocket. He had probably lost the opportunity by now.

The telephone rang, and Rob reached out for it with a wry smile, covering the mouthpiece to mime, 'Sorry.'

The call finished. 'I don't know how you cope without a telephone,' he said, 'but I suppose at least you get some peace. Anyway, I suppose your booking agent manages all that?'

'I expect I shall need to get a phone installed.' Gad ignored the bit about the booking agent. 'We're thinking about moving, though.'

'Are you?' Robert sounded astonished. 'Isn't it good to live centrally? Easy to get back home late at night, and so forth?'

'It has its advantages, yes.'

'M-m-m.' Rob seemed lost in thought on the subject, till, 'Well, anyway, to business,' he said at last, sitting up as though about to chair a board meeting. 'Elspeth and I were wondering – before you get inundated with offers – we were wondering if we could persuade you to give a concert here.'

Without warning, Gad's throat constricted and he was filled with enormous gratitude, despite the inaccuracy of this supposition.

'We can pay you a small fee,' Robert went on. 'You know all about our finances. And I don't suppose your travel expenses would be very high?'

This made Gad smile, and immediately calmed him. 'I don't suppose they would be,' he said, 'unless we move to Land's End.'

'Oh! Is that likely?'

'You never know.'

Rob looked at him quizzically. 'Well, at least the piano is an old friend!'

There was a moment's pause.

'You'll give me a few days to think about this, won't you?' Gad said at last.

'Well, of course,' Rob said easily, though on a questioning note. 'You won't leave it too long, will you? We need to fix dates soon.'

'Right,' said Gad, 'but don't count on me.' He got to his feet, frowning. Rob said no more, so Gad made a small 'see you' gesture and left.

*

Gad went no further than the square: that was where Londoners went. It was towards noon, and the early autumn sun was high enough to show for an hour or two over the tall buildings. Already the benches were occupied by bunches of young women in their neat outfits and smart court shoes, gossiping as they ate their sandwiches.

He found a bench for himself and sat, staring at the little grey stones under his feet until a mauve and grey pigeon with its pink eyes and pink talons edged into his line of vision, invading as close as it dared. Man and bird stared at each other without recognition. A new pair of highly polished shoes moved in, the pigeon fluttered off and Gad lifted his head to see Ronald, of all people. Of course, he had rooms nearby. Everybody he knew seemed to end up in this square sooner or later.

'So, howdy,' said Ronald. He sat beside Gad.

'Have you been out West, or something?' Gad challenged, laughing.

'Never. Trying to raise a little cheer. What makes you so gloomy?'

'Gloomy? Me? On a day like this?'

'Yes. It smells good, doesn't it – those leaves. Makes me wish I had a garden.'

'Yes.' Gad smiled, thinking with relish of blazing fires that he would one day light and tend, Guy Fawkes' bonfires with excited children.

'I'm going to drop in on Elspeth,' said Ronald. 'Did you know it's her birthday? You coming?'

'No,' said Gad to both questions. 'I've just come from the House.'

'Oh?'

'Yes. Rob asked me to give a concert.'

'Wonderful!'

'Yes, isn't it?' But his head was low.

Ronald looked at him as if doubting his sincerity. 'When is it to be, then?'

'I don't know yet. We haven't made definite arrangements. Of course I want to do it; after all, I owe them.'

'I suppose – all those hours of practice we put up with!' Ronald smiled, remembering.

'Oh – nobody said it was a pain!'

'Of course it wasn't. I'm joking. It was a pleasure. Of course, we've already heard all your pieces, heard them often – over and over – but there must be people in the world who haven't.'

'No need for the sarcasm!'

'Will you be hiring tails again?' Ronald enquired. 'I can't wait to see you all togged up.'

'No!' Gad exploded. 'I can't stand wearing tails!'

'Your *lungyi*, then? We'd love that. You'll look adorable.'

'Stop it, will you? We're not in Burma. And I'm not a penguin either. I'll play as I am, or not at all.'

'That's the stuff. Attaboy. You will do it though, won't you? Of course you will,' Ronald pressed on, a trifle anxiously.

Gad sighed. 'I expect I will. I can't stop now. I have to find a way of doing it that...' He trailed off.

'You've got a problem, then? What's the matter?'

'You really want to know?'

'Of course.'

Gad tried to gather his thoughts. He felt unsettled, and couldn't work out why.

'I need a break, you see. I'm sick of people wanting me to be this or that.'

'Better than not wanting you at all, isn't it?'

'Ah! Well, yes, you would think so. I just don't want to fall out of that frying pan into a half-baked fire.'

'Not to mix your metaphors!'

'Ronald, you live in your own little world – try going outside it! Jokes! Patronising jokes! They're everywhere. Everything's all right if it's a joke. It's sapping my energy, just when I need to keep strong.' For the first time Gad himself understood the danger of turning everything into a joke. 'There's Thérèse now – I've got to think of her, and our children if we have any. You don't know anything.'

'No, I don't see it. I suppose I do live a sheltered life.'

'I can't even go back home now, you see?'

'Since your mother died? I am so sorry.'

'Yes, that. And Burma's hopeless anyway, you know. Don't you read the papers?' He heard James saying the same to him.

'Yes, but...'

'I know. There's not much about it. You should look at the inside pages – the little columns down the edge.'

'Yes, I should. But you're all right here, surely?'

'Oh yes, I'm fine here, provided I keep to my station in life – as a clerk, say?'

'Who have you been speaking to? I've never heard you talk like that before.'

'To James Wilby, actually.'

'Oh, him!'

'Yes, and you know? He made me think – never thought much about politics before; the wider picture. And you know what? I'm not going to live out my life hiding in a corner – will not do it. It's middle of the stream or nothing!'

'Good for you!' He clapped Gad on the back and got up to go. Then, as though coming upon something important: 'If you want to do things your way, remember your Gaderace performance?'

Gad groaned. 'Oh, don't! I don't even want to think about that!'

'No, but listen – think how enjoyable that was. Of course, I don't mean the way you played – that was horrible. But the way you managed to include us all in the performance. Suppose you worked out something serious along those lines – even take some requests, perhaps – but give us the music straight and classical, the way it should be? Only speak to the audience about the pieces, too – say what they mean to you. I don't know, Gad. I'm not a musician. Just a thought – I must be off.'

Gad watched him stroll away, disappearing through the trees on his way to the House.

Maybe... he thought. Maybe...

CHAPTER 50

AIR MAIL
8th September 1955

Dear Wilma,

Thank you very much indeed for your letter. You sounded so different from when Mummy passed away. I feel as if a new chapter is opening in your life.

You were always my clever big sister, and loved music, but you never had the chance to study as I did. I am so very glad you have already been to two symphony concerts, and hope you will enjoy many more in the future, and make some musical friends of your own.

You are right that there is a great variety of music-making in London, though it is not so obvious or easy to find as the big orchestral concerts. Perhaps you will discover San Francisco is the same.

I do realise that it will be hard to make my living by music alone to begin with, so I have been increasing my hours of work at the London County Council. Luckily, they are such a big organisation that they are able to be flexible with their employees, so I shall be able to vary my hours to allow for concert bookings. And listen, I have been having ideas about different ways of presenting my own concerts, instead of just waiting for others to invite me. Many people have told me that I should speak to audiences as well as play; introduce the pieces and explain why I have chosen them. What do you think? Also, I am wondering about approaching my violinist friend

Pyotr, and Valerie (who is pregnant, by the way), the singer I accompanied in Hampstead, to join me for performances. Apparently I am a good accompanist! We could build our experience in small venues for small fees since my main income would come from the LCC. The only problem is, when would I sleep??

It is so nice to be able to discuss things with you like this – in a way I never could with Mummy.

With love and God Bless,
Your brother Garrard

CHAPTER 51

September 1955

The sound came at them like a tidal wave – big, brash, and swinging – as they stood at the massive double doors giving entry to Chelsea Town Hall. Gad took a deep breath. The impact of the music was unfamiliar and yet moving; it reminded him of something that lurked at the back of his mind, momentarily inaccessible but nonetheless potent.

'Come on,' said Thérèse, turning towards him with an impatient swing of her hips, and grabbed his hand to pull him in.

They moved across the foyer to look into the hall. It was cavernous, filled to capacity. There was a great moulded ceiling with chandeliers hanging by long chains. Walls blazed crimson. White and gold were everywhere, light bouncing off glossy paintwork and brass doorknobs.

A couple swivelled past them, joined by one hand, the girl spinning, her ankles flashing white between her black pedal pushers and her ballerina shoes. The boy, sporting a glossy DA haircut, navigated her expertly amongst a tangle of moving limbs, through which they could make out a wall of musicians.

Gad panicked. 'I can't do this!'

'Yes, you can! *Allez!* Listen to the music – and don't let go of my hand!'

They moved on to the floor. He hung on like grim death, standing still while Thérèse began to move, watching her respond to the rhythm, trying to anticipate where she might fly off to next, not letting go. There were so many people round them! When he saw that the dancers had a kind of radar that prevented collisions he began to relax, became less watchful. Horns blared, drums beat, his feet moved and he found he was a dancer after all. It took a while for their steps to synchronise, but as drums and bass syncopation began to work on his ear, he got it. His body became loose; the tune ran through from head to foot; he crouched; he was jiving! The only fixed point in the universe was his hand grasping Thérèse's. His eyes saw only the yellow skirt, flying out as she turned, spiralling round her thighs as she twisted back, her long legs quick and accurate.

Just as in his first days in the West End, Gad's was the only 'black' face to be seen. The difference was that here, nobody cared. Here, nobody patronised or judged, or made it their business to insult you; there were no curtains to twitch, no property to protect. As for the boys, they were intent on getting their lives together: the music, and their moves, and their girls. Each couple was in a world of its own. If you were here for the same reason as the rest, then you belonged.

The music stopped. The bandleader turned and bowed to the applause, his black hair gleaming and his neat moustache jaunty above the black bow of his tie. The band rose to their feet, ranks of instruments dazzling as they caught the light.

It was this that took Gad straight back to something forgotten for years – the sweaty open-air festivals held in the country parts of Burma, the *nat pwes*. Light had reflected from their instruments too, but it had been from flares, living flames. The d'Silva children were strictly forbidden to be there, but it didn't stop them. They yearned to hear the thunderous drums, to see the *kadaw*, elegant master of the *pwe*, carrying out the rites that would propitiate the local *nats* – the green ghosts, spirits of place, protectors of the land, and guardian angels to his grandmother.

Memory came singing through to him: dancers possessed

by music. He looked at the faces around them and saw the same dazed look. He leaned against a wall, mopping his face with a clean handkerchief – the one for show, not the one for blow. And there was the voice of his childhood again; Mummy whose words they were. In this noisy horde he could barely hear it; his heart beating to another pulse. Thérèse's warmth rested against him amongst the exuberant people.

★

Eventually they stumbled out into the soothing cool air of the King's Road. There was only intermittent lighting. Thérèse looked at Gad and laughed.

'You look a mess!' she said. His hair was a tangle and his shirt damp. Her own hair stuck lankly to her cheeks, and her shoes were scuffed.

They found a bus stop, and stood propping each other up. As always, the number elevens were running in packs, but they were saved from a long wait by a stray two-one-one. They climbed on board and set off towards town.

She sighed, 'Oh, I'm so thirsty,' and leaned her head on Gad's shoulder.

'Are you? We could try Victoria.'

They stopped off at the station to see if there was coffee to be had by the cab stand, and there was. Thérèse drooped wearily while Gad fetched the drinks.

'Been dancing, 'ave yer?' said the stallholder, dishing out watery fluid in smeared mugs – but it was hot and sweet, anyway.

'Yes. It's thirsty work,' said Gad, and added with admiration, 'She never stops for breath!'

'Good for 'er. Ta.' The man turned away to the till.

They sat down on a bench and began to sip the scalding stuff.

'I'm not ready to sleep yet, are you?' Gad asked her.

'Well, I'm – whacked, do you say?'

'Yes, you do.' He smiled.

'Just give me a minute. This is good.' She gulped the coffee. 'Let's go down to the river to cool off; have a proper look at the Festival Hall.'

'I don't know – it'll be closed, and it's a bit of a desert round about. We could look over from Westminster Pier. It won't be so far home then.'

They picked up another bus for the short ride to Big Ben. It was nearly midnight and the streets were deserted.

From Westminster Bridge, they started down the steps to the Embankment; but Thérèse suddenly began to cling to the handrail, frowning. Gad heard her call his name, and put his arm round her waist to steady her as she struggled to hold her balance. Finally she sank down on the grimy bottom step with her head between her knees. He crouched beside her.

'Thérèse! What's wrong? You feel faint?'

Big Ben above them began its deliberate chimes, before midnight prompted twelve solemn booms.

'No, it's OK. I'm fine,' she protested, but in that moment she pulled herself to her feet to throw up violently.

He held her while she retched again and a thin dribble ran from her mouth. At last the spasms stopped, leaving her mouth sour and the back of her nose aching.

'*Mon dieu*,' she said, embarrassed, gulping to steady herself. 'I am so sorry.'

Gad handed her his damp handkerchief. She wiped her face and blew her nose, then went over the road to throw the sodden result into the river. Gad watched her with a small nagging irritation at the waste. His sister had been just like this when – oh my God! – when she was first pregnant. *Can it be…?*

She moved away to lean her forehead against the Embankment wall, and he followed her.

'I'm cold,' she said, and waited with a pinched face while he threw his rough tweed jacket over her shoulders and hugged her to him, rubbing her back and upper arms. He gave her a moment to warm up before asking the question that was uppermost in his mind. 'Are you sick, or – do you think you might be pregnant?'

She turned to face him, looking into his eyes. He saw there hope and trust and excitement.

'I think I may be,' she said simply, holding his gaze. 'What would you think?'

'What would I think?' The ferment in his chest and head threatened to choke him. 'Darling, of course this is wonderful – fabulous – fant-...' He couldn't keep still.

She cut him short with a finger on his lips.

'Don't!' she murmured. 'Not yet. I didn't want to tell you yet in case it was a false alarm.'

'Even if it is, we can have a false hope together – you and me. Oh sweetheart!' And he kissed her sour mouth, taking her lips into his and hugging her fiercely. His eyes shone. He had had no idea he wanted this so much.

'This changes everything!' he shouted, throwing his arms open to Thérèse, to the night, to the river and to the shining building across the water. 'Anything's possible now! Look at that!' he said to her, waving at the radiance with its luminous reflection. 'Remember when we last looked at it? That was when you said "yes" to adopting. No need now! No need at all!'

His eyes were full of white light and dazzle. Perhaps, he thought, perhaps I might still play there one day. And if not me, then our children?

'We'll have beautiful children!' he exulted.

'Uh – more than just this one?'

'A dozen at least!' He was in extravagant vein. 'And a big house for them and for our piano! And our door will always be open!'

She laughed again, at his mad enthusiasm. 'And what will you do, while I have babies?'

'I will find a way of music that will be properly mine, and earn lots of money to buy you diamond earrings, and we will go travelling; we'll all go to Brittany, and you will show me the great standing stones, and I will get to know the organs in all those little churches…'

'And my mother and father will adore you – and the grandchildren. And you will learn to play Breton drums.'

'Some hopes! Or, we'll stay in London, and I'll get a job as a humble clerk, and we'll live on porridge and coffee…'

'So what's new?'

Gad came to his senses. 'Seriously, though, sweetheart, this is what I've been waiting to hear. And you are not to worry. I will find a way. I love you and I will never let you down – you know you can count on that. We will make the dreams come true.'

He drew breath, aware that it was not often he made such speeches. He could see that Thérèse believed him. She gave him a quick kiss and leaned back against him, wrapping his arms around her.

The streetlights were not so bright as to obscure the stars, which were mirrored in the calm, greenish-grey mass of water moving steadily past. Gad's eyes followed the flow till it went out of sight. Not for the first time he thought about where the great river was leading, its waters pouring into the sea, a link with the world.

Now at last he could let it go.

Author's Note

Marjorie Lazaro was born in Dorset, read for an Honours degree in London and stayed to work in music and book publishing whilst travelling widely. A violinist and singer, she performed in London-based orchestras and choirs under talented young conductors. Married with three children, she taught in new comprehensive schools, and now lives in a Hertfordshire village. She has written a full-length opera libretto, short stories and pieces for music, artwork and voice, performed in St Johns Church, Bethnal Green and in Hoxton Town Hall. *A Person of Significance* is her first novel.

ACKNOWLEDGEMENTS

I would like to thank the following for help and advice freely given during the making of this book:

Caroline Natzler and members of her writers' group, for sensitive and constructive reading; Joan Deitch, for a rapid pub edit; Debi Alper, for knowledgeable guidance; Andrew Wille for an inspirational workshop on the tarot; Rose Tremain, for writing *The Road Home*; Jane Campbell, of the Dacorum U3A Railways group, for advice on railway journeys in the 1950s; Dr Doreen Jewkes for input about agricultural practice in Brittany; Jill Heller and the Dacorum U3A 'Testing the Waters' group, for critical listening; Clare Lazaro and Roger Ramsden respectively for their input into cover design.

I warmly appreciate all their involvement.